# Light in the Dark Forest

## by

## Gency Brown

**Light in the Dark Forest**

Cover Art by *Teddi Black*

The Wild Rose Press, Inc.
PO Box 708
Adams Basin, NY 14410-0708
Visit us at www.thewildrosepress.com

Publishing History
First Edition, 2025
Trade Paperback Print ISBN 978-1-5092-6337-0
Digital ISBN 978-1-5092-6338-7


Published in the United States of America

## Dedication

For those who held the flashlight for me throughout this journey.

Advisory: This work of fiction contains themes and depictions related to war and Post Traumatic Stress Disorder. Included are flashbacks, trauma responses, and emotional distress including suicide. Reader discretion is advised.

Chapter 1

The crunch and dust from gravel filled the air as Ava Hardy pulled into Simmons' General Store along highway 270, outside Wilburton in Southeastern Oklahoma. Weathered signs advertising everything from chewing tobacco to automotive oil to sliced bread and more littered the exterior walls of the business. It was nothing like the stores she frequented in Tulsa. Feeling at home right away surprised her. The lush green forest of the Kiamichi Mountains on the horizon filled her eyes and heart. The photos she'd seen online could never capture this beauty. A step down from her four-wheel-drive vehicle brought a cool June breeze to her weary back after the two-hour drive from her home in Tulsa. She stretched to the sky and headed inside the building.

Her voice called out strong and friendly to the man on the porch as she climbed the steps. "Pleasant afternoon, don't you think?" She scolded herself for jumping when he spat over the side railing as his chair thumped down onto the wooden porch where it had leaned against the clapboard wall.

He raised a sleeve to wipe across his smiling mouth. "Hi stranger. You must be the lady rented the cabin."

"Uh, yes, Ava Hardy. That would be me."

"Your application said you're a reporter for the *Tulsa Herald* newspaper. That so?"

"Yes, but I'll be doing some personal writing while

I'm here. I want to create a second novel."

With a folded newspaper under his arm, he rose from the chair and said with a wave, "Come on in and we'll get you set up."

She handed him her shopping list and watched as he stuffed one bag, then another with everything from crackers to lunch meat, jams, chocolates, and insect spray. He announced with a grin, "Those are my wife's jars of canned goods over there, if you'd like to add some."

Ava couldn't resist the green beans, peaches, and corn relish in quart mason jars. "They look scrumptious." She paid the total in cash.

He joined her at the front of the counter. "My name is Charlie, by the way. Charles Simmons. It's summer in these mountains, and the area is crawling with visitors. Good thing I had a cabin available. We call that one The Kiamichi Retreat. You want it for a three-month vacation, right?"

She liked his friendly manner and found him easy to talk to. "Yes, a sort of vacation. This is my time to answer questions about life, career, and that novel to write. I won't bore you with details, but let's just say I want to look at my life goals and evaluate where I am with those. I guess I'm wondering if there's something more for me."

The grocer shook his head. "Good luck with all that. Now, you know it's a solid two miles up there with all the switchbacks? Electricity, but no internet or cell phone signal. Well, the kids say sometimes you can get a text through. A quarter mile from there to the nearest neighbor. That's Marvin Cameron, a veteran who is a little, well, let's just say it's best you know he likes his privacy."

After they loaded bags and boxes into her car. Mr. Simmons snapped his fingers and declared, "I almost let you get away without your linens."

Before they could get back inside to retrieve the items, a large, black pickup slid to a stop at the foot of the steps. She saw a tall, middle-aged man in denim overalls and a tee shirt exit the truck and make his way inside. He carried a rifle at his side and favored one leg as he climbed the stairs.

Mr. Simmons let out a sigh. "I've told him not to bring guns in here."

Ava's blood pulsed and her eyebrows drew together. "What's going on? He goes around armed?"

"No, not usually." Mr. Simmons waved her to the porch steps. "Come on. Let's finish up and get you on your way."

Inside, he filled her arms with sheets, towels, a pillow, and a quilt. Ava turned from the closet area to leave. The man from the pickup rounded a counter stocked with cleaning supplies and the two shoppers crashed together, her soft goods tumbling to the floor. He repelled from her and took a crouching stance behind a display of canned goods. Ava froze only feet from the barrel of his rifle, aimed at her face.

Mr. Simmons stepped toward the man, palms pushing ahead in a stop motion. "At ease, Marine. Friendly encounter."

The man sat rigid, leaned back against the cooler, never lowering the rifle. "Stand back, Sarge. I'll take 'em out."

"Put your weapon down, Cameron. That's an order."

The shaking man persisted. "No, this is one of those civilian bombs. Enough ordinance strapped to her to take out the village. Out of the way, Sarge. One clean shot is all I need."

Ava whimpered and glued her eyes on Mr. Simmons as he tried to calm the man. His steady voice carried comfort and friendship. "Marvin, it's me, Charlie." He inched forward.

The rifle wavered as the troubled man squirmed on the floor. Sweat dripped from his face and glistened in the sunlight from a transom window above. His body fell limp with eyes that held a fire only his tears could quench. "Charlie?"

"That's right, buddy. Now calm down. No harm done here. You okay, Ms. Hardy?"

A nod of her head was all Ava could muster.

Mr. Simmons moved to take the gun away, then embraced the man until he stopped quaking. "Okay, Marvin. It's over now. Pull yourself together. Is that gallon of milk on the floor what you came for?"

"Yeah. I'm sorry. It's just when we made contact…"

"I know. I know. If you think you're all right to drive, then grab your things. I'll put the milk on your tab."

Marvin Cameron stepped over the linens Ava had dropped to the floor and called back as he pushed open the screen door to leave, "I'm real sorry, ma'am." The door slammed behind him.

She braced herself on the counter. Deep breaths steadied her with arms now full again. "Wait. Is that guy the crazy neighbor you warned me about? Wow, is he a loose cannon, or what?"

"Now, just a minute, young lady. I called him no

such thing. He's a nice but troubled man who wants his privacy is all. See, he's a Desert Storm veteran, and has these flashbacks. PTSD, he says. He's hurt no one, but can be unpredictable, so that's why I thought it best you steer clear."

Ava turned to see the man climb into his pickup and watched the over-sized tires throw gravel behind as he left. Her mind went back to difficult times with her dad. She'd never thought of his Vietnam memories being the cause. The wheels were turning in her writer's mind. "Well, I'm sorry he has it so rough. He's certainly interesting"

"Are you sure you're okay? I know that was scary. What a welcome to our mountains. You know, you'll be alone up there on the mountain."

"Don't worry about me. I'm tougher than you might think. My family had a cabin at Lake Keystone until my dad died when I was eleven. I wanted to do everything he did, and even so young, I chopped wood, cooked over an open fire, shot varmints as needed, and bathed in the creek. Nothing in the woods scares me. Not even odd neighbors." Then she added to convey her resolve, "I can take care of myself."

The store keeper tilted his head and raised an eyebrow as he walked back to his work. "By the way, I had our youngest, Davis, sweep out the place and chop some wood for you in case of a cool night or two."

"Thanks. I'm happy to pay him. Is he around?"

"You don't have to do that. You just missed him. He's working in town at the pizza place this summer. He'll be a senior next year and been saving for college. I'll have him run up to check on you come Saturday. That is, if I can keep him from his little girlfriend that long."

"Teenage boys always have girls on their minds." She wondered about a man with heavy gray around his temples and stooped shoulders having a teenage son, but held on to her manners.

He chuckled. "I see a question on your face. Yes, he was our miracle baby when we were both a little shy of fifty. As folks say, it was a cold winter in the woods that year." They shared a laugh.

Ava looked around the room. "And your wife; where is she?"

"She volunteers at the senior center in town at lunch time. Otherwise, she's here. By the way, the propane tank up there should be in fine shape. I had it filled in May."

"Good to know. I have the map I printed out. Just stay on the dirt road up the mountain, right?"

"Yes, almost exactly two miles. You'll see a big charred pine left over from the fire three years ago and blue check curtains on the windows of the cabin. Now listen, there are loud sirens to alert us to fire danger and tornadoes. Don't even think you can wait it out. Get down here to shelter right away."

"I hear ya. Well, I think I have everything, so I'm off." As she pulled onto the road to her cabin, she wondered what awaited her there. Adventure or the quiet writing atmosphere she craved? Did this mountain and its people hold answers for her? One thing was for sure; nothing could surprise her after what she had just witnessed.

## Chapter 2

Ava entered the cabin coughing from the stale air inside. She carried the mattress out to freshen it up. The small pad covered with a blue and white striped ticking lay on the porch steps as she beat it within an inch of its life with the broom from the kitchen, then returned the fresh cushion to the bed frame.

She spoke out loud. "There, now, I'll unload and make this place a home. How nice to know I can speak without worrying about who is around to hear. I'll be able to try out my words before committing them to the program on my laptop. Can't do that sitting in a coffee shop."

Ava spent the rest of the afternoon familiarizing herself with her summer home. The cabin was one large room. In a corner was the six-foot kitchen counter with a large crockery bowl converted into a sink. She pushed aside the calico curtain below to reveal the hoses, which brought water in and back outside. She remembered reading online about a pump used to bring fresh water from a nearby spring. The faucet had one lever to turn water on and off. Not hot and cold, just on and off. "Interesting, but I guess it works."

The two-burner cookstove was propane powered. Storage was open shelving above and cabinets below. There were enough glasses, bowls, and plates for four. "Either I have guests or only wash dishes every four days." Her laughter filled the cabin. Pots and pans and cast-iron cookware rested on the lower shelves.

A small mahogany gate-leg table stood next to one wall with leaves folded down to conserve space. "I'll put this by the front window for light." She moved it with ease and lifted one leaf for more work space. "Yes, this will be my writing desk. There's an electrical socket right behind. Perfect."

She put sheets on the bed and covered it with the quilt. "Wow, someone spent some hours on this beauty. I think Grandmother would call it a Dresden Plate pattern." A rainbow of colorful small diagonals made up the pinwheels placed across the white background. "So beautiful. I wonder who wore the shirts and dresses, later used for the warmth of the quilt?"

The hand-crafted table beside the bed, made from limbs of a willow tree, held only a lamp, too small to read by. A free-standing closet stood in the corner. It looked large enough for the jacket, jeans, shirts of denim, and tee shirts she unpacked. "Plenty of room below for boots and sneakers. Hey, I can use the basket from the gift of cheese and fruits the gang at work gave me to hold my socks and underwear in here."

In front of the fireplace lay a braided rug, which mimicked the colors of the forest. A wooden love seat and padded rocker sat in the rug's circle with another handmade table and a floor lamp. "This is great for reading or those three guests." Again, she giggled.

Only one room was missing, but she knew the website had advised, "Personal facilities available just outside your door." She walked out to discover the structure behind the cabin at the edge of the woods, which was a little larger than expected. "Okay, here we go." She opened the door and peeked inside to find a composting toilet and an open shower with a pair of hoses. Knowing those wouldn't be for hot and cold, she supposed one brought water in and the other fed it back out into the woods.

"You've got to be kidding. And this all works? Great. That must be a heavy-duty pump." She followed the hoses outside, where she found them attached to the oversized equipment.

At sundown, her work complete, the grumblings from her stomach announced meal time. She opted for a ham sandwich, chips, and an apple from her gift basket collection. At the small cook stove, she steeped tea in a two-quart sauce pan. "A successful day. I've got to use my time here to my advantage. I've writing to do and answers to find."

****

After a night of strange dreams, she shook from seeing the ghostly image of her father in the dark, at the foot of her bed. "You didn't have to come tell me what a risk this is, Dad. I keep thinking someday you'll come to say you're proud of something I've done." She shadowed him as a small child, in a kind of hero worship. She endured his occasional gruffness, because of a daughter's love for him, though she didn't understand. Their relationship suffered as she grew and developed a mind of her own.

The sun shone through the window to blanket her face. Once she had her feet on the floor, she remembered the long walk to the facilities.

"Oh, crap. As soon as I hit the cool morning air, I'm done for."

She donned her robe and shoes and took a deep

breath before starting a fast walk to the outdoor bathroom.

"Ah, success." She questioned the shower again. At this height in the mountains, it was much too chilly in the mornings for bathing in the cool spring water from the hose. She'd have to figure out something else.

Back inside, Ava opened her laptop on the makeshift desk. A stack of pads, pencils, and a sharpener occupied one corner. With her coffee in hand, she stepped out to the porch to enjoy the morning.

She had brief thoughts of what might happen in the news room, but didn't miss it. She rarely asked for time away from work, making this respite a treat. Her apartment location near the bus line and restaurants made subletting easy. Had she remembered to cancel the newspaper delivery? "Oh well, it'll be a nice perk for the traveling nurse who leased the place."

Her head snapped around and up to a rustling in the oak tree beside the porch. Two squirrels ran down to the ground, where they continued their chase. One wanted the acorn the other had found. She laughed as they squealed and fought until the loser ran off in a flurry. "It's like in any life, fellas. Someone always wanting what you have but not willing to work for it."

She remembered how her heart sank when her boss, Matt, announced Pete's promotion. Not the first time he passed her over, though he always praised her work. "Hmmm. Get to writing, Ava. I should scrap what I've been working on all those nights. Yeah, clean the slate and start a new story line. Something like what these squirrels and I go through in trying to get ahead might work." She went back inside to her laptop.

With a fresh cup of coffee at her side, she started an

outline for her new manuscript. This would be something right out of current events. A man of substance facing an angry takeover of his business. She decided on names, ages, and location. New York City would be likely. His son-in-law, the surprise antagonist. The year would be…no. Her hand rubbed her eyes, as she knew the outline wasn't working for her. She wanted more creativity from her writing.

A small notepad and pencil went into her pocket for a hike in the woods in hopes the fresh morning air would help. A colorful array of wildflowers lined the sides of a well-worn path. Pinks of the Common Yarrow and Wild Blue Indigo. Reds, yellows, and oranges of Indian Blanket blooms. She surprised a raccoon washing in the small waterfall from a spring which fed into the shallow creek.

Ava sat on a large boulder at the water's edge doing deep breathing exercises. Her mind freed and the muscles at her neck loosened. She brought out the notepad to record her thoughts. A new try filled the first few pages. She didn't like it. "I'm pressing too much. Relax, Ava. Something will come when it comes." After dangling her feet in the water for another hour, she headed back to the cabin for lunch.

A salad along with cheese and grapes hit the spot. She ate at the laptop until frustration at not finding the right words overtook her. The sun had been high long enough to warm the water in the hose for her shower. She stripped down and donned her robe, gathered her toiletries, and walked to her outdoor spa. No way she could call it an outhouse.

She hung her robe on the provided hook and reached for the lever, which controlled the shower flow. Water sputtered, then ran only a little faster than molasses before it gave a full stream. The liquid felt warm to her hand, so she stepped in. Her slippers stayed behind on the dirt floor as she stepped onto the wooden platform facing the showerhead. She rushed to rinse, but when the warm water from the sunbaked hose turned cool, the lather still ran down her body. Now the cold water made her body shiver. She made a note that speed would be of the essence.

She stood for a moment, wrapped in her towel. The sun beat down through gaps in the roof and helped some. The robe clung to her damp skin as she ran to the cabin. Inside, jeans and a tee shirt caressed her body. This would be her daily attire while here. As she laced her boots, she continued to plot a story.

The click of the keys on her laptop mingled with the sounds of nature the rest of the afternoon. Her character, Adeline, became a woman from Phoenix and introduced her family and friends. This was genuine progress. The sun had gone behind the trees when stiff back muscles advised Ava to stop. She rose to stretch and moved to the kitchen for food.

As night fell, she read in the yellow glow of the porch light. She had brought several paperbacks along for company. The action novel couldn't hold her attention as the sounds of the night surrounded her. There was melody and rhythm to the calls, whistles, and stirrings of forest creatures who shared her evening.

The crack of a rifle startled her out of her chair. "What was that?" She looked from side to side, craning her neck to see in the darkness. Wasn't it late for someone to be hunting? The sound didn't seem so far away, but what did she know of gun shots in the woods?

It could be someone killing a snake or other varmint. She had her dad's hand gun along for just such a purpose. Nevertheless, her reading would continue indoors where she remembered Mr. Simmons' son, Davis, would be there Saturday. "I'll ask him more about my neighbors."

Chapter 3

The next morning, she explored farther from her doorstep. She walked a quarter hour before she heard the whack of an axe driving through the heart of a log, which brought her father to mind again. She remembered him at the cabin as wood split with each stroke of his axe and fell on either side of a stump platform. As she crept toward the sound, the aroma of a campfire filled her nostrils.

An opening in the trees gave way to a bright tunnel of daylight, which guided her to the edge of the forest. She stayed low behind a large elm tree, still fifty yards from the cabin before her. Beside a butterfly bush, a few feet in front of the porch stairs, the man who caused the excitement at the store stirred a cauldron atop a fire edged in small boulders. An American flag hung on end from the eave over one side of the porch. He split another log and tossed it onto a pile, then leaned his axe against the stump and returned to stirring the contents of the cast-iron vessel. She jumped back as a rabbit ran out of the woods and across the meadow between her and the cabin.

A large black German shepherd stood on the porch, ears moving like radar, targeted forward. The man turned to survey the meadow. "Stand down, Major. That's only a small animal and we have our dinner for tonight." He peered toward the edge of the forest as the dog continued to growl, stiff hair raised on his neck. "Is there something else?" He stood still to watch and listen. The rifle leaned against the stairs close by his hand.

Ava froze in place. Mr. Simmons had warned her to stay away, but she had thought a neighborly visit might be acceptable. After all, he couldn't be all that bad. He'd taken time and effort enough to apologize for his actions. Her nosy-reporter mentality pushed her to learn more about him. A memory flashed before her of her father yelling at her for sneaking up on him when she was little. Much like the time she interviewed a prisoner and stood to walk around the table. His stiff body jerked around when she stood behind him. Come to think of it, his defensive explanation had included his PTSD. "Maybe this man won't see me creeping in like this as friendly. I don't want to be a bother to him." The attentive dog also made her question being there. She stayed put while the man continued his work. The dog returned to his nap on the porch. She thanked her lucky stars the breeze blew toward her today. One muscle, one foot, one step at a time, she executed her silent retreat.

Back on her porch, she made notes about what she had seen. She was determined to find out more.

\*\*\*\*

Mid-morning on Saturday, Ava came outside to find a lanky young man on the porch reading from the stack of books she left there. "Well, you're a quiet one. I didn't hear you pull up. Hello, are you Davis?"

Her visitor dropped the book on the side table and rose to remove his Oklahoma University ball cap. "Yes, ma'am. I knocked. I guess you didn't hear me."

"Sorry. I had music playing in my headphones while I washed dishes."

"My dad sent me to check on you. Everything okay?"

"I'm doing well, thank you. Sit down, please."

"You take the chair, ma'am. I'll sit here on the steps. I guess you figured out how everything works?"

Ava thought he was a nice-looking, wavy-haired young man at six foot one or two. "Yes, I have, thank you. You're a tall drink of water, as my grandpa would say. Do you play basketball?"

"Yes, ma'am. I'm on the varsity team one more year."

"Davis, it's fine you call me Ava, if you like. What were you reading when I walked up?"

"I'm sorry. They're all back now."

"You can borrow one if you like. Are you an avid reader?"

"Yes, ma'am, I mean Ms. Ava. I read all the time. The library here in Wilburton doesn't get much new like this. The college has a big library but, of course, I can't use that. They have everything."

"That's right. I forgot Eastern Oklahoma State College is in Wilburton. You'll go there?"

"Yeah, Mom thinks it'll be best for me to start there for a couple of years. I'm not sure where after that. I need a good writing program since I want to be an author someday. My dad says you're a writer and already have one book published. That's awesome."

"I work as a journalist, but I've been lucky enough to get a novel out there. I'm here working on another one. My dad was a writer, too, and used to go to our cabin all the time. He said the peace in nature helped him put the right words down on the paper. I hope it works for me. I like your name. You know, Davis Simmons will look good on a book cover some day."

He blushed. "Thanks. It sounds kind of old-fashioned to me. My folks named me after a great grandfather on my mom's side. Most of my friends call me Davey."

Her head cocked to one side. "Since you told me you have a desire to be a writer, I believe I'll stick with Davis. Take the book you were looking at. I finished it last night. It's not a new one, but I enjoyed it. Or have you read it?"

"No, but I like the author a lot. Okay, thanks. I'll bring it back. Is there anything I can do for you while I'm here?"

"Yes. Maybe you can tell me a little about my neighbors. I'd like to meet them."

"Most are nice. Mr. and Mrs. Jenkins are pretty close to you over there." He raised an arm to direct her vision. "They come every summer, so I've known them all my life. And over there is Mr. Cameron and his dog." He turned back to her with forehead furrowed. "You need to stay clear of him. Our cabins are all rented, so there are plenty of folks you can be friends with."

Her reporter ears perked for information. "Something more I should know about Mr. Cameron? I ran into him at the store the other day. For real. Your dad said he's a war veteran."

"Yeah, I guess so. Dad doesn't like me carrying tales, but…" he scooted toward her on the step and looked from side to side as if to make sure the coast was clear for storytelling. "He still thinks he's over there sometimes. Like he's in a dream and can't get out or something. Even though he retired as a cop over in Ft Smith, you wouldn't know it by how he acts sometimes."

"He causes trouble?" Ava's memory of their meeting kept her on the edge of her seat for his answer.

"I guess not so much. Sheriff Jim Carson has been up there a few times, though. Dad says he's pretty harmless, but I still think there are others you can meet."

Ava sat back to think out loud. "Marvin Cameron. A police officer, hmm?" She retrieved the notepad and pencil from her pocket to make notes.

"You're not going to do like I said, are you, Ms. Ava?"

"I don't want him to think I'm too nosy, but I told you, Davis, I'm a writer, always searching for a story."

When he was ready to leave, he tossed the book inside the pickup, then turned back to her. "Ms. Ava, if it's not too much trouble, I mean, since you're an actual writer, could you read some of my stuff and tell me what you think?"

A grin broke across her face. "Oh my. I haven't evaluated someone's work like that since my student teaching days, but I'd be happy to read for you."

"My teacher says I have talent, but so far, I haven't gotten an A on anything. So, you're a teacher, too?"

"I have a minor in education, but went with the paper after a couple of years in the middle school system. I'd been in a classroom most of my life and had the desire and degree to use my writing skills. Bring something next Saturday and we'll talk about writing." She'd like to share with him and thought it a chance to learn more about the interesting veteran.

After Davis's visit, Ava reviewed what she understood about her neighbor and started a new outline. Even with so little information about him, she recognized an interesting story waiting for her. She'd have to be careful about how she approached him, though.

****

Ava continued to mull over her new story. She had changed direction again, but at least she was writing. Her Masters of Fine Arts professor at Oklahoma State always said, "Just keep writing." The mystery man and his dog challenged her to do just that.

After lunch, she grabbed her pencil and notepad and left for a walk. She felt alive and her steps light in the woods. The sounds and smells of the forest enveloped her as she strolled through the cool shade of the trees. The scurry of a small animal through the carpet of leaves and pine needles on the forest floor broke the silence. Her chosen path took her to the north at a higher elevation. When she came upon a cabin, she stopped to check out the surroundings.

A man's shirts and a few feminine under things waved in the breeze from a clothesline, which told her two people lived there. Could it be the friendly couple Davis told her about? Wooden rockers sat side by side on the porch. Thirty feet in front of the cabin were four Adirondack chairs surrounding a fire pit. A tree on one side held a child's swing swaying in the gentle breeze. A dusty, older SUV sat along the south side of the cabin.

The screen door opened and a woman in jeans and a tank top stepped out onto the porch. After securing her long salt and pepper hair back from her face, she stretched, turning at the waist to the right, then the left. Ava watched as she bent to touch her toes as if her spine were a limp piece of pasta. She rose and both arms reached straight up for a full minute, then settled into a prayerful pose. The woman went to the clothesline, and

19

ran her hands along the garments, then took them down and into the cabin.

Ava felt comfortable enough to venture forth to meet the neighbors. She halted at the steps of the cabin and called inside. "Hello. I'm new here and came to say hello."

The woman came to the screen with a big smile. "You arrived last week."

"Yes, I'm Ava Hardy. Is it all right I came?"

"Of course. It will be fun to have company. I'm Maggie Jenkins. John is off traipsing in the woods somewhere. Would you like something to drink? I have tea." She moved down to the yard where a large glass jar full of the dark liquid steeped in the sun.

"Anything cool would hit the spot. I enjoy nature so much, and I've walked myself into a real thirst in this heat." Her hand moved the air back and forth at her face. "Another warm one."

"Yes, I'm afraid so. Come on up to the shade of the porch. I'll be right back." Maggie soon returned from inside the cabin with two glasses of ice and a bowl of artificial sweetener packets and lemon wedges. She set them all down on a log, leveled at both ends, to serve as a table between the comfortable rockers. "How long do you plan to stay, Ava?"

"About three months. I'm on a break from my job at the *Tulsa Herald,* and I hope these beautiful surroundings inspire me to write another novel."

Maggie smiled. "You're alone? No young man with you?"

Ava felt her face flush. "Right. Here I am thirty and friends say I'm married to my job. How long will you be here?"

"Well, let's see. John and I have owned this place for over twenty years. We come after the spring semester ends and stay until classes pick up again in the fall. My husband is an ecology professor at Tulsa University. He says he'll retire after this next session, but then, he says that every year. Our dream has always been to live here full time."

Ava relaxed with her tea. "Sounds wonderful. You wouldn't miss some comforts, though?"

Maggie's head cocked to one side. "I'll admit I miss my children and grandchildren when we're here, but I go into Wilburton to use the computers at the library once in a while to email them or do a video chat on special occasions. Otherwise, I get along just fine."

Ava grinned. "And the swing in the tree?"

The woman's face turned red. "I'll admit to a midnight swing a few times, but it's really for the little ones. Our daughter will be here for a visit with her family next Saturday."

Ava measured the cabin in her mind, not much larger than hers. "That sounds nice, but how do you have room?"

"Kids love a tent and sleeping bags." Ava liked Maggie's laugh.

A mustached man with a long gray ponytail hanging from under his cap came walking, almost skipping, out of the woods. "Maggie, look at this beautiful yellow Southern Lady's Slipper. The meadow east of here is full of them. I dug these up to take home for class." He halted. "Oh, we have company. How nice."

Maggie rolled her eyes at Ava. "Only my husband gets so excited about a wildflower." Ava giggled with her.

"Now, Maggie, you know…oh well, excuse me while I get this potted in the greenhouse." He cradled his treasure and disappeared behind the cabin.

Maggie put another lemon in her tea. "He knows I'm just teasing him. Our love of nature and passion to save the planet drew us to each other all those years ago. We met at a used book store in Berkley in 1969. We were both searching for a copy of Rachel Carson's Silent Spring."

"So, you might say it was love at first read? How did you get from Berkley to the Oklahoma hills?"

"The university wanted to ramp up their ecology department back then and asked John to head the effort. It's top notch now."

The man came around the cabin using his jeans to wipe his hands before reaching for Ava's. "Hi, I'm John, and you are?"

"Ava. I have the cabin down the way, on the main road up."

"So, are you just here to relax, Ava?" John sat on the railing of the porch.

"Well, as my boss jokes, I'm here to write the great American novel. Something like that anyway."

Maggie's face perked with excitement. "What do you write about?"

"My first was fantasy, but just whatever fiction comes to me, you know? I have some ideas outlined since I've been here. For instance, can you tell me anything about Marvin Cameron? Mr. Simmons and his son told me a little, but it almost seemed like a legend."

Her new friends gazed at each other before John spoke. "Marvin's okay. He and I get along fine. He's troubled, is all. You'll write about him?"

Ava sat back. "Not him specifically. Davis said he was in Desert Storm. PTSD or something?" Ava was aching to get her notebook out but thought casual conversation might garner more information during this first visit.

John laid his cap at his side. "I guess that's what they call it these days. Post Traumatic Stress Disorder. I remember my older brother came back from Viet Nam and was never the same, but I'm not sure we knew what to call it back then. The family lost track of him some years later."

Ava whispered, "Oh, I am sorry."

Maggie joined in. "Like John said, most days Marvin is fine, but you never know. He only wants to be left alone with his dog. Some beautiful furniture comes out of his workshop, though. Like these rockers."

Another hour of enjoying her new acquaintances, and Ava was ready to return to her writing. She had more information about her character for the novel's outline. As she typed, her father's unexplained mood swings and outbursts of anger came to mind. As a child, she thought she caused it, but what if it was his war experiences which haunted him?

She continued to shape a character inspired by Marvin Cameron. It had not occurred to her yet how she might convey his story. What is the story that people would want to read? A man hidden away intrigued her. She yearned for more.

Chapter 4

The following afternoon, Ava paced her small living space as she pondered if this would be the day. If he was to model someone in her novel, she had to go. The tense memories of interviews with prisoners and angry politicians made her ask, "Why is it so hard to walk up and meet a man and his dog?" The cautions from the locals who knew him rang in her ears as she turned to go.

She stopped at the edge of her desk. As she stared out the window, her hand reached for a notepad and pushed it into her pocket with a pencil. Deep breaths filled her lungs with each step toward the door. She was on her way to meet him.

Ava practiced her introduction while walking along the now familiar path. When she reached the creek, she kneeled down to splash cool water on her face. A moan and desperate whine came to her ears. She sat rigid to listen. Was someone there? Then a louder, pitiful cry. This time, she recognized it as an animal. She knew to be careful. An injured animal can be dangerous.

At first, stillness seemed her ally, but then she had to shift or endure the cramp overtaking her leg. She moved as slowly as a clock on Friday afternoon as she straightened her leg, then stood. Again, the cry of pain came from the other side of the creek and to her left. Her standing motions didn't seem to bring the sound closer, which told her the injured couldn't move. This was her clue to either run in the opposite direction or offer help.

Her feet skimmed through the shallow water until she reached the other side. She followed the faint sounds, then caught sight of a furry leg and tail. A dog? She spoke low in what she imagined were comforting tones. "Now, hush, be still. I'm going to help you. What have you done to yourself?" The dog growled and tried to get up, but two large boulders held his paw captive under the water. Blood was flowing into the creek as he floundered. "Take it easy. I won't hurt you. You're his dog, aren't you?"

She yelled out to the cloudless sky. "Help. Somebody, help." As she looked in the distance where the roof of Marvin Cameron's cabin came into view. "That's where you live, isn't it? You stay still while I get help."

Ava didn't hesitate to run as hard as she could toward the man she had feared only moments before. As she got closer, he was not in sight. Her legs churned like a paddle wheel on a riverboat. She called his name all the while. "Mr. Cameron, your dog. He needs help. Mr. Cameron, are you here? He's hurt. "

She stopped at the base of the steps as he opened his screen door and moved out onto the porch, yelling. "Who the hell are you? Get off my property."

She had to stand her ground. "I found your dog at the creek, sir. He's hurt." That was all she could get out with hands on knees as she labored to catch her breath.

He asked in a rough voice, "What do you know about Major? Present yourself, woman. Who are you? How do you know my name?" In her doubled-over position, he was close enough for her to recognize the butt of the rifle by his foot.

Still, she stood straight and declared between labored breaths, "I'm your neighbor, Ava Hardy. We met at the store, remember? I was coming to say hello when I found him hurt at the creek. Hurry, he's too big for me to handle."

He started running with the limp she had seen at the store, which didn't slow him. He left her in his dust. As she gathered herself to take off after him, her curious mind wondered again about the leg. As she reached the creek, she heard the dog scream out in pain and watched the muscled man hoist the hundred-pound canine over his shoulder. He took determined steps toward the cabin, rifle in hand, leaving her behind with no word of recognition.

She stood there wondering what would happen next. Her feet propelled her after him.

The dog squealed again as she reached the porch where the man kneeled over his friend. "Can I help, Mr. Cameron? I know some first aid."

His voice was impatient. "No. We've been through worse."

"I only want to help." She stepped back with a start as he stood and turned to her with a growl.

"Why are you still here?"

"Well, I intended to have a friendly visit with you, but then I found…what did you call him? Major? Is he all right?"

"He'll be fine. Thank you for your quick action, ma'am. Now, how is it you know anything about us?"

"Others told me your name. I just wanted us to have a better meeting than what happened at the store."

He looked at her hard. "That was you?" He turned away and put medical supplies away in a metal tackle

26

box. "I'm sure those others told you I rarely have visitors."

"I guess since Major brought us together, we could be neighborly."

His voice became a roar. "Did you not hear me? I don't need anyone. Major and I are just fine." His chest rose and fell, rose and fell again as he grabbed the porch railing and took deep breaths, eyes closed. His voice calmed. "Now, you'd better go."

She had come too far to give up. "I understand you make furniture. Was it some kind of finish you had boiling in the pot the other day?"

He stared at her long enough to make her heart race. The dog tried to get up. The man swiveled to face him. "Stand down, Major. You're off duty for the rest of the day." He jerked around as she moved toward them. "Are you nuts, lady? Never sneak up behind me. Ever. Now, I said thank you. It is time you leave."

She stumbled back and said, "I'm sorry. I've done it again."

"What do you mean, again?"

"My dad used to yell at me something awful when I'd do that to him. He said it was something from his combat days. I didn't understand then."

His eyes seemed to soften as he repeated, "You'd better go now."

Before she headed to the stairs, she glanced at the splint on the dog's leg. "You're right. This is a bad day for a social call. We'll try it again another time."

She ran to her cabin and sat on the porch for a few minutes until her shaking stopped. She still wanted to meet Mr. Cameron on better terms. He was unsettling, but seemed somehow familiar. She'd seen him in action.

How would she ever get close enough again to even talk to him? He had a story for her to uncover. One she might tell to the world and would be worth some uncomfortable times. She had hours of work invested in him and couldn't give up.

****

The next day, she sat at her desk, filling her outline with emotions and movements she had observed from Mr. Cameron. He appeared to be in his fifties, graying at the temples, and about six foot three. Arms like fence posts and a barrel chest told her he kept himself in shape. His actions were military and formal. At the sound of a vehicle pulling up next to hers, she peered out the window to recognize John and Maggie's SUV. A smile stretched her cheeks at the sound of her new friend's voice.

"Ava, are you in there? Come on out." Maggie's powerful lungs let out a playful laugh.

Ava walked up to the window of the car. "What are you up to, Maggie?"

"I'm heading into town. Wanna come along? I can show you all the hot spots in Wilburton, such as they are." She had a laugh like a kid on a carnival ride.

"Sure, let me change my shoes and comb my hair. Be right out." She sprinted back to the car and asked as she settled into the passenger seat, "Can we go by the library? I have research to do."

"That's my first stop, to send a birthday greeting to my sister's kid. Researching something for the novel?"

"Yes, I want to learn more about PTSD. I mean, I know some and even wrote a brief article on it in a college journalism class, but I want to know everything I can." She told Maggie about her adventure with Mr.

Cameron and Major. She listened again as Maggie warned her about putting herself in difficult situations.

Ava kept talking. "Somehow, I think he's okay, and I can't get him off my mind. There's a story there and I'm trying to piece it together, but I can't pressure him. There's so much about what he's going through I don't understand."

"Fine. We'll get you a library card and then you're on your own while I email family."

After she found books on her subject, the women had a fun lunch of burgers and frozen custard at a local stand. In the cute downtown, Ava bought an extra box of pencils, a package of clothespins, cotton rope, and a galvanized tub for doing laundry. Her heart jumped at finding four bars on her cell phone and called her mother.

"Hi, Mom. I got here a few days ago. Sorry I didn't call before I went up the mountain."

The familiar voice responded, "You told me there wouldn't be cell service there, but I have been worried."

"I gave you the number to the little grocery. If you have an emergency or something, they'll get word to me. I haven't tried it yet, but they say we might be able to text."

"This is like when your father would go off to the woods. I never got used to missing him. You know, we had our honeymoon at Robbers Cave State Park north of where you are. Your dad thought camping on a honeymoon was the greatest thing ever."

Ava laughed. "And, of course, you went along with the idea."

"You know I would have followed him to the ends of the earth."

"I'm not sure why, but I've been thinking a lot about

Dad since I got here."

"In what way, dear? I know you miss him. I wish you could have settled your differences before he passed."

"Yes, I do, too. I don't mean to worry you, Mom. I'll figure it out. Goodbye for now and I'll call again soon."

On the ride back, Ava thumbed through the books she had checked out. "Maggie, did you know there are four major symptoms of PTSD? It says here, intrusive memories, avoidance, negative changes in thinking and mood, and changes in physical and emotional reactions. Boy, I experienced that when I stepped up behind him. He was like a cornered animal."

Maggie lowered the volume on the radio. "Ava, promise me you'll be careful. Like I said before, he wants to be left alone."

Ava set the books on the floor board at her feet. "You know, like when I saw Major laying there, bleeding in the water, crying and afraid of me, I couldn't let his fear or mine keep me from helping him. Not that I imagine I can help Mr. Cameron, but I want to understand his story so I can write mine."

Maggie nodded, and they rode in silence until the vehicle parked outside the Simmons' store. She turned to Ava to make her point. "We lived through what John's brother did to their family. I know there wasn't much treatment back then, but he became violent with their father. Not only did they exchange blows, he pulled a gun on John. He left and never returned."

Ava lowered her voice and spoke at the risk of sounding like a know it all after so little study. "It could be he realized what his illness was capable of, and leaving was the only way he knew to protect them." She made a mental note of the statement for her manuscript. She gazed up at Maggie's caring eyes. "Don't worry, I won't go back until I understand more. I'd like to think he and I could be friends."

Harriet Simmons greeted them inside the store in a calico bib apron. She straightened her hair back into the bun at her neck. "You ladies come on in here. Maggie, good to see you. Is this Ava? The famous writer Davis goes on about?"

Ava felt her face turn crimson. "I don't know about the famous part, but I am Ava. It's nice to meet you. I hope you don't mind I spend time with Davis on his writing. He is talented and such a polite young man."

"No, we don't mind. He has a dream, for sure. He is a good kid and thinks he's John Boy Walton or something with that journal he's always writing in."

"That's wonderful. Journaling is important for him to develop his skill."

The store keeper moved behind the counter. "What brings you ladies in today?"

Ava stepped to the counter. "I need some bread and a few things."

Maggie chimed in. "Did you get in those cinnamon buns John likes? Better give me two packages and some milk."

After dinner, Ava started the arduous task of reading what she had checked out from the library. The personal accounts taxed her emotions and the text books were dry but full of information. She recognized so much of Mr. Cameron in what she read, and her heart ached to acknowledge his pain. Would he let her near enough to befriend him, or was he determined to remain locked away with his haunting memories?

Ava knew research was important to her writing. Her time with the trauma survivors she read about was an investment in realism. She wanted to know what made her character do and say the things he did. How would he interact with others? The idea this man displayed some of the same stressed qualities she remembered in her father nagged at her. With all the research, was she finding answers to his moody behavior?

Chapter 5

Davis's long frame stretched upward as he stepped down from his truck parked in front of Ava's cabin. "How has it been up here at Kiamichi Retreat?"

Ava gave him a big grin. "Delightful. I had to shoo a squirrel out of the bathroom one morning. Other than that, I'm enjoying the place a lot."

He found his spot atop the step, "I finished the book you loaned me and you were right. I couldn't stop reading."

"I thought you'd like it. Now, tell me what you liked. Describe his style. How did it flow? Anything you would change?"

They discussed writing, the young man hanging on her every word.

"So, how much writing have you done, Davis?"

"Aw, most of it in school. I won a poetry contest in fifth grade. So, I've been at it awhile."

"Have you heard the saying, the only way you become a better writer is to write? Your mother mentioned your journal. It's wonderful you've started at a young age. Do you have a specific genre you lean toward?"

"Maybe mystery or action. Just different things right now. I brought a few short stories. You said you'd read them."

"Sure, let me see what you have there."

While she skimmed over each, he sat drawing in the dirt with a stick.

"I recognize the talent your teacher talks about. I'll read them more thoroughly before we meet again. Your first goal is to find your style. These are kind of all over the place. Don't try to sound like other writers, even if you enjoy reading their books. Just keep writing and, over time, your writing will sound like you, regardless of genre."

"Yes, ma'am." His pencil moved with ease across the pages of the notebook she gave him for recording the tips she offered.

While they took a cookie break, she asked for more information about Mr. Cameron. "Davis, do you know if Mr. Cameron has a family somewhere?"

"Yeah. Dad said he asked him one time. He has a daughter in the Oklahoma City area. I guess he's divorced or something. I mean, he's so cut off up there. Him, his dog, and woodworking. Why would someone want to live all alone like that?"

She wondered, too. "I'm sure he has his reasons."

As Davis readied to leave, she gave him a writing assignment, and he squirmed before responding. "I'm sure you'll find plenty of mistakes."

She hoped her smile was reassuring. "Don't worry. Being willing to have someone critique your work is part of the process. Remember, you asked me to help. Anyway, my review will be fair and intended to help you learn."

"Thank you for all this time you're giving me. I can tell you're going to be an outstanding teacher for me. I'd better get home."

"Here. Take another paperback. It's important you

read all you can, then write every day if possible, to help find your own voice. This action novel should be to your liking."

He read the title and said, "Oh yeah, I saw this movie."

"Aha, then be able to describe what they did with the screenplay. This has been fun. How about 1:00 next Saturday?" If she set their meetings later in the sunshine, it allowed her a shower before greeting company.

She waved as he drove away, then went inside to prepare a light lunch. After washing her few breakfast and lunch dishes, she recorded the additional bits Davis had shared about Marvin Cameron. Her outline was growing.

\*\*\*\*

By studying the library books, she understood more about why Mr. Cameron leered at her with suspicion, and possibly why he preferred to be alone. There were heart-wrenching stories written by and about specific veterans. After learning what causes the disorder and how it manifests itself in humans, she found less written about how families, partners, and friends could help. The world still has a lot to learn. She read passages over several times, feeling herself a little girl again with questions about what went on in her family.

Armed with her new knowledge, she decided it was time to check on Major's recovery and make another attempt at conversation with the reclusive veteran. The fresh air scented by pine and wild flowers rejuvenated her as she walked. No wonder John and Maggie wanted to live here full time. The question to her was whether Mr. Cameron was also here for the beauty, or hiding from something ugly.

She slowed at the edge of the woods to survey his place. Major stretched out on the porch alone. She took three steps forward before the dog rose, ears pointed to the sound, his muzzle twitching, searching the air for identifying scent.

"Mr. Cameron. Yoo hoo, Mr. Cameron. Are you there? It's me, Ava Hardy."

He appeared, hands on hips, at the corner of the cabin. "You don't give up."

Her anxiety caused hesitation, but resolve carried her on. The canine moved down one step, staring at the intruder.

She marveled at how he showed such restraint at not charging toward her. Half way to the cabin she could see his leg, still bandaged. Was he saving himself in the event he decided he must attack? She didn't question whether he would act through the pain to protect his home and master.

Ava approached with her eyes never leaving the wounded dog. "Hey, Major. It's okay, I'm a friend."

His ears moved at the sound of her voice, but his lips split just enough to bare teeth at her continued movement.

"I should have brought you a treat, I guess. Now, now, it's me. I helped you. Remember?" She kept her focus on the dog as she heard the man's voice to her left.

"Stand down, boy." Marvin instructed in a calm voice. "Now approach real slow, ma'am."

The dog began his painful trek down the steps to sit at attention in front of her. She squeaked out the words, "Now what?"

"Put your hand out to him, palm down. He'll smell to recognize you." The dog sniffed, then gave her hand one lick before limping to a shady place under the stairs.

Ava let her head sway from side to side as she wiped her brow and faced the man. "He's amazing, and would have protected you through all his pain."

"It wouldn't be the first time. What are you doing here, after I thought I made myself clear the other day?" He walked around the side of the cabin.

She rushed to catch up to him, then remembered not to crowd him. "I wanted to check how Major was healing. Did you take him to a veterinarian?"

Mr. Cameron kept walking to a workshop beside the cabin. "Didn't need one. He's mending fine. I have to get back to my work."

"What are you building? I find it fascinating how you can take part of a tree and make something beautiful."

He spun around. "You don't listen well, do you? Or is it the understanding part you're slow on?"

Ava stopped in her tracks. "You don't have to be rude. I have done nothing but try to be friendly. Even Major warmed to me a bit." After a moment, she thought he might suppress a smile.

"That's how we're different. Deep down, he likes people." He reached for his axe and walked toward her. She made no sudden movements, her eyes glued to his. He laid the instrument on a table at her side. "I have to say, you've got nerve. Stay back out of the way."

Relief engulfed her at what she decided was almost an invitation to stay. "I will, and I won't stay long. What is it you're making?"

"A child's rocking chair." He straddled a bench with a clamping mechanism in front of him, which held the work piece. He used a two handled cutting tool to make a firm drawing motion back to his body. With this movement, the blade shaved away curls of wood. She noticed how his eyes almost closed and he breathed in air as his muscular arms pulled the slices from the naked limb. He shaped a part of his project with care.

"What tool are you using?"

"It's called a draw knife. I don't use power tools unless I have to."

"It must be sharp. I'm surprised I've never seen one before. My dad had a nice shop in our garage."

He turned the tool over and back in his hands. "Having the handles on each end of the blade gives me control over the depth and direction of the cut as I draw it to me. The wood gives off a sweet aroma with each slice." He went back to work in silence.

"I love the smell of the wood, too. The chair is a custom order?" She inched closer. "How do people find your work?"

"The mountain rumor mill didn't fill you in?" He shook his head. "I take a few things down to the farmer's market some Saturdays."

She chose her words with care, then sensed his comfort at talking about something he loved so much. This seemed a start to him opening up. She excused herself around lunch time. "I'll see you another time, okay?"

He didn't stop his work. "Hmpf. Doesn't seem like I can stop you."

"I'll take that as a yes." She waved at Major as she passed on her way to the woods, and ran all the way back to her cabin. This had been a break through. Patience was the key.

The afternoon gave way to dusk as she worked at the

laptop, adding ideas from her contact with Mr. Cameron. She knew her manuscript had to take better shape soon or time would get away from her. After supper, she heated water to wash her hair in the sink and again to rinse. She sat on the porch, combing through her wavy tresses to dry them naturally in the evening heat. Her own manuscript was never far from her mind, as she read her favorite mystery author.

Chapter 6

Ava wanted something more substantial to fill the pages. Her study of PTSD and the few encounters with Mr. Cameron gave her a direction. Her outline gave her organization. She was ready to start the story.

*The Novel*

*"Pull your head out and get in line there, boot." The drill sergeant shouted across the field at all within earshot. In case he was yelling at him, Maxwell Archer thought he should do as the man said and stay out of trouble. His first day in the Marine Corps, and already he questioned his decision to sign up at eighteen.*

*He should be leaving for UCLA with Beth, his high school sweetheart. He considered her the only good part of the life well-planned by his parents. The controlling plan which drove him to leave. He had to prove himself a man on his own terms and without his family's money.*

*Thirteen weeks later, he enjoyed his after-boot-camp leave, alone on Malibu Beach, close to home. Another six months of training and the Marines considered him sufficiently ready to arm, pack, and ship off to play in the devil's sand box in Iraq. He was part of the United States-led forces in the conflict aptly named Desert Storm. He'd heard the stories about enemy mines and scud missiles destroying tanks and lives alike. There were dark tales of death due to friendly fire, as well. By now, none of it deterred him. He was all Marine. "Ooo-*

*rah!"*

Ava's character mirrored thousands of young men and women caught up in war. Max was valedictorian of his class one day, thrust into life-altering events the next. Had Marvin Cameron felt the same fears as this recruit?

Four chapters of adventure filled her day on the porch until the waning light of evening drove her inside.

\*\*\*\*

A few days later, Ava took a break from writing and returned to Mr. Cameron's cabin. As she approached, she heard a growl but didn't see Major around the cabin ahead. A twig snapped behind her and she turned around to his big brown eyes, staring up at her. His ears relaxed as he stepped toward her.

"Hi, Major. Are you following me?" She held the back of her hand to him and talked in soothing tones. He inched to her and sniffed. She must have passed inspection because he trotted to the cabin with her close behind.

She called out to announce her arrival. "Hello, Mr. Cameron. It's me, your neighbor, Ava. I've been talking with Major and he seemed to invite me in."

The man peered around the side of the cabin. "He could have been bringing you in closer for the kill, you know." He wiped his hands on a rag, then walked toward her.

She swallowed hard. "Well, maybe so. After all, he didn't lick my hand this time."

Her try at humor caused one side of his mouth to rise ever so slightly. He walked onto the porch. "You need to get smart. These woods are full of hunters and nervous pot growers. You know, you could get yourself shot if you don't know the area." He poured two glasses of tea and sat.

She took it as an invitation to join him. The iced tea was most welcome to her parched throat. "Marijuana growers, really?"

"Sure, off to the east. It's legal in the state now, you know. There was a day we'd be up there rousting them out and burning the stuff. Times change."

"You mean when you were a police officer?" She didn't look at him as she sipped her drink.

"You have been getting the scoop, haven't you?"

"I've met a few people. John and Maggie Jenkins, for example. They seem nice."

He looked toward their cabin. "They're decent folks. John and I have fished some downstream where the creek feeds into a little lake." He chuckled. "Left over hippies, I call them."

"I kind of picked up on that, too." Ava remembered she had to be careful not to push for information. "It's beautiful here. I've lived in Oklahoma all my life but never been in these mountains." She thought her story might prompt something from him about his background. It didn't.

She tried again. "Was Major a police dog? Is that where you got him?"

His hand reached down to touch the head of his friend. "We patrolled the streets of Ft. Smith until he took a bullet for me. They said he couldn't serve anymore, but what do they know? I had enough years in to muster out with him, so I did. We've been here six years now."

Her heart beat faster. His words captured her. He was telling his story. She prompted, "Major is sure a fine animal and a good friend. Have you finished the little rocker?" A safe enough question, she thought.

"Yes, they picked it up." He took slow steps off the porch.

She followed him to another structure out back. Inside, her eyes grew large at the sight of his work stacked and hanging in the storage unit. "Oh, my. Are these all spoken for?"

"The ones gathered over here. They'll pick them up at the market next weekend."

She looked through the chairs, tables, and toy sleds. In the back, she saw what she thought to be the roof of a doll house. He pulled a wall shelf out of the way to reveal the Victorian styled structure.

She moved to get a better look. "My niece would flip for something like this. How much?"

"Around $300, depending on style and size. I start this time of year, making enough for Christmas orders. He pulled a rag from his back pocket and swatted at dust on an alder table.

"I'll see what you have when I'm ready to leave for home. I for sure want one." They moved back out into the morning sun. "I guess I'd better go so you can get back to work. Thanks for the tea."

As she walked away, he called after her. "Like I said, be careful."

How could she know if he worried about her out in the woods or what she might find with him next time?

After crossing the creek, Ava ran most of the way back to her desk. There, her fingers moved with speed at the keyboard as her character, Max, continued to come to life.

*The Novel*
*Unsteady hands held the rifle up to his shoulder. His*

troop inched its way toward an enemy-held village, where reports stated they would find the leader of a terrorist group hidden. Even from a safe distance, he heard music and people talking and laughing. In the next few moments, either he or the people behind the sounds would likely be dead.

He spread out on his stomach, ever vigilant, awaiting orders. In the darkness, he heard his friend, Allen Corson, whisper ten feet away.

"Max. Hey, Max, are you scared?"

Max didn't answer, but motioned for his friend to be quiet.

"I'm scared, Max. I'm not ready. Max? You hear me?"

Max swatted the air toward the frightened private as he whispered, "Shut up, you'll get us all killed." He thought he could hear a sniffle. No time to worry about him. He'll be okay when it starts.

The scout who'd gone ahead was running back toward the troop when the firing started. Max could see the flare from rifles in the windows of the building ahead. The returning Marine lunged forward with the force of bullets riddling his body and fell a few feet in front of Allen. As the scout hit the ground, Max felt himself thrown away by the blast of a mine. He saw his captain's mouth move as if to yell, but for Max, there was only the deafening ringing in his ears. In the vacuum, he looked over to the place where Allen and the scout had been. The cavernous hole in the ground smoldered in its emptiness. He forgot the bullets whizzing past him and got up on all fours to vomit.

As the muffled sounds of gunfire returned to his ears, he felt his leader's hand grab his uniform at the *shoulder. "Get up, Marine, find your weapon."*

*It was then he realized, not only was he knocked away from his rifle, he had taken shrapnel in his right leg. Oddly, he felt no pain, only anger. He was determined to do his job and avenge his fellow Americans.*

*The captain ordered artillery strikes which hit on target. Max and his remaining brothers moved in to secure the area and eliminate anything left alive.*

Ava trembled as she reviewed the words on the page. Her body went limp with exhaustion from living the scene with her characters. She wondered what else he must have endured.

Chapter 7

"Maggie, come on, you're the one said we have to leave so early." Ava rapped on the screen door again. Maggie and John exited their cabin and followed her, toting a large cooler between them.

Maggie was smiling and chipper, as always. "Good morning. It's my fault we're running behind. John has been up and ready to go to market since six. He loves talking with the growers. Not only do they learn from each other, but they discuss and solve the world's problems." She laughed and sat in the front passenger seat while her husband settled beside the cooler in the back.

John thumped his wife's arm playfully. "If man would only recognize how nature sustains us, we'd be okay. A lot of these young folks are trying to do what they can to care for Mother Earth."

Ava glanced at him in the rear-view mirror. "You're right, John. I love how passionate you are about it all. I bet you're great in the classroom."

Maggie kicked her sandals off and turned toward her companions. "Ava, how is the writing going?"

"Pretty well. For a first draft, of course. I finished chapter five last night. There's more research to do, though. I want to build my main character, so he's believable. What made him join up? What made him change over time? How he handled everything after coming home. After the farmer's market, I want to return my books to the library and see what else I can find."

John leaned forward to lay his arms on the back of Maggie's seat, her ponytail brushed his skin. He mused, "I wish there was a good bookstore close by. You have to drive a ways for that. Anyway, we'll stop by the used bookstore to see if you find something there."

"Sounds like while I'm on the internet at the library, I'd better see what I can find to order online. Okay, we're coming into town. Who's my navigator today? Tell me how to find the market."

Maggie pointed to a convenience store. "Pull in there first. We'll get some ice for the cooler. The market is in the park a couple of blocks farther down the street. You can't miss it."

She was right. The crowd of shoppers and a sea of vehicles surprised Ava. The closest place she could find to park was in a lot across the street. They walked through the main entrance under a hand painted archway which invited them to Latimer County Farmers Market. John and Maggie spoke with everyone they passed. The rich colors of the produce and aromas of Indian tacos, empanadas, and funnel cakes frying surrounded her. Pop up tents formed the large oval shape of the event space. To her left were the growers, offering selections of vegetables, fruit, fresh breads, meats, and preserves. To her right were crafters. Everything from aprons, jewelry, and stained glass hung from the struts of the tents. At the far end, a bluegrass group provided background to the chatter of the crowd. Children ran to the petting zoo behind the corn dog and smoothie trailers.

"Maggie, this is amazing. I go to the markets in Tulsa and they're great, but I love the community feel here. Everyone seems to know each other. Don't let me buy too much. I have to remember how small my refrigerator is."

"Yes, it's a real gathering spot for the county. We've known some of these growers since they were kids."

Ava's eyes tried to take it all in at once. The morning sun shone on wooden crafts she recognized from Mr. Cameron's shop. As she approached, a carved sign hanging above his space cried out Legacy Trees. "I'll find out what his interesting business name means."

His craftsmanship pulled at her heartstrings even more than when she first peeked into his dusty workshop and storage. She wanted to take one of each polished table or chair home to her apartment. A bronze-skinned man with a braid down his back stood with Mr. Cameron talking as she approached.

When the two men stopped to acknowledge her, she said, "Good morning, Mr. Cameron. Your things are beautiful in the sunlight."

"Good morning, thank you. Meet Gerald Rainwater. He has the booth with his uncle's carved walking sticks down the way."

She shook the man's hand, and the sun caught on a silver and turquoise bracelet on his arm. "It's nice to meet you. Sorry to interrupt."

"The pleasure is mine," he said. "And I must get back to my tent, anyway." He turned to Mr. Cameron and said, "We'll talk more, brother, and don't forget the meeting."

Mr. Cameron walked to a director's chair at the back of his booth and sat. Major lay at his feet, ears aware of all the foot traffic, with shoppers looking over the smaller items inside the tent.

"I see Major came along. Hi there, boy." She kneeled before him. "How does he like all the city commotion?"

"He manages. I wonder sometimes if the noise brings back frightful memories of our work on the streets for him, too. There was always a lot happening. Yelling, gunfire, someone crashing into something. He stays hunkered down right there until I say it's okay for him to venture out. Like I said before, he likes people and interacts with them so I don't have to so much." A slight smile appeared.

Ava looked across the way at the man she just met. "You've known Mr. Rainwater a long time?"

"He's a kindred spirit. Gerald and I met at a group session at the VA Center in Talihina. I don't go much anymore, but he does."

She pointed to his sign. "I notice the name of your business is Legacy Trees. Does it mean something special?"

His face took on a thoughtful, almost reverent pose as he talked. "The trees give us so much, like beauty and shelter. I never want to be someone who just cuts them down to clear space or for firewood or something. I figure my furniture helps the wood live on. A new life and legacy."

She was stunned by his heartfelt response "Nice. A fitting name for what you do."

As she shopped the rest of the market, she looked back to Mr. Cameron's area. Customers paid for items, then he returned to his well-hidden seat. Once, she saw him at the front of his tent talking with a man wearing a Navy veteran's cap. They shared, laughed, and shook hands before the man left. The fact he was more relaxed and friendly with a fellow veteran became clear and made sense to her. "Such an interesting guy. Today, he seems downright likable."

At the library, Ava found more books about war and even some about Desert Storm. She ordered three more from online sources. After, the trio visited the downtown area where Maggie perused boutiques and a spice shop while John entered the garden store. Ava saw the newspaper building and went in. The man at the desk turned to greet her. "Hello, young lady. You want to place an ad or something?"

"No, I'm just visiting. My name is Ava Hardy and I write for the *Tulsa Herald*."

He rose to approach her. "Oh. I'm Stanley Wyatt. What brings you to our little berg?" He opened the swinging gate at the end of the counter. "Will you sit a spell?"

"Thanks, I will. I'm here on a kind of sabbatical, I guess you'd say, to write my second novel."

"Never got around to that myself. You might say I'm more suited to the brief articles and editorials I do here."

"You run it all alone? That must be a lot of work."

"It is, but I get help from some of the locals. Every once in a while, somebody wants to report on the ladies' club or a sporting event."

"If there's some way I could help like that, I'd be happy to while I'm here. It would keep my reporting skills fresh."

"Well, there is a Fourth of July event coming up. You want that story?"

"Sure, and I could get to know people while I capture some interviews." They worked out the details, and she left feeling more like a local all the time.

Chapter 8

The next day, the excitement she felt at Saturday's market and her interaction with Marvin fueled her steps on her morning walk. In the afternoon, she sat on her porch to read. One book the librarian had suggested was by a mother relating what war had taken from her and how she moved on. A short but powerful tale which said, "It's not only soldiers who suffer during and after wars." The story inspired Ava to move on to her own writing.

*The Novel*

*"Nurse! Nurse!" Pain stabbed deep into the muscles of his leg like a hot poker. Max struggled to raise himself in the bed.*

*A nurse came to his side. "Hold on, Corporal, I'm coming. It's too soon for more meds. How about we roll you onto your side for a bit?"*

*"I don't care about the clock. All I know is it hurts like hell. Wait. What do you mean, corporal?"*

*"A field promotion. They said a detail would soon be here with papers and some colorful hardware for your uniform."*

*"How long have I been here?" He reached to scratch the material wrapped around the wound.*

*"Four days. You know, if you had been able to come in right away instead of having to walk on it, the infection wouldn't have been so bad. Doc said the surgery was tough."*

*Maxwell turned his gaze out the window at a scene only he saw. "Ma'am, I had a job to do."*

*After helping him roll onto his side, facing her, she fluffed a pillow and placed it under his bandaged leg. "I know. I've heard all the Marine bravado before. And the Army and the rest." She sat next to his bed, her hand on his arm. "You know, while you did what you had to, I'm sure there's someone back home who is proud and happy you made it through."*

*His heart sank to his stomach. "I haven't heard from anyone in a while."*

*"That's not unusual when you're down range. A few letters caught up with you yesterday, as a matter of fact. Want me to read them for you?"*

*He couldn't hide his smile. "I guess so."*

*"The first one is from Mr. and Mrs. Maxwell Archer, Sr. Your parents? From Malibu, huh?"*

*"Yeah. Wish I was there now. Hey, I'll be able to surf again, won't I?"*

*"Doc says you'll be just fine. It will take time, though. Your mother has beautiful handwriting." The nurse moved closer to him and read the loving words of encouragement and day-to-day news from home.*

*Max fought back tears as his mother's words flowed over him. She always ended with, "We love you, son. We're counting the days until you come home."*

*The nurse put the pages back in the envelope. "What a pleasant letter. The next one is from a Beth Miller."*

*He reached for it as she tore it open and pushed it under his pillow. "I'll read this one later. Sorry, I didn't mean to grab."*

*The nurse stood and laid the letters aside. "A special someone. I'll leave these on your table and read the other two later if you like. You seem tired now anyway, and I have other patients."*

*"I'd like that. Thank you. What's your name?"*

*"I'm Cynthia."*

*"Lieutenant Cynthia, I see. Now I'm really sorry I yelled at you."*

*"We're going to see a lot of each other over the next few weeks, Max. We'll forget the salute for now." She had made him laugh, which eased the pain.*

Ava leaned back from the laptop, pleased at what she saw on the page. Her goal was to show that these soldiers and nurses have families and feelings and their stories need to be told. She jumped to her feet at a gunshot and scream in the distance. Inside, she locked the door behind her and stared out the window into the dark mystery.

****

On Monday morning, Ava drove down the mountain to Simmons' store to make a phone call. Her breath caught, then she let out a yelp of surprise at the sight of a dead bobcat tied to the hood of a pickup at the front steps. She asked as she entered the store. "Is that the awful sounds I heard last night?"

Mr. Simmons looked up from his inventory papers. "Yep, they scream like that when they're hit. Ted Martin, back here on the pay phone, he bagged him. His wife, Margaret, keeps chickens at their place a quarter mile northwest of you, so Ted stays busy controlling the wildlife up there."

"What will he do with it?" Ava shuddered at the picture in her head of blood running down the side of the truck. At least the shots hadn't been Mr. Cameron acting out as Davis had described.

"If he ever gets off the phone, he'll take it into town. Some guy there buys them and gets them ready for museums and such. You had enough of our mountain life yet?"

"No, not at all. It's different from what I'm used to, though."

"I still have some copies of the Sunday *Tulsa Herald* this morning. You interested?" He moved one across the counter to her.

Ava laid her hand on the front page. "I guess I should be, but no. I'll check in with my boss, though, when this Ted gets off the phone." She examined the well-stocked shelves behind him. "While I'm waiting, I'll get some crackers, and more of your wife's green beans, too." She gave and received a short greeting from her sharpshooter neighbor as he left.

She settled to stand by the phone. "Matt? Hi, boss, it's Ava. What's new back in the big city?"

The familiar voice teased her. "Well, she comes out of hiding. Of course, you left me in a pickle here. How's the writing?"

"I'm sure you're fine without me. Listen, I may be onto something here. A story fell into my lap, but it's going to be a lot of work. Have you got a minute?"

"Sure, I only have a paper to get out on time. What's the story? Something good for us?"

"Hmmm, it's my novel. We could work out some excerpts for the paper, though." Her voice quivered with excitement as she relayed the details of what she was writing. "This whole thing about these veterans is so interesting."

"Hold on there, Hardy. You may have hit on something. It's timely for sure. What do you need from me? No more time. You're already killing me."

"No, my request is for help with research. I'd like statistics. You know, how many people have PTSD after war? Do they also have physical injuries? Male to female numbers. How many succumb to suicide? That kind of thing."

"Sounds like you need an assistant."

"So, I was hoping you had someone in the research department there. I'd pay them, of course. "

"What's in it for the paper? I can't just loan you somebody. I do have a paper to get out."

"No way you'll let me forget that. I told you, bits of it in a Sunday feature for a few weeks would help promote the book and build circulation. What do you say?"

He grumbled on the phone. "Oh, okay. I'll put you through to Eddie. Tell him what you want. You can have him for an afternoon."

"I appreciate the help." She arranged for Eddie to email his results. It meant a trip into town to use the computers and printer at the library, but it would save her time and the information would be worth it.

Mr. Simmons said as she hung up the phone, "Big doins next weekend. Fourth of July celebration in Wilburton. Food, crafts, music, games. Folks will be there from all over the area. The wife wanted to make sure I told you. Starts 9:00 a.m. at the city park."

"Yes. Mr. Wyatt asked me to cover it for the paper. I'll see you there."

Chapter 9

The Independence Day event in the park was even larger than the growers' market. Not only were there more food and craft vendors, but added local businesses and area politicians. A large stage showcased different musical performers each hour. Ava used her reporter status to stop by Gerald Rainwater's booth. Something was drawing her to this handsome man.

"Hello, Mr. Rainwater." She looked down to hide the color that filled her cheeks.

"Hello, and it's Gerald, please. How are you enjoying our event?" Sounds of a local country band and the aroma of fried foods and cotton candy filled the air.

"I find it as beautiful as the area. I'm enjoying myself. Your booth is amazing."

"My uncle thanks you."

After a few minutes of timid sharing and pictures taken with her phone, she moved on to Mr. Cameron's area. His vendor booth held the best of his woodworking. They shared friendly greetings.

Ava made inquiries for her interview of him. "If it's okay to ask, how did you decide these mountains would be your home?"

He waved at someone across the park. "I had been over here fishing on weekends. The quiet and nature were exactly what I wanted. The city got to me after being on the force for all those years. Don't get me wrong, Fort Smith has a lot going for it, but I wanted peace and privacy more."

She offered to share her roasted peanuts. "I get it. Sometimes Tulsa is too much for me. I thought you came for the trees. Do you use the ones around here in your furniture?"

"Not much. Most of this area is the Ouachita National Forest. You can only cut what you can use to survive, like firewood. I have sources from McAlester to Little Rock to keep me in business."

She leaned forward in her chair. "How interesting. Is part of it Choctaw land, too? Am I right in thinking Mr. Rainwater is native?"

"That's right." He raised one eyebrow. "Are you interested? He's single, you know."

She felt her face turn the hue of strawberries adorning the funnel cake a young girl carried by. "No, no. I was just asking. What's your favorite piece you've built?"

He walked to the front of his booth and watched the children at the petting zoo. A far-off look overtook him for a silent moment. "A dollhouse. Three-foot Victorian with all the gingerbread trim and bright colors."

"Oh, that sounds amazing. Was it a special order?"

"I made it when my granddaughter was born. She's three, and old enough now to enjoy it."

Ava tried to be careful with personal questions, even though he seemed in a talkative mood. "Do you see her often?"

"No. They live in Oklahoma City to be near my ex."

Ava felt like sinking into the atmosphere. This was almost too personal. "I guess I'll move on to an Indian taco. Nice talking with you, Mr. Cameron."

"You know, why don't you call me Marvin?"

"Fine, Marvin. And remember I'm Ava. You and Major enjoy the rest of your day."

Marvin called to her as she turned to go. "Uh, wait a minute, Ava. I've been wanting to ask you something. John tells me you're a writer. What are you working on?"

A weight pressed on her chest. This was the question she dreaded and made light of the subject. "Oh, you know, all writers are working on a best-selling novel. We're always dreaming of that big prize."

"So that's why you're here? To finish a novel about…what?"

She took a deep breath and dove in. "After meeting you, I have become interested in the difficulties returning veterans experience."

His shoulders stiffened and at first his voice came through as a raspy whisper, then almost a growl. "So, I'm your guinea pig? Your model? Did it occur to you I might not want you writing about me?" He stepped up, his voice surrounding her. "My life is nobody's business. Especially not to some wanna-be Virginia Woolf, young enough to be my daughter."

She rose to her full five foot six inches. Her words coming in a flurry of disdain. "Woah, I didn't say I'm writing about you. What I've seen in you has inspired me to learn more about what we put our young men and women through in the name of peace and supposed harmony in this messed up world. I've read, I've studied, I've tried to understand you, your pain, your solitude, and even your occasional outburst of being an asshole. As a matter of fact, my dad was a combat veteran and I now realize I've dealt with some of this crap all my life. I was hoping my words would help someone else down the road. So don't flatter yourself, Mr. Cameron. No, sir, don't you bother." With a puffed-up attitude, she left to continue work on her newspaper article. He sat down, in a daze.

****

The next day, Ava listened on her porch to a mother bird feeding her squealing young ones. Two chipmunks chased across the yard. Her festival story stalled as she ruminated over her encounter with Marvin. She hadn't dealt with it well, but he didn't have to fly off the handle either.

Just then, Davis's pickup pulled up to her steps. He got out and helped a young lady out as well. Ava thought her about his age and cute in cut-offs and flip-flops.

"Hi, Davis, come on up. Who is this with you?"

"This is Brandy. I figured it would be okay she came. We're going to the lake after you and I finish."

"Of course, come sit down, Brandy. I guess you go to school with Davis?"

"Yes, ma'am, but I'm only a sophomore."

Davis beamed with pride. "She's a cheerleader and on the honor roll."

Ava handed the girl a glass of tea. "No need to blush. Those are good things to have on a college application. Do you have a major selected?"

"Yes ma'am. I love history, and I want to teach at the university level."

Ava's eyebrows raised. "That's wonderful."

The young people sat at the top of the steps. "How've you been, Ms. Ava?" Davis asked.

"A little out of sorts. I had a run-in with Marvin Cameron. Seems he doesn't like the subject of my manuscript."

"See? I told you he's a different one. Want my dad to talk to him or something?"

"No, I just have to figure out how to get back into his good graces. My problem. How did you do with your assignment, and did you finish the book?"

"I did. Boy, they sure change things for the movies, don't they?"

"Something else you have to learn if you want your work to go that direction. It's all about the contract you work out. Otherwise, how did you like the writer?"

"I liked her style. She kept me on the edge of my seat, for sure. Even more than the movie, and I really liked it."

"Anything you would have done differently?"

He scratched his head. "Gosh, I don't guess so. Like what?"

Ava thought about her answer. "Well, what if the main character was a guy instead? Or perhaps another location would have suited the events better."

He shook his head. "I have so much to learn."

She felt a rush of satisfaction in teaching so willing a student and confidence in her ability. "Start reading like a writer. You'll see. Now, for your writing assignment." She grinned and opened the folder which held the type-written pages Davis handed to her. "Nice. Very professional."

He paced in the yard with Brandy as Ava read.

When at last Ava laid the folder on her lap, he made his way to the porch steps, notebook and pen in hand. "Well, how bad is it?"

"Not bad at all, Davis. I'm impressed with your creativity and the engaging main character. There are a few grammar issues to discuss, and I have to ask you about the abrupt ending."

"I was running out of words. You said one thousand words, so I had to keep it short."

"Yeah, sometimes for magazines, contests and such, you have a word limit. We'll go over my notes, then would you like to try again? Finish it this time. Use your words wisely. I know you can make it a lot stronger. I can't wait to see what you come up with."

The two talked about writing and screen plays for a few minutes more before Ava noticed him looking at his watch. "You two kids go ahead. You don't want to miss the best sun at the lake. Brandy, you come again, okay?"

"Thank you, Ms. Ava. It was nice to meet you."

Ava waved to the two as they drove off. She finished work on her story and delivered it to Mr. Wyatt. "Could I watch you print the paper? I never get to see that side of the business back home."

"Of course, I'm sure the equipment there is newer and more sophisticated than mine. You come in tomorrow afternoon and we'll work it up. Your story looks fine."

"I think I'll enjoy this setup better. All that technology takes the romance out of it. I'll be here."

****

Ava sat on the porch the following morning when a rustling of leaves and a snap of a twig alerted her to company. Major bounded from the forest, with Marvin making slow progress behind. Her heart fluttered like the blades of a windmill turning in a prairie wind. Her hand stroked Major as Marvin walked up to the steps. He used his voice in a friendly firmness. "That'll do, Major. Stand easy."

Ava said with a tinge of sarcasm, "Oh, he's okay. At

62

least he and I get along. You're welcome to sit, if you like."

He settled on a step halfway up. "Thanks. Warm morning, huh?"

She nodded. "It sure is. Taking a break from work?"

The friendly chatter did little to cut through the tension between them.

"Yes, the workshop was already as hot as the inside of an old Quonset hut."

Ava thought it was only right to offer him something cold to drink.

He stood and called for the dog to follow. "No thanks. We were just out for a walk and Major wandered over to say hello. Later."

She felt amazed at his departure, then stood to walk the porch. "What was that? Does he suppose it serves as an apology, expecting me to forget the angry words? Not likely. I was wrong, too, though. I should make it up there to work things out with him."

Ava peered over at her laptop, sitting idle on the table. "I must get to writing. It's not like he holds the key to the whole thing." She lifted it onto her lap and added to her story until time to leave for the newspaper office.

*The Novel*

*"Come on, Marine, you can do better than that. Step, step, Max, push, push."*

*"Are you my physical therapist or just enjoying torturing me?" Maxwell bent over in pain.*

*"If you're going to get back to where you were, you've got to put in the work. Enough for today. We'll pick up again tomorrow. Get a cold pack from the nurse and stay..."*

*Maxwell grabbed a towel to wipe the sweat from his*

*face. "I know. Stay off it for fifteen minutes. Like I'm gonna run a race."*

*Nurse Cynthia pushed a wheelchair up behind him. "Your chariot awaits."*

*"Thanks, I'm done for today. He had me going this time."*

*She laughed. "You looked pretty good on the treadmill. Not bad for your second week, anyway. You want to sit up a bit or hit the rack?"*

*"Pull up to the bed and we'll see if I can fall in." Maxwell winced as he transferred.*

*Cynthia offered, "You settle in while I get you a cold pack for your leg."*

*When she returned, she positioned the cold bundle on the healing leg. "There you go. Keep it right there. It will help with the pain. Try to relax enough to nap before dinner."*

*His hand rubbed his face. "Yeah, I didn't sleep much last night."*

*She settled beside him. "Those dreams again?"*

*"Nightmares, you mean. I can't shake them. Will it ever stop? I can't take much more." His hand beat hard into his mattress.*

*She reached to pull his hand back to his side. "It's okay. I know your pain is more than physical."*

*He glared at her. "Really? You think you know? So, you have the same bloody scene running through your brain all the time? One you can't leave behind? You have the demon in your ear telling you to give up? How about when he says everyone around you is the enemy you see in the dreams? I can't shut him up."*

*She spoke with compassion. "You've been seeing Dr. Malcom?"*

*"The shrink? Like clockwork, Tuesday and Thursday 10:00 a.m. For all the good it does. I want my damn leg fixed so I can get out of here."*

*"I know you don't want to hear it again, but it's going to take time."*

*He made a mock salute. "Yes, Ma'am, Lieutenant, I'll be the fine, upstanding Marine."*

*She stood in silence by the bed, then turned to leave. "Tomorrow then, Corporal."*

Ava left Max to stew and whine while she showered and dressed to meet Mr. Wyatt. Her afternoon was satisfying for her as together they worked the old equipment to get the news out.

She pushed the hair back from her face. "This gives me a whole new appreciation for the small-town newspapers still struggling to stay alive. This has been fun for me."

He watched her wipe down the press. "So, you think you'd like this life? You know I'm going to be retiring soon."

"Oh, don't tempt me, Mr. Wyatt. I have a good job in Tulsa. This will probably always be an unfulfilled dream for me." Still, she thought about his words through the night.

Chapter 10

Her manuscript took shape as Eddie's research back in Tulsa filled in a lot of the gaps for her. Disappointment ate at her over not having Marvin's personal experiences and she missed their friendly chats. She may have to get used to never getting the help from him her novel needed.

Instead of writing on the porch, this time she ventured through brisk winds onto the trail. At the creek bank, her feet moved the cool water back and forth. Squawking from a flock of birds raised her eyes to the sky. The pages of her notebook flew back and forth in the breeze as she tried to write. A buck, then a doe splashed through the shallow water. A rabbit family scurried from the bushes. "What the heck? Where are you guys running off to?"

She headed to her cabin when the gale became more intense and the sky darkened. That made her think it was bad weather moving in to upset the animals this way. Half way there, her nostrils and eyes burned from smoke. It wasn't a tornado, but wind fanning the flames of fire. She held her ears as the siren filling the woods called out its warning. Her legs churned faster.

When she arrived at her cabin, a man's voice called to her over her coughing.

"Ava, where are you? Ava Hardy, answer."

She stopped at the sight of Marvin's pickup. "I'm

right here." She saw him then, mouth and nose covered by a bandana. "The siren must be for fire. The smoke is terrible." She kept one hand over an ear, the other covered her nose and mouth.

He spoke through his coughs, "Yeah, the wind is blowing a fire and its smoke in this direction. We have to get to safety. Jump in your car and meet everyone else down at Simmons' store. Major and I will follow in my pickup."

Ava started for the cabin. "I have to get my laptop. My manuscript."

He swung around to grab her. "No." he yelled through the make-shift mask. "That's crazy. Get out of here."

She struggled, but couldn't break away from him. "I haven't backed up the last four chapters. You'd love for everything I've written to get trashed. You can't stop me." His grip on her arm tightened like a vise.

"You'll get in your vehicle or I'll drag you to mine, and I'm already dealing with an excited dog in there. Don't fight me, I mean it."

The intensity of his voice and the glare in his eyes alarmed her. The warning signal shrieked on. She got in her car and headed down the mountain, tears streaming down her face. She screamed at the windshield and beat the steering wheel. "I hate you, Marvin Cameron. You make me furious and I wish I'd never met you. "

At the store, Mrs. Simmons welcomed her with a face mask. "This will help with the smoke."

Behind the counter, Charles Simmons talked on a ham radio. Maggie and John were there, as were neighbors she had yet to meet.

Maggie motioned for Ava to join her. "Here, sit

down. Charles is talking to the ranger station. We're okay for now, but last time this happened, we had to caravan south to Hugo, and the year before, east to Mena, Arkansas. Depends on the wind direction at this point. Have you been crying? We'll be okay, I promise."

"I'm so mad I could spit. Marvin Cameron, damn him, wouldn't let me go in the cabin for my laptop. If I lose even part of my manuscript, so help me, I'll never forgive him."

John joined in. "Is he coming? He knows the drill."

Ava's angry words surprised her. "I don't care if he gets stuck up there."

Charles stood before the group. "Ranger Stanley says to stay together here, but be ready to move. The front line hasn't reached the county line to the north, but the high winds still have it pushing in our direction. Weather folks are telling him they expect the winds to change to the northeast tonight or tomorrow and there's a slight chance of rain. Let's pray for lots of rain."

John stood to speak to the crowd. "We have all the doors and windows secured to keep most of the smoke out. With your air filter running, Charles, we should get some better air quality in here soon. Keep your masks on for now, people."

Ava wiped away a tear. "Why do we have to stay here? Can't they blow the sirens again if it gets too close?"

Maggie shook her head. "No. You can wait too long. These things move fast. With so little communication available, it's best we stay together. At least this way we know everyone is safe."

Ava still had questions. "Is this because it's been so dry this summer?"

John had the answers. "That or a careless camper. With this climate change, though, everything is upside down. There's not enough rain. We had three significant fires last season, and we're lucky this is the first one this year. It used to be we might see one every five years or so. If the government would only—"

Maggie jumped in. "That's enough, Professor. No ecology lectures today."

Just then, Mr. Cameron and Major rushed in, reeking of smoke. The dog laid down, rubbing his eyes with his paws. Marvin tucked something under his arm while he replaced his bandana with a real mask.

Though his back remained to her, Ava's anger boiled over. "You sure took your sweet time. We might have all been on our way out of here by now. Not that I would cry over leaving you behind."

He stood motionless for a moment, then turned and walked toward Ava. He held her laptop out to her.

Stunned and red-faced, she accepted it without looking up to him. Her throat opened enough to whisper, "Thank you." He found a chair on the opposite side of the room.

Ava didn't dare look at Marvin. "Maggie, I'm so ashamed. I talked awful about him. Why would he risk looking for my computer to bring it down to me?"

"You never know what people have inside. You're not quite used to seeing him let the good guy out. Don't worry. You two will patch things up right away."

"I hope so. Deep down, I always felt he was a nice guy."

After a day and a half of sitting in chairs and sleeping on pallets and in vehicles at the store, word from the forest ranger released them to return to their homes.

At least she had met more neighbors over the sandwiches Mrs. Simmons prepared. The red sky of fire moved deeper east into the Ouachita Mountains, while they got into their vehicles to leave. Ranger Stanley advised them to stay alert. He wouldn't sound the alarm again unless danger was eminent.

During that night, Ava ran outside to see if she was imagining the sound of raindrops on the cabin's tin roof. With arms outstretched, she allowed the welcome water to hit her cheeks. If only this would help the fire fighters. She returned to bed, able to sleep better than before.

****

After breakfast the next morning, she stared at the screen of her laptop. Focus was hard, and the words weren't coming. The air still carried the odor of burning forest as she worked on the porch. She heard movement in the woods. Major bounded up to her porch, where she kneeled to rub his thick coat. He smelled of a dog covered in smoke that had recently made his way through a wet forest.

Marvin emerged from the trees. "Stand down, Major. Don't bother the lady."

Her hand stayed on the dog's back. "That's okay. I enjoy his company."

Marvin moved a little closer. "I checked with Charles, and the ranger told him we're safe. They only have it thirty-five percent contained, but the winds continue to push it northeast."

Ava squirmed. "That's great. I guess that bit of rain helped."

"Yes. They got heavier moisture around the immediate fire area than what we saw here. It'll still take some time to put it all out." He looked out into the trees.

"Look, I've done a lot of thinking since our talk. I owe you an apology. One reason I moved here was privacy, and I guess I'm overly protective of that sometimes."

Ava swallowed hard before speaking. "That's understandable. If I'm honest, I thought you wouldn't like it. That's why I said nothing earlier. My intentions are good, though. It's fiction, but I want to make sure the story is realistic. It would be great if someone who has been through what you have, or maybe a family member, would find some comfort or understanding from my humble words."

"Right, but it's hard to talk about. I went to group sessions when I first got back, and we all thought nobody else could understand. So, it's easier to block people out."

Ava looked over to her notepad, but left it lay there. This was two neighbors talking.

"I should have told you what I was working on, but didn't know how to ask for your help. Then when you found out, I was mad at myself and felt embarrassed. I lashed out at you to cover my anger at my stupidity. It's not like I'm writing about you, but about the things that vets with PTSD go through."

She broke the awkward silence, which held them captive. "I didn't thank you properly for getting my laptop to me the other day. I was just scared, upset, and over reacted. The cloud holds most of my writing. I wouldn't have lost that much."

Amid the gentle sounds of nature, Marvin filled his lungs, then reached for the stair railing to pull himself up without turning around. "I can't promise anything. I just wanted to apologize." He snapped his fingers for the dog to follow. "Let's go, Major."

Ava watched the two companions disappear into the trees. "Well, anyway, that wasn't a definite no. I'll have to go easy until he's ready, and remember I'm not interviewing some stranger for the paper. It's possible he's becoming a friend." The screen door creaked as she went inside to her laptop.

Chapter 11

Ava left early to visit the Veterans Center just outside Talihina, thirty-eight miles to the southeast. She had many questions that neither books nor Marvin could answer.

Her 11:00 appointment with the director left time for breakfast at a local diner. She slid into a booth and craned her neck to look at the vintage décor until the server brought a menu and hot coffee.

"Your first time here, sweetie?" The woman stood back with the pot steaming.

"Yes, I've never had the pleasure. It smells like my grandma's kitchen."

"Have any idea what you want? Joe's at the grill this morning. He's the best."

"Well then, I guess I'll have the works. Two eggs over easy, bacon, toast, grits if you've got 'em."

"I'll have it out here before you can finish that first cup."

Ava watched the woman stop at a table in the front window to pour coffee for a group of men she thought must be regulars. Another example of the warmth of a small town.

Hunger satisfied, she drove two miles northeast of town to the 600-acre facility that served veterans in the area. As she started up the long driveway through abandoned buildings and warehouses, once-plush lawns and a lake surrounded by cattails and colorful wild flowers greeted her. A cracked and unlevel sidewalk led her to the entrance of the sizeable brick building. The interior looked much nicer. She approached the reception desk. "The director is expecting me."

A young attendant gave her a shining smile. "Ava Hardy? Yes, ma'am, have a seat and I'll let Mrs. Braxton know you're here."

Ava observed men and women walking the halls or moving in their wheelchairs. A stout woman with red hair walked to Ava with hand extended. "Ms. Hardy, welcome. I'm Milly Braxton. Come on in the office so we can talk and I'll get a better idea of how I can help you today."

Ava took a seat across from the woman at the desk. "I appreciate you seeing me. Like I said when I called, I'm writing a novel about a man who comes home from war and has PTSD. I've been studying, but I'm sure there's a lot I don't understand."

The woman shifted in her chair. "May I ask how you came to this topic?"

Ava felt the stare of skepticism. "I've met a man who survived Desert Storm but still has mood swings, and well, let's say, occasional difficulty getting along with others because of it all. My writing is fiction, but accuracy is important to me. A reader might learn from something I've written." She sat straighter. "I want to honor these veterans, not exploit their pain."

The corners of the director's mouth hinted at a smile. "We help them deal with it by getting them to talk through pain and memories. Some require medication to handle stress, or simply to sleep. I find getting them involved in social activities is key. And, of course, not everyone here has PTSD."

Ava had questions. "The place is nice, but I noticed several abandoned buildings on my way in. Is it mostly a medical facility or, more like a senior apartment they might find in town?"

The woman straightened things on her desk. "We work hard to provide a suitable home. We think they deserve it. The center is set up for all veterans, but fewer take advantage of the services than when it was built after WWI. As insurance and social services are more readily available now on the outside, not all buildings are needed anymore. We have more of an advanced age. Some need full-time nursing care and others choose this as the place where they live out their lives." Mrs. Braxton stood and motioned for Ava to follow. "It's time for chow around here. I'll introduce you to some of our residents. Have you eaten? You're welcome to join us."

Ava's hand went to her belly. "Oh my. I had the biggest breakfast ever in town. I'll have a tea, though."

As the two women entered the dining room, heads turned and a few hands went up in a wave of greeting. Silver hair dominated the room, with attire that varied from men in sport shirts and pajama bottoms to women in matching blouse and slacks. So many questions came to Ava's mind.

"I suppose they come from all walks of life. That must make your job a balancing act."

Mrs. Braxton smiled. "Each person is different."

"May I speak to some of them?"

"Yes. Of course, you understand the use of their names and stories would be up to each resident. I can't provide information about them because of the HIPPA regulations. Let me introduce you to a few. Some will talk to you and some won't. I'll get my tray of food while you get to know them."

She introduced Ava to two men huddled over their food at the first table. "Jimmy Allen, Butch Davis, this is Ava Hardy. She's a writer and may have some questions for you."

Ava inched toward the men and attempted to calm her awkwardness with small talk. "Mr. Allen, your lunch sure looks tasty."

"Now, young lady, you call me Jimmy. We don't stand on rank at this table. One thing is for sure, they feed us good all right. Are you visiting someone in particular? What did you say your name was again?"

She kneeled closer as he cupped a hand around his ear. "I'm Ava Hardy. I came to meet folks who might talk with me about serving. Thank you for your service, by the way."

The man across the table looked up from his meatloaf to proclaim, "I'd do it again if they'd let me."

Jimmy chuckled. "Yeah, Butch, you with that stiff leg and my bad heart. We'd give 'em hell, anyhow, wouldn't we?"

Ava chose her words to keep the conversation going with the second man. "I'm sorry. Butch is your name, sir? When did you serve?"

He raised to attention in his chair. "Butch Davis, Corporal US Marine Corps WWII. Jimmy here was Navy in Vietnam."

Her heart beat like a cavalry drum. "I guess you guys had unique experiences coming back home. Can we talk about some of those?"

The two proud veterans shared a glance as both pushed their empty plates away. Butch spoke first. "Yes,

Ma'am, Jimmy doesn't talk about it much, but it was tougher returning from those jungles to this one. They welcomed my buddies and I back from Europe with hero parades, and Jimmy and his guys were spit on. Can you believe it? That's just not right."

They sat in silence until Jimmy took a toothpick from behind his ear and chewed as he formed words around it. "It made it tough for sure, and a lot of us still share some of the hard stuff."

Ava almost whispered the words. "Like what, Jimmy? What do you mean?"

"The nightmares, alcohol, losing family, you name it. Remember, we were kids over there. Some handled it better than others, but the point is, after what we saw, we have a bond others can't understand."

Ava sensed this might be enough for them for one day. She rose to thank the men and excuse herself. "I'd love to hear more of your stories. Can I come visit you again sometime? I can't make any of it up to you, but I can listen. And if you don't mind, what you share will help me build the main character in my novel."

Butch reached to shake her hand. "Fine with me. You should talk to old Frank over there, if he's having a good day."

She held his hand tighter. "He has some good stories, huh?"

"Oh yes, ma'am. He used to be my roommate, but he'd wake me up screaming about incoming and crying for his mama. I couldn't handle that. They found him a new place."

She shook her head. "I'd better move on. Thank you for talking with me."

Butch gave a quick salute.

The hallway walls full of photos of men and women in uniform caught her eye as she made her way back to the office. Down the way hung a bulletin board with snapshots of groups fishing, sitting in the stands at a baseball game, or a picnic on the grounds of their group home.

Mrs. Braxton's voice came over Ava's shoulder. "We take them on outings when weather and health matters allow."

"I'm glad to hear it. Do their families come often?"

The director brushed a speck of something from one of the picture frames. "Most come as often as they can. Some only see family once or twice a year. Others don't have anyone left." She smiled and asked, "Have you met Ms. Amanda? We'll find her in the library about now. She straightens the books every day after lunch. At least, the ones she can reach from her motorized chair."

Ave stopped. "Wheelchair? Was she wounded?"

Her host grinned. "Follow me. I'll let her tell her story."

The library was small but well stocked. The petite woman dusting books looked around when Mrs. Braxton raised her voice to call to her.

"Ms. Amanda, I have someone who wants to meet you. This is Ava Hardy, and she's a novelist. Someday you might see her book in here."

A smile stretched the old woman's wrinkled face as she extended her hand in greeting. "I'll take care of it, too. Come on in, young lady. Closer. I won't bite."

Ava took the frail hand in hers. "I'm glad to meet you, and thank you for your service."

The elderly woman looked Ava in the eye. "What branch were you in, hon?"

Ava felt warmth come to her cheeks. "I never signed up. I went to college and then got right to work."

The old woman settled back in her chair. "That's okay. We all have our path to follow. You know, I'm going to be one hundred and two next week. They're having a big party for me. A newspaper reporter was here yesterday or the day before. I can't remember which."

"But you don't look a day over eighty, MissAmanda." The time-worn eyes lit up. Ava asked, "So, you were there for WWII?"

With shoulders set back, she answered, "Yes, I was. I did my part to patch them up for return to duty or get them on the train back to Mama. They were so young and most had never been away from home. Our work was important. We were there to take care of them." She blushed. "I married one of the cutest. Sixty-three years and two children." Her face turned dark. "They're all gone now."

"Oh my." Ava's heart ached for her. "Grandchildren?"

The smile returned. "Six. Three great-grandchildren and two great-greats. Everyone's so busy, I don't get to see them often enough."

"I'd love to visit you again. Would that be okay?"

"Of course. You'll bring me your book."

"Before I go, may I ask, did you have trouble acclimating to civilian life when you came back from the war?"

The old woman let out a sigh, then looked right through Ava to a scene from memory. "It was different back then. We did what we had to and didn't complain. I mean, you just didn't. Like when I lost the use of my legs to MS a few years ago, I adapted. Just glad to be alive."

Ava finished her tour with Mrs. Braxton and reviewed what she'd learned as she drove to the cabin. She wanted to record it all. There'd be a lot of writing to do to complete her day.

*The Novel*

*"Beth, I don't want to go tonight."*

*"But Max, my parents are expecting us. I'm running out of excuses." Beth pleaded.*

*Max paced. "Don't you get it? I can't sit there over your mother's pot roast and listen to your father talk about how great the Air Force was for him for twenty years. Like I ducked out on purpose or something. I don't know what he wants me to say."*

*"That's not it. He wants you to be as proud of your service as he is of his. Maybe he's just trying to connect with his future son-in-law." Her eyes searched his for the needed answers about their future.*

*"Proud? By God I'm proud. I'd go back now, but they won't take me. See, nobody understands. They made me a Marine, a warrior who did every hellish task assigned. Then it seemed so simple for the system to toss me aside like an empty box of shells. Proud? The darkness of what those tasks were hasn't dimmed my pride. It's all I have left." Max folded into her arms.*

*Beth ran her fingers through his hair until he calmed. "Baby, I know it's hard. I wish I could help, but I know nothing to do except help you move forward. Your leg is so much better and the doctor said physically you're cleared to get work, or how about university?"*

*"I can't seem to focus on anything. I don't know what I want to do." He raised up, kissed her, and said, "Except marry you." He grinned. "What time is dinner?*

*I'll be ready."*

*"Thank you. I promise we'll make an early evening of it." The touch of her hand sent chills through him.*

Ava stretched back from the computer to think about what she'd written. "Okay, we're seeing some of his turmoil since he's home. I have to add a lot more about his day-to-day life." She stood to stretch and move around the room. After rinsing her tea glass at the sink, she looked at her watch and declared aloud. "It's midnight already." Her time in the mountains ticking away weighed on her. "I'd better get a little sleep and hit this hard in the morning."

## Chapter 12

At Simmons' store, Ava dialed her mother's number. "Hi, Mom. How's things in Sand Springs?"

"Good. However, the air conditioning man just left. Looks like the old unit is about done. How are you?"

"It's wonderful here, Mom. I get so much writing done, and I'm finding I take after Dad more than I thought. Not only the writing, but loving the outdoors, too."

"You were his little sidekick when you were young. I was about to leave to pick up Madeline for a movie. Did you need something, honey?"

Ava's heart dropped. "No, not really. Well, yes. I have a question if you've got a minute."

"Shoot."

"Dad never talked about his time in the army, but I saw his medals and he attended those reunions a couple of times. Was he ever diagnosed with PTSD?" She felt a fist gripping her chest as she waited through the silence on the phone.

"Your father was a good man."

"I know, Mom. He always took care of us. There were times, though, I wasn't sure he was with us, even though we sat at the same dinner table. We always said he was in one of his moods." Silence again. "Mom? I'm sorry. I guess this isn't the time."

"It's okay. I was texting Madeline I might be late.

Listen, when he came back from 'Nam, not too many knew what to call what he was going through or how to help. We had some rough times, but we worked through it together. Of course, we tried to keep it away from you girls. The anger, tears, trips to the cabin, nightmares, and yes, a lot of therapy for both of us after they offered it. Why ask now?"

Strength drained from Ava. "My novel. This syndrome is playing a big part in the story. I know you're supposed to leave now. I'll call later."

"Yes, we can talk again if you have more questions."

"You've given me a model for a strong female character who stood by her man. Thanks."

Ava hung up the phone and spoke to Mrs. Simmons. "I'm having dinner at the Jenkins' tonight and should take something. I'll have some of your green beans."

Mrs. Simmons moved to the shelf holding her filled jars. "I'm afraid I didn't put up enough this time. We're all out. How about some corn or carrots?"

"I'll sure miss those green beans. My favorite snack at night. Okay, give me one of each."

"How's the book coming along?"

"It's going well. Lots more work than I expected, but I'm enjoying it. I wanted to tell you Davis is sure making our sessions fun. He is so eager to learn."

"He told us you're a fantastic teacher, and he's going to get you to apply for a job at Eastern. It's a good college."

Ava couldn't hide her smile. "He's too nice. Yes, working with him has got me thinking about teaching, but I have a job."

On the short drive to the cabin, Ava couldn't stop pondering what Davis had told his parents.

\*\*\*\*

"Maggie, do you think it would be okay to invite Marvin for lunch or dinner? Would he come?" Ava paced the neighbor's living room with her tea.

"Honey, it would be fine. All he can do is say no. Are you still worried about your little tiff with him?"

"Yes. We apologized, but I haven't had the nerve to visit him up there since. Even if he doesn't help with the book, I don't want to leave it this way."

Maggie adjusted the ribbon, holding her hair back. "Here's what we'll do. I'll have John go up and ask him here for hamburgers over the campfire. Nothing unusual there. Then you can meet in neutral territory. How about it?"

"That would take some pressure off. Thanks. I'll bring something for dessert." Ava relaxed as they planned the event.

\*\*\*\*

When Ava arrived on the arranged night, John's face reflected the glow of the orange flames as he stoked the campfire. She greeted him as she approached. "This looks great. I brought the makings for smores. I'll grab some sticks for roasting the marshmallows." She almost ran over Major when she turned to go into the woods. She kneeled to accept his kisses and looked up to see Marvin walking toward her.

He stopped, then looked from Ava to John and back. His smile surprised her. "A party, huh? Nice night for it."

She took a deep breath and her heart pumped at a normal pace again. It was going to be a good night after all.

Maggie brought the meat, bread, potato salad, and chips to the small table by the fire. The group talked and laughed until the moon shone full. John opened the cooler. "Another beer, Marvin?"

"No, two is my limit, even though I'm walking home." He chuckled. "John, it doesn't mix well with my meds, you know?"

Ava could have filled her notebook with the silence before she said, "I want a chair for my porch like you made for them. A place for guests to sit."

Marvin grinned. "I have some made and can bring one over for you."

Ava gave a child-like giggle. "Oh, I can't wait. It will perk up my place for sure. Come by anytime." She was enjoying his company, and wondered who this guy was and where he'd been hiding? She chose her words with care. "How did you get into police work, Marvin?"

Maggie's eyes cut to Marvin's face. Her voice wavered as she stood to say, "Anyone want more tea? There's plenty"

He smiled to calm his friend. "It's okay, Maggie. Yes, I'll have a glass." After swallowing hard, he said. "I bounced around for a while, going from job to job. It took me a while to realize I missed the regimented lifestyle the Marines gave me. The police work offered that, and I'd like to think I helped people. The wife couldn't handle it, though. You win some, you lose some, I guess. I'm not sorry about the career I chose, though."

After enjoying her friends and more discussion, Ava left with a new view of the man, Marvin Cameron. At two in the morning, she put her laptop away and enjoyed a satisfied sleep.

**** 

Ava sat outside the Wilburton library eating an ice

cream bar and waiting for Matt to answer her call. Even with the air conditioning on, the car felt like an oven. The rough voice of her boss came on the line.

"What is it, Hardy? You coming back soon? You know, I've still got a newspaper to put out."

"Don't start. I still have time left. Hello, by the way."

"How's the novel coming along? When can we publish some of it?"

"Whoa, not for a while. I have the start of something exciting, though. I'll send it through my editor as soon as I get back."

"You know, Billy Jackson has been eyeing your desk. Left me a sample of his writing the other day. You'd better be careful about getting back here on time."

"The kid from the mailroom? You're trying to scare me with a high school intern from downstairs? Give me a break. Of course, it is beautiful here. If you decide to fire me, it might not be so bad. I've gotten a ton of work finished." She grinned at the phone.

"Hey, now. Not funny. You get yourself back here on time. How am I supposed to run a newspaper like this? Why did you call, anyway?"

"I wanted to check in with you and thank you again for Eddie's help." She licked the ice cream before it dripped on her lap. "You know, they have an opening in the English department down here at Eastern Oklahoma State College? Maybe I'll check it out." She grinned into the phone.

Matt's voice roared through the phone. "Now you listen to me, Hardy, I'm not kidding. You get yourself back here."

"Ha ha. I was just making sure you're listening. I'll

let you get back to putting out a newspaper." She laughed as she ended the call.

Ava finished her treat while imagining what fun it might be to stay in the mountains. With the last bite, she brushed the thoughts aside and got her mind back on task before she entered the library to use their internet connection for more research.

A rush of air conditioning stopped Ava in the entrance to the library. She stood and let the cold air wash over her while she pulled her damp shirt away from her back. Small children running to story time jolted her back to reality.

The friendly reference librarian came to her. "I found some more books to help you. Do you want to see?"

Ava followed the woman to her desk, where the half dozen books lay stacked at one end. "Thank you. I'll look them over."

She headed to her usual table in the corner, where sunlight shone across the room from a large window. The man Marvin had introduced as Gerald Rainwater was there surrounded by books, paper and pens. Her chair scraped across the floor as she prepared to sit down. He looked up and nodded a greeting, then returned to his work. His dark hair shined in the light from the window, and the polished silver of his turquoise and coral jewelry gleamed each time he moved.

She skimmed the new books, then opened her laptop to work.

After an hour, Gerald sat back to stretch. "Pretty tough reading you have there, Ms. Hardy. "

She glanced at the volumes before him. "I see we have similar choices. I'm writing a novel, so this is research for me. And you, Mr. Rainwater?"

He straightened his books, then said, "I'm studying to be a counselor at one of the veteran centers. They sure helped me. I want to pay back."

Her hand raced to her pen, sensing the possibility of an interview. "May I ask some questions about all that?"

He cocked his head to one side. "You just met me and already writing things down? How about a cool drink at the sandwich shop across the street?"

She responded with a tease in her voice. "Oh my, Mr. Rainwater, aren't you forward, though?" They shared the humor as she packed her laptop and rose to gather her books. "Let me check out a few of these and I'll meet you there."

Ava left her vehicle parked at the library and walked to the meeting place. That gave her time to plan questions she might ask him. She pushed the door to the cafe open and looked around for her new acquaintance. He waved from a booth on her right. She fanned herself with a small notebook as she joined him. "Sorry it took so long. I put the books in my car, but I brought something to take notes, if you don't mind."

He shrugged. "Let's order something and see how it goes."

She got out of the booth. "I'll get the drinks. What would you like? I'm having sweet tea."

"That suits me. Here, my treat. After all, I invited you." He handed her a ten-dollar bill.

After a while, they fell into an easy banter. She detailed her background and learned he was taking classes at the local college while working part time at a Jiffy Lube. After a refill of tea, she described her manuscript and her wish to have veterans' tales give her book authenticity. "Do you mind some questions?"

He didn't hesitate. "I don't mind. After all, telling my story will be part of counseling others."

"Right. So, tell me, what drew you to the service?" She opened the notebook and readied her pen.

"I enjoyed high school and lettered in football and baseball, but I didn't know what I wanted to do with my life. The only job I held was at the tribal car wash between sports seasons. The day all the armed forces recruiters came to our high school, I saw opportunity I would not have otherwise. Being native in Oklahoma isn't always all it's cracked up to be unless you're a famous artist, musician, or politician The men in my family have always served. I know as far back as my great-grandfather who was one of the twenty Choctaw code talkers for the army in WWI. So, I followed in their footsteps."

"I guess that means you're of the Choctaw tribe?"

"Yes, I am."

Ava thought a moment before saying, "I've only heard of the Navajo code talkers in WWII."

He shook his head. "Not unusual. First, the government instructed the men like my great-grandfather not to talk about what they had done in the war. Then, the Choctaw are a humble people. We let others brag about us. I knew little about it until President Geo. W. Bush awarded them the Congressional Medal in 2008."

She wasn't sure what to say. "Better late than never, I guess."

"Yes, but what's sad is the French recognized and thanked them long before their own country. Not surprising when you realize the US didn't even give natives citizenship until 1924."

She took a sip of tea and calmed her embarrassed heart before asking, "How were you received in the Army?"

"Some called me Okie and others Kemosabe. It was okay. I'm proud to be from Oklahoma and especially of my Choctaw heritage, so they couldn't take those from me. It wasn't all bad either. Some are still my friends."

"I'm sure it didn't keep you from doing your job. Where did you see action?"

"Afghanistan, two tours. I'm thinking you want to know about coming home. Right?"

She felt her face flush. "Yes, if you don't mind. Thanks."

He moved his glass aside and leaned forward. "I had issues like a lot of men and women. You can't unsee the things we saw or change the outcome for those who didn't get to come home. At first, I fought the help that was offered, like most do."

She took more notes. "What made the difference for you?"

"A counselor took a genuine interest in me. I mean, he came to the house to find me when I didn't show up for sessions, and I could call him anytime to help me out of the darkness. I want to do these things for someone else."

"So admirable, Gerald. Am I keeping you from something? I'm enjoying this, but I didn't mean to take over your afternoon."

He sat back. "You mean evening? It's almost six o'clock. How about we order dinner? Then you'd better start your drive before dark sets in. Will burgers be okay?"

"An onion burger for me. If you'll order for us, I'll visit the ladies' room." While washing her hands, she looked at the joy on her face and heard her words coming back to her from the mirror. "I like this guy. He's so handsome, too. Stop it, Ava, you're here to work."

Back at the cabin, her fingers flew across the keyboard of her laptop. Finding someone to assist her with authentic experiences thrilled her. She had found a friend, and they planned to meet again. The anticipation kept her awake late into the night.

****

"Maggie, he's so interesting." Ava's words came fast, like an auctioneer. "Marvin introduced us. He's proud of his heritage and his service. We're having dinner next Tuesday. I have a hundred more questions for him."

Maggie waved her hands for Ava to catch her breath. "Whoa, girl. Is it about the questions or something else? Maybe a new romance?"

Ava lifted a hand to cover her face. "Oh, I don't know. It doesn't make sense. I just met him and besides, I won't be here much longer."

"You shouldn't limit your feelings, though. Have fun with it and see what happens."

Ava leaned in. "He's so nice, Maggie, and easy to be around, you know? That's hard to find these days."

Her friend grinned, "And it doesn't hurt that he's easy on the eyes."

Now Ava's face was all red. "You know it."

Chapter 13

Ava approached Marvin's cabin with care. After calling out to him, she heard Major barking as he ran toward her from the workshop. He slowed as he recognized her. A gentle rub of his head was her greeting.

Marvin joined them. "Hello. You found the chair I left for you the other day?"

"Yes, it's gorgeous. I'm sorry I wasn't there. I brought cash for you."

He motioned for her to sit. "I can use a break."

"You work out there every day?"

He settled back and fanned himself with his ball cap. "Have to. Most of my sales come in the fall for Christmas gifts. I'll start pushing the kid's furniture and doll houses this month. You'd better choose the one you want so I can put it aside for you."

Ava turned to him. "Oh, thank you for remembering. Next time I'm in town, I'll hit the ATM so I can pay you."

He shook his head. "No rush, and anyway, I'll take your check."

Ava's words came out with a chuckle. "I must have wanted to leave civilization behind because I didn't even bring my checkbook, just a debit card."

"So, has living out in the wild lived up to your imagination?" Marvin brushed his hand through Major's coat.

"Oh, yes. I've been able to write like never before. I've met some interesting folks, too." Her eyes cut to him.

He grinned. "Yeah, I guess you have. John says you've been to the veteran's center."

She couldn't hide her excitement. "The men and women there are amazing. Some are friendlier than others, but none have asked me to mind my business and leave."

Marvin squirmed. "Like me, you mean?"

"We're beyond all that now." She rose. "I'd better let you get back to work. I was out for a walk and thought I'd say hello and drop off the cash. Thanks again for the chair. It's lovely. See ya later."

On the way back to her cabin, Ava thought about their growing friendship. Indeed, she had met some interesting souls here. Even Marvin Cameron.

\*\*\*\*

Two days later, she walked to Marvin's place again. Half way there, she heard Major delivering his most intense protective bellows. Stepping closer, she could make out his form, chained to a tree. A quick look across the property revealed no other activity. She wanted to run to release the dog, but held her stealth position behind a tree. Something was wrong. After what seemed like an eternity, Davis's pickup pulled up to the cabin and he and his father got out. The dog pulled against the chain and bared teeth at the intruders.

Davis cupped his hand to his mouth and yelled, "Ms. Ava, are you here? Where are you?"

She left her hiding place in a run toward the men. "I'm here."

Charles Simmons stood with hands on hips. "Anyone ever tell you about the awful chances you take? Were you here when they took him?"

"Took him? Marvin? What's going on?"

Davis said, "We stopped by your place and when you weren't there, I told Dad you'd be here."

Ava brushed the hair from her eyes. "Well? Are you going to tell me what happened?"

Charles answered, "In town, I heard some scuttlebutt, so I called for the sheriff and they said he was already up here on official business. We met the sheriff's car with Marvin in the back seat on our way up here."

Charles took her arm and directed, "Come on, we'll head to the station and find out more. The desk sergeant told me he thought the sheriff was coming to question Marvin."

Ava ran to the vehicle. "Question him? About what?"

Charles hesitated. "Murder."

\*\*\*\*

This was not the first time Ava had been inside a law enforcement facility in her role as a newspaper reporter. It wasn't even her only interview of a murder suspect, but this was different. Her heart raced and her fingers tapped her knees until the sheriff came out to talk to the trio.

"The doc has him calmed down now. I'm not sure you should see him tonight, though."

Ava stood. "I have to. It's important."

The sheriff looked her over. "You family?"

"No, he's a friend." Her mind sped to a plausible story. "I have to find out what he wants me to do about his dog."

The sheriff considered., "Okay, for a minute or two, but I don't want him upset again."

The walk down the dark hallway made her shiver. This wouldn't be her usual conversation with a prisoner. The sheriff called for a deputy to bring a chair for her to sit outside the cell where Marvin lay with his back to her. He moved only when she called to him to sit on the edge of his cot. "You shouldn't have come."

She scooted closer and grabbed a bar of the cell. "I'm here as a friend. What happened?"

He rubbed his neck and face. "I'm not sure. I remember a vehicle coming toward the place and then Sheriff Jim calling out to me. Major was going nuts. Jim got back into his car until I could get the dog in the cabin. As usual, I had reached for my .22. He started asking my whereabouts two nights ago and why I would shoot some guy. A guy I never even heard of. Then, he says I started aiming the rifle, calling him the enemy, and firing."

"You don't remember any of that?"

He rubbed his face again, as if to clear his thinking. "No. I guess he disarmed me. I know later he took the cuffs off just long enough for me to feed Major and secure him to the tree."

"Yeah, Major was awful mad when we got there. Will he be okay? Will he let me feed him?"

"He'll be fine 'til morning. You're probably the only one he'll let near him, but he's terrible upset, so be careful. His food is in the black tub on the porch. Thanks. I don't know how long I'll be here."

"Is there anything else I can do? A lawyer?"

"Already called. This is so crazy." He paced the cell. "They say I killed a guy. I haven't been over to the grow farm in months."

Ava's heart jumped in her chest. "The marijuana farm? That's where it happened?"

"Yes, or close by. They say the guy worked there. I didn't do it, Ava." He looked at her with uncertainty in his eyes. "I couldn't have, right?"

On the ride home, Charles repeated what the sheriff had told him. "The investigation revealed witnesses who say Marvin threatened the guy some time back. A Latino guy that worked at the farm. They found him a short distance from the headquarters. The body had a bullet straight through the heart from a high-powered rifle like he knows Marvin owns."

Ava thought she had the answer. "Ballistics will show it wasn't his though, right?"

"Maybe, if they could find his rifle."

Davis chimed in. "Right now he's only being held for questioning on the murder, but firing at the sheriff, then resisting arrest? He'll have to face those charges no matter what else."

\*\*\*\*

The next morning, Ava made her way to feed and care for her canine friend. She hoped he still saw her as a friend. Her approach was slow with a soft, calming voice.

"Hi, it's me, Major. Are you hungry? I can fix that for you. Now, no growling, and you put those sharp teeth away. That's it, you know me."

She retrieved his bowl from the porch and put a healthy portion of kibble inside. Cautious steps took her to the end of his chain, where she could place the food before him and still make a quick getaway. He sniffed, then moved to the bowl without taking his eyes from his visitor. By the time he devoured the food, he was ready to accept the tub of water she set in the shade under the tree which held him prisoner.

"I hate to leave you here, but it's best for now. If I turned you loose, you'd run all the way to town looking for your man. That wouldn't be right." She kept talking to him until mid-morning. "I have to go now and see what I can do to get Marvin back home."

On the walk, she stopped at her favorite place along the creek. She recorded events in her little notebook. There was a lot she didn't understand, but she recognized another episode brought on by the turmoil inside a man consumed by awful memories. It all brought on another scene in her manuscript.

*The Novel*

*Beth brought coffee to Max as he shaved. "I wish you wouldn't go today, but I understand you want to support your friend."*

*He spoke as he held the razor under the steamy faucet. "Johnnie and I were in basic together. Now that we've reconnected, we'll be there for each other no matter what comes."*

*"But being in court can be stressful. You know what the doctor said about staying away from triggers? Stress the biggest one."*

*"Johnnie never would have hit that officer if it weren't for the guy calling him the n word. Then he told him being a veteran didn't get him a free pass, either. Why couldn't the guy pull him over, give him a ticket, and go about his business? Johnnie saw the officer's hand go toward his holster and it set him off."*

*"Do you have an idea what will happen today?"*

*Max finished dressing as he answered. "If only he got the right public defender. Otherwise, he could be looking at some time in county. I'm not sure he could stand it."*

*Beth straightened his tie. "Call me when it's over. Remember, I'm here for you."*

*Max took a seat in the back of the courtroom. Windows on one side sent morning light across the pew-like benches. Families huddled together, awaiting their loved ones to appear. As the accused entered the room, Max shook, seeing his friend cuffed with head bowed low.*

*A uniformed officer of the court stood at the front of the room. "All stand for Judge James Thompson."*

*The people rose like a congregation standing for the singing of an opening hymn. Max's fingers gripped the back of the bench before him until the judge sat and told them all to do the same.*

*The judge called out, "Bailiff, call our first case."*

*She recited. "The State of California and Johnson's Grocery vs. Mavis Shipley on two counts of shoplifting." As the bailiff presented each case, Max waited. An hour passed, then two. The pounding in his head grew stronger as each minute ticked away. Each rap of the judge's gavel brought an earthquake through him. His leg and shoe tapped a rhythm on the wooden floor until the seat under him shook.*

*Finally, his friend's time to face the music came. Max stiffened when Johnnie idled up beside his attorney.*

*The bailiff handed the paperwork to the judge, who read it over with care. His eyes locked on Johnnie. "John Calvert, why is a decorated veteran with no priors in my court today?"*

*Johnnie stood at attention. "Not sure, sir, uh, Your Honor. Something he said I found offensive, and well, things got out of hand."*

*"Does this happen often with you?"*

*"More than I'd like, Your Honor."*

*The judge referred to the paperwork again. "It says here you've been attending therapy and anger management sessions since your discharge. Are you taking them to heart? Is that helping?"*

*Johnnie shrugged. "Sometimes."*

*The prosecutor interrupted. "We have the arresting officer here to relate the events to you, Your Honor."*

*"Sit down Barry. This is not a trial, and I can read the officer's report. Mr. Calvert, while your actions were over the top, I'm sorry the officer was, shall we say, less than professional with you. I will suggest he rethink his tactics in the future. However, you must recognize your aggressive response is unacceptable. I am directing you to complete six months of community service and I insist you continue the therapy until such time it is determined you can control your anger in these situations. So ordered." His gavel came down hard, then he said, "Mr. Calvert, I thank you for your service."*

*Max felt his body relax and his breath settle into a smooth rhythm. He went to his friend and shook his hand. "Community service isn't bad."*

*Johnnie moved his head from side to side. "That was close. Max, I can't miss any more meetings. I've got to lick this thing."*

*Max put his arm around his shoulder. "I'm with ya, man. We'll get through it together."*

*Later, when Beth got home from work, Max met her at the door. He wrapped his arms around her in a bear hug. "Thank you for understanding today."*

*She whispered in his ear, "I'm glad you called to*

*say it went well for him. Is he okay?"*

*"He's pretty shook up. I have to admit it scared me, too. Beth, it could have been me standing before the judge. Things have to change. I drove over to the campus and spoke to a counselor about taking pre law classes. People get into situations like Johnnie's sometimes and only need a little understanding and someone to be on their side."*

*She kissed his cheek and hugged his neck. "I'm so proud of you, and I'm beside you all the way."*

*"Beth, another thing, I know I should get a better job. Stocking store shelves at night won't cut it. Would your dad hire me for something at his firm? After all, I need to support his daughter. How about we get married right away?"*

*They laughed and jumped around the room in celebration until out of breath, then Max proclaimed, "Now the real work begins."*

\*\*\*\*

Ava entered her friend's cabin. "Maggie, I can't stay long. I wanted to talk about what's going on." She gave Maggie what she knew. "There has to be some way I can help. No way Marvin did this."

Her friend poured coffee. "You say he doesn't remember being at the farm at all?"

"Not for months. I want to ask him when he knew his rifle was missing."

"Now, Ava, you let his lawyer handle everything. You don't want to be tied up in all the mess."

John returned from Simmons' store and parked the Subaru. "Here's the milk and rice you wanted. You'll never guess what's happened."

"Yes, Ava filled me in." Maggie went inside to put

the groceries away.

Ava pressed John for more. "Does Charles know anything new this morning?"

"He said the sheriff was interrogating everyone. I guess he'll be here soon. You are staying out of this, aren't you, young lady?"

"Not on your life. I feel like I have to do something. If this is from another of his episodes, I'm afraid nobody is going to understand."

John sat next to Ava. "So, you think he did it?"

Ava couldn't answer fast enough. "No, but I'm saying we don't fully know what he goes through. When the time comes, will the legal system be ready to listen and learn?"

Maggie returned to her chair. "Have they found the rifle yet? That seems important."

John took off his cap and smoothed his hair back into his ponytail. "No, but they have deputies and dogs combing the woods around his place and the crime scene."

Ava jumped to her feet, eyes wide with an idea. "I have to talk to the sheriff."

Maggie's shrill call followed Ava to her car. "You be careful."

Chapter 14

"Now, Ms. Hardy, I don't have time to listen to your theories and help you get a story for your book. This is serious." The sheriff slammed the file cabinet closed and took a seat at the desk.

Ava settled across from him. "I know how serious it is. He's my friend, and I also know he couldn't do such a thing. It has nothing to do with my writing."

He held up his hand to stop her. "Okay, okay, but we're doing everything we can. We've got to find his rifle. I can't hold him much longer."

"And what will the rifle tell you? Only that it might have fired the shot. Here's my thought." Her wide eyes and raised eyebrows looked like someone revealing a great scientific concept to the world. "He wouldn't toss his gun away."

The sheriff rocked in his chair. "You can't be sure of that."

She leaned forward, elbows on his desk. "Listen. Were you in the service? And now you're in law enforcement. Officer friends have told me one of the first things you learn is to never put down your weapon. Even if something bad happened, he wouldn't."

He paused. "Hmm. Plausible. I suppose you have an explanation for its disappearance?"

Ava straightened up with confidence. "Someone stole it, used it in the crime, then got rid of it somewhere."

He grinned. "Simple, huh? Fine, you make a good point, and he doesn't remember the last time he saw the rifle. I'll keep an open mind."

****

Ava stood deep in thought at her kitchen counter late that afternoon while making preparations for her dinner. As she put a meat loaf in the oven, she heard a knock on her door. She turned to see Marvin and Major through the screen. Her mind raced as she wiped her hands and went to greet her visitors.

"What on earth? Last I knew, you were behind bars." She reached down to the excited dog. "Come on in. What happened?"

He shook his head. "I knew they didn't have enough to hold me. Jim said I'm still their only suspect, though." He removed his ball cap. "I understand you visited the sheriff. Not sure what you said, but it must have helped."

Ava waved away his comment and motioned for him to sit. Major found a comfortable spot on the braided rug. "How did you get home?"

"Charles came to my rescue. He's a good friend. And I must admit, so are you. Thanks for taking care of Major."

She looked over at the calm canine. "He was pretty stressed, even with me. I know he was glad to see you home."

Marvin hung his cap on the back of his chair. "Yes, and to get off that chain. I detest doing that to him."

She set a glass of tea in front of him. "I wanted to bring him over here, but thought he would try to run off to find you."

Marvin nodded. "You did right. I can't thank you

enough."

She moved to the kitchen. "I just put a meat loaf in the oven. I bet you could use a decent meal."

"Yes, thank you. I won't stay late. I didn't get much sleep last night."

They moved her writing equipment to make use of the drop-leaf table for their meal. Marvin held her laptop. "Will you tell me something about what you're writing?"

The look on her face reflected the shock of his question. She composed herself to say, "Of course. Would you like to read some while I finish dinner? Remember, it's rough at this point."

While she worked, an occasional glimpse of his struggle caught her eye. With each page he turned, a new twitch or shake appeared. He rose twice to take deep breaths and pace a circle back to the manuscript.

She set the platter on the table. "Dinner is ready. Are you at a stopping place? I can keep this warm if you want to read more." She washed the baking dish while he finished a chapter.

At last, he leaned back and let out a full breath. "Wow. I mean, well, wow. You're a talented writer, Ava. Some scenes were tough for me. Maybe you should warn the reader. A note at the beginning about triggers and such? I want to read more sometime. Let's eat and then we'll talk."

Her heart pounded as she set a fresh glass of tea next to his plate. "I'm sorry. I should have thought about how it might affect you, but I welcome your comments."

After the meal, they moved to the porch. Marvin spoke first. "There's something about sitting out here in the evenings enjoying nature. A peacefulness." He turned to Ava. "Don't you agree?"

"I do. I could stay here forever if I didn't have to go back to the job." Her hand waved away the thought. "It is what it is." She braced herself for his thoughts. "What do you think of what I've written?"

Marvin left his chair to step to the porch railing and looked across the night sky. "Good." He spun around to her. "Sorry. I know you want more." His hand raised to shuffle his cap on his head. "I was there with Max. You hit on some memories for me. I see what you mean about making it real. Boy, you got it in most of those scenes."

The hammer in her chest beat faster and her eyes became salty pools. "You have no idea how that makes me feel. But you sound like I'm missing something."

He smiled. "Have you got a pen and paper? I can help with your homecoming scene."

Her hand reached into her back pocket for the notebook and pencil. "I have them right here."

He let out a laugh that woke Major lying next to him. "Of course, you do."

For the next hour, he paced and every few steps spoke words about family, battles, nightmares, and emotions, while her pencil stood poised and moving. When she asked a question for clarification, he stopped for a drink, then started again. He spoke with a tremor in his voice and fists clenched.

As the moon rose, the silence expressed his fatigue. He savored the last drop of tea. Ice hitting the bottom of the glass rang through the night as he set it down. "I'd better get to the cabin. I'm exhausted. This was good for me, though." He smiled and rubbed his stomach. "Thanks for the meal. I owe you one. I cook a pretty mean steak myself."

Ava shook his hand. "No, it's me who owes you. Let

me know what I can do to help with your legal troubles. Should we go out to look for the rifle ourselves?"

His words were fast. "No. I don't want Sheriff Jim saying I tampered with evidence. You stay out of it, too. You hear me? Don't get mixed up in this. I haven't seen the rifle since I last cleaned it, maybe two months ago. How someone got to it, I don't know, but there's no other answer because I don't have it." He started down the steps. "Before I go, my daughter is coming this weekend. I want you to meet her."

"Oh, I would love to. She's concerned about you, right?"

"She's an attorney and wants to make sure how things are going. I can't wait to see her. If only something other than this situation had brought on her visit."

"You'll enjoy the time together."

\*\*\*\*

Tuesday afternoon, Ava moved around the cabin in a flurry, preparing for her evening date with Gerald Rainwater. Was it actually a date? Maybe he only wanted to help with her story. She tried on the fourth shirt before she stopped at her mirror and decided on one. "Ava, tee shirts? That's all you brought? Really? This will have to do." She grabbed her trusty writing implements, then ran to her car for the drive to a restaurant in Wilburton where Gerald met her at the door.

The casual talk over dinner turned to concern for Marvin. Gerald read about the murder in the newspaper, but not that Mavin was a suspect. "Are you kidding? How is he dealing with everything?"

Ava swallowed her last bite and pushed the plate away. "Like a trooper, but he doesn't understand how it could happen. The sheriff hasn't charged him, but he's keeping him in his sights."

Ava watched Gerald sit back in the booth, face up to the ceiling, eyes closed as if to calm his thoughts. "I'll have to go see him tomorrow." He lowered his gaze to Ava. "This kind of stress is hard for someone like him to handle."

Ava tilted her head. "What I don't understand is how he managed as a police officer all those years. I mean, you talk about stressful."

He ordered coffee for them. "I asked him once. His answer was that it was like being a marine. It was his job and he could put the voices and demons aside long enough to do what had to be done. At least most of the time. He had a couple of negative citations in his folder he's not proud of. I'm sure he could answer better for you, if he will."

A smile filled her face. "We had a nice dinner together. He read some of my manuscript, even though I wasn't ready for anyone to see it. It was hard on him, but he gave me some great tips to strengthen it."

Gerald's eyes widened. "You must have powers beyond being a pleasant dinner partner. I'm surprised he did that."

Her cheeks warmed red. "Maybe he's trusting me."

He reached for the check and his wallet. "We didn't talk about your novel much tonight. Is that okay? I enjoyed getting to know you better. Thursday is free for me. What if we could work at the library and then burgers later?"

"Sure, I'd like that."

They planned their Thursday meeting. then she started the drive home, stopping at the only store open, on the way out of town. The colorful blouse she bought was perfect for their next date. "Yes, by golly, it is a date". Her spinning head told her to ignore the flutter in her chest. She liked him even more now. "What are you doing, Ava?"

Chapter 15

Ava worked at her desk, until she heard a vehicle pull up to her cabin. Through the blare of the auto's horn, she greeted her friend. "Maggie, you're out early."

"I'm headed into town. Want to ride along?"

While she ran a hand across her tired neck, Ava leaned down to look through the car's open window. "I can't. I'm behind on my work after worrying about Marvin. Have you heard anything new?"

"John spoke to Charles, who said they're still looking for the rifle. He also visited Marvin, who is staying busy making furniture as fast as he can."

Ava stepped back from the car. "I've made a fresh batch of tea. Can you come in for a bit?"

The women sat inside next to a small fan, which moved the warm air around the room. Maggie saw the new blouse hanging on the end of the portable closet with price tags waving in the breeze. "What a cute top. When did you get this?"

Ava felt blood rush to her face. "After my dinner with Gerald last night. We're meeting again on Thursday."

Maggie moved forward in her chair. "Really? Tell me everything. I want details."

"We're going to work at the library then have burgers after. Nothing special."

"Yeah, only new-blouse-special." Maggie put down

her glass to continue the interrogation. "So, you like him, huh? When do we get to meet him? Is it going somewhere?"

Ava jumped up to wave off her questions. "Stop, Maggie. It's a friendly date. Don't make too much of it. Besides, it can't go anywhere if I go back home."

Maggie's eyes grew large as she asked, "If?"

"Oh, don't start. I meant when. You know my life is in Tulsa."

"Yes, and if I read between the lines of what you say, a job that doesn't seem to suit you."

Ava's hair waved back and forth across her shoulders as she made her point. "That's not true. I mean, I like the writing and my name on a byline is cool, but I can't seem to get ahead. These days, women are climbing the corporate ladder all around. Why not me? I guess that's one question I want to answer while I'm here. How do I climb that mountain? I sure see why you and John love it here, though. Until this thing with Marvin, I felt a wonderful peacefulness here."

Maggie stood and delivered her glass to the kitchen. "I'd better get moving or I'll never get my errands done today. Ava, if this guy interests you, and I can tell he does, don't shortchange yourself. Go for it."

Ava walked Maggie to the door and said with a certain glow in her voice, "It may be too late to do anything else."

When she returned to her desk, Max and Beth came to mind.

*The Novel*

*Max rolled and tumbled until he fell from the bed. As he hit the floor, it started.*

*C'mon Buddy. Stay down. Don't give up our*

*position.*

*"You're not real, only the nightmare I had all night, tearing my guts out." His fists churned through the air, hitting nothing. "Leave me alone."*

*No, no. They're coming to get us. I hear the tanks rolling in. Be ready, Marine. Kill 'em before they get you.*

*"God, help me. I can't do it anymore. I've got to get home to Beth." His body shook with a knocking at his door. With the demon controlling his brain, he recoiled to the corner of the room, sweat soaking his pajamas.*

*God's not here. You hear the rat-a-tat? That's enemy fire. Get up, Marine. Do your job.*

*Now a fist banged at the door. "Max, it's Johnnie. Open the door. Come on, we'll get through this."*

*Don't fall for it, Marine. Get up and fire. Get up, you coward.*

*At the sound of his friend's voice, his muscles relaxed and his mind exited the fog. He shook his head and rubbed his eyes. His legs felt and moved like lead, and an arm raised to wipe away tears and the demon. "Johnnie? Wait, I'm coming." When he opened the door, a face of concern, then a smile, greeted him.*

*Johnnie took his arm and guided him back to a chair. "It's okay. It's over. Sit down and let me get you some water."*

*Max smothered his face in his hands. "It's too hard. I can't do it."*

*Johnnie returned with a full glass. "What can't you do? Marry the prettiest girl around? Come on, man, she's waiting at the church. Everyone is there." He straightened his tie. "You can do this."*

*Max looked up at him. "When I asked you to be my*

*best man, I bet you never bargained for this."*

*"Part of the job, partner. Now get in the shower. I'll lay out your suit."*

*When Max stepped out of the shower with a towel around him, he said, "You know she's too good for me, right?"*

*Johnnie chuckled. "I agree, but she sent me to find you, and somehow, I don't see Beth as a woman I want angry at me. I trust her with my best friend, Max. She's got your six. Now get dressed."*

*Johnnie parked the car with Max jumping out before it stopped rolling. He ran through the back entrance of the church and bumped into his soon-to-be father-in-law.*

*The man's expression said it all, but still the tenseness in the man's voice shook Max. "Young man, you're not off to a worthy start."*

*"I'm here to fix that, sir." Max sped past him and into the bride's dressing room. The bridesmaids surrounding Beth let out a scream, then a sigh.*

*Max locked eyes with the woman he loved. "Give us the room, ladies. Please."*

*When they were alone, Max spoke to his bride. "I'm sorry. It's not enough, I know, but it's what I've got. Beth, I'm afraid.*

*"And you think I'm not?" She walked to him and started tying his bow tie. "We're in this together, Max."*

*When she stood back to survey the results of her work, he took her hands. "I-I have to ask if, you know, if you're sure."*

*She kissed him the long familiar sharing of emotion they knew so well. "The fact you ask me tells me I've found my man. Now, go out there and let's get married.*

*It'll be a breeze."*

*As he reached the door, he turned to say with a grin, "That's easy for you to say. I still have to pass your father in the hallway again. By the way, honey, you are gorgeous."*

Ava stretched as she reviewed the words on the screen. "Happy wedding, you two. I hope it works out." She gazed out the window.

****

Their Thursday meeting came and Ava wore the new blouse. Work at the library was productive and fun for them. When hunger overtook them, they deposited their books in their cars and walked to the cafe across the street.

He stopped her at the door, "I didn't ask you if this would be okay."

"It's perfect. You know how I love my onion burgers."

He chuckled and opened the door for her. "Sit wherever you like. I'll get some menus. Or shall I just order for us?"

"Sounds fine to me."

He ordered and brought the drinks to the table. "I swear, I don't know how you keep your figure with all the onion burgers you eat."

Ava looked down at her glass to hide the crimson taking over her cheeks. "I'll take that as a compliment. I try to eat pretty healthy, but I can't resist this treat."

"You look great. Shoot. Now I'm embarrassed. We got work done today. Didn't we?"

"Yes, your story about threatening your cousin during a drunken night was just heart wrenching. I appreciate you being so open about everything."

113

He took his straw from its paper cover, then drew a long drink before he asked, "How will you use the things we talked about?"

"I try to use the basic scenario, but alter it some to fit my characters. You may only recognize small bits of your story in mine."

"It's an honor to know I helped. And you're teaching the high school boy about writing?"

"He makes it easy the way he soaks up everything I say. I have to admit, it's fun."

Gerald went to the counter to retrieve their dinner. He continued when he placed the burger baskets before them and took his place in the booth again. "Have you thought of teaching as a career?"

She had to grin and laugh about the question arising again. "Even though I majored in journalism with an emphasis on creative writing, I carried a minor in education. You know, a female thinking I might need a backup. I taught middle school for two years but decided to take a job which utilized my writing skills. I love the writing and journalism."

He reached with a napkin to wipe mustard from her chin. "You up for a movie tonight?"

"Don't you have a test tomorrow?"

"That's what I was studying at the library today when you arrived. I'll be fine."

Her face faked disappointment as she announced, "Well, heck. I wouldn't have eaten so many fries if I'd known popcorn was in my future." She gave him an impish grin.

"We can always split a small bag. Deal?"

"You bet, if the movie and snacks are on me. You picked up this ticket."

Gerald shrugged his shoulders as if resigning himself to the independence of his new friend. "Agreed."

After the comedy, Gerald drove her back to her car. With the engine off and radio on low, they talked until almost midnight. She listened to him chatter about his upbringing and goal as a kid of getting away from the small town he still called home. Ava loved his passion for community and his plans for helping others.

He placed his ball cap on the dash and wiped his hand down his face. "I shouldn't have kept you out so late. Please let me drive you up the mountain."

"No. You have to get up early. I'll be fine. What a great day it's been."

He answered by taking her hand. "I want to see you again, and how about we don't pretend we need the library or your novel as an excuse to get together?" He moved close to her.

His arms warmed her skin as they surrounded her. Their lips met in a tender first kiss.

She asked, "How about I cook dinner soon?"

"It's a date." He kissed her more intimately.

When she washed her face that night, she said to the mirror, "This guy is too good to be true. I can't believe I felt like a teenager when he took my hand in the dark theater. Be careful, Ava."

Chapter 16

On Saturday morning, Ava took her usual journey into the forest. Songbirds welcomed her from tree limbs above. Her head raised to them. "You never fail to bring me back to beauty, no matter how dark things get down here." She looked forward to meeting Marvin's daughter at dinner. Maggie made it more comfortable for everyone by creating a cookout at their cabin. Marvin told Ava he'd invited Gerald, which she saw as another opportunity to discuss her novel, and get to know him better.

That night, Marvin led Major and a nice-looking woman, who looked to be in her late twenties to the gathering around the campfire. He introduced her to the group. "Everyone, this is my daughter, Jennifer."

Casual chatter back and forth addressed questions about her family and law practice back in Oklahoma City. "I have a three-year-old daughter and my husband, Robert, is an accountant. Dad tells me you're with The *Tulsa Herald*, Ava."

"Yes, I'm here on a leave of absence to work on a novel. Which has turned into something more than I bargained for."

Talk through dinner was friendly and casual, with no mention of the murder case that brought Jennifer to them.

Maggie brought out small plates and plastic forks.

"Time for dessert. Tea or coffee?" They each made their request. "Jennifer, the cake looks luscious."

"Store-bought, of course. It surprised me to see your store here so well stocked. I thought Dad was living in some remote campsite or something. I haven't been here before. It's lovely."

Ava brought up the question everyone had been thinking about., "You came to help with his defense?"

Jennifer put her coffee down. "I thought I should see first-hand what's going on after the story on the evening news. His attorney, Jasper James, met with us today. He seems a capable fellow."

John joined in. "But you could help Marvin's case?"

"I offered my services, but like I said, Mr. James seems on it already."

Marvin beamed and bragged on his daughter. "You should have seen her with him. Talking all the legal jargon and not letting anything slip by."

Her response showed a shyness. "That'll do, Dad."

The laughter of friends rang through the night.

Gerald whispered to Ava, "Perhaps she could help with the book?"

"The family aspect? Of course. I'll find the right moment to approach her."

John moved his chair closer to Marvin. "Is there any new word on the case?"

Marvin shifted in his chair. "No. They're focusing their efforts on finding the gun. My fear is they overlook something in this guy's past that would be a lead."

Jennifer stood to pace as if in the courtroom. "Ava, the sheriff told me this morning you said maybe it was one of his episodes and so he doesn't remember it happening. I'm not sure that will be the right defense."

Ava's eyes glassed over in the moonlight. "I didn't say I believed it, but it's a possibility. If, however, they decide that's what happened, everyone involved has to have some recognition of what he goes through. It will take some preparation to present the medical and psychological side."

"The court may want to see it entered as an insanity plea. Others tried it with mixed success. Those are tough."

Ava bristled. "Excuse me, but your father is not insane. He may be moody and gruff, but he's one of the most clear-thinking men I've ever met." She felt Gerald's calming hand on hers. "He has flashbacks and nightmares we don't understand, is all I'm saying."

Jennifer moved to her father's side. "Maybe you should represent him. No, he's not insane. It's the only way our judicial system has to deal with a temporary disassociation with reality. He says your book includes someone with PTSD. How's it going?"

"It's going well. I continue to do a lot of research, and I've found people around here willing to talk about their experiences. Like Gerald and John gave me stories about family dealing with the same things. I could use more." She noticed the eyes of the group all turned to Marvin's daughter.

Jennifer took her place again and let out a sigh, hands gripping the chair arms. "What would you like to know?"

Ava's heart stuck in her throat, and she wished for her notebook. "Uh, well, things like how it was for his child to deal with the way it was? H-how was it?"

"He was my dad. Like any other little girl, I followed him everywhere. The ballpark, fishing, movies, and him enduring our little tea parties. Then there were those times a different man came home from work. There was yelling and throwing things. I hid in my closet more times than I care to remember."

The woman's voice wavered, and Ava sank back into her own childhood. "If it's too hard…"

"No, it's okay. Dad wants to help you, and I can see you're trying to do the right thing. Anyway, I was eight when they divorced. He stayed in Arkansas and we moved to Oklahoma City. My mother wanted nothing to do with him, and I didn't get a choice. Over the years she mellowed some, but by then I was a teenager feeling deserted and unloved by him and pretty much cut him off."

Maggie looked at Jennifer with a pouting face. "You didn't see him at all?"

"Funerals, graduations, sometimes holidays. When I got out on my own, I was busy and by then I was used to being without him."

Marvin reached over to take her hand. "We've agreed to do better. Both of us."

John spoke next. "I rebelled when my brother left the family, blaming my folks as much as him. But there had been such hurt and violence with him there. Twelve years later, we got word he died homeless in Washington, D.C. of all places. After learning that, I felt guilty for a long time because I was glad when he left. It took me years to recognize his pain and deal with mine. I never got to see him again to forgive us both.

Gerald added his story. "My mom had six of us kids and raised most alone. When I came back, I was a handful. It took me a while and a lot of alcohol and drug abuse before I saw the light. She was tough while supportive, but finally told me to get help or get out of her house." A nervous gasp ran around the campfire.

"You see, in the old days, before the white man led Choctaws, and some say forced, to Christianity, we followed a special ritual when someone died. Some still do. They built a fire on the site of the death or more often outside the deceased's dwelling and kept it blazing four days to light the way to the person's happy place. This was also a time of grieving for close family members to begin their psychological process of dealing with the loss. I came home one night to see her sitting at such a fire. The boy she raised and sent off to war was dead to her."

A silence fell over the group. Ava wiped a tear from her cheek. "Your mother knew you'd get the message."

Gerald grinned. "She knew tossing my baseball card collection into the flames would wake me up." He led the group in laughter.

"The next day, I drove out to the VA Center, and they helped me so much. Now, as some of you know, I'm studying to go back and help others."

The murmurs of "Great." "Fine man, Gerald." and "Way to go," ran through the night air.

Ava pressed on, "You all mentioned violence after returning. Can anyone take me through one of those times?"

Marvin volunteered. "I know for me, I didn't remember much after it happened. Like Jennifer said, another man was in the house. It was like watching things as they transpired, not recognizing the beast causing the pain. My wife dealt with so much and had to protect our daughter. I don't blame her for leaving."

Gerald shared more. "Mom said the same thing. It

was like a devil inside the man before her. She could stand her ground, but was afraid for the other kids. There were voices filling my head with crap and taking over. It helps to talk about this with those who understand. That's why sessions at the center help me. A lot of people think we're making excuses for our behavior, but that's not it at all."

Marvin warmed his hands over the campfire. "I haven't talked this much in years."

Maggie, always the hostess, asked, "More coffee, anyone?"

They all declined and rose to leave. Jennifer suggested lunch in town the next day with Ava.

"Sure. There's a little place called Josie's on the highway out-of-town that serves Sunday brunch. Is 10:00 okay? I know you want to get on the road back to The City."

\*\*\*\*

The women talked over quiche and coffee. "Ava, thank you for taking such an interest in my dad's case. He seems to have some fine friends here."

"I have to admit at first it was hard to separate my need for a story and seeing that he's a nice guy. We've worked through a lot and now he's a good friend who's in trouble."

"I'm excited about your manuscript. Dad says what he's read is fabulous."

"He's too kind. It's the first draft for sure. Do you like to read? You could be a beta reader for me to make sure I get things right. I mean, I know you're busy, so it's okay if you can't."

"I'm never too busy for the stack of next reads beside my bed. Send what you have when you're ready, and I'll put it first on the pile."

"Did I pelt you with too many questions last night? Your view of how this affects the family is important."

Jennifer became somber. "It was fine. Ava, do you think it's possible he did this? Even under some spell? The cop in him keeps telling me the sheriff will do his job. It will all work out like it's supposed to."

"No, I don't. After he fought for the right for so many years, it wouldn't make sense."

After paying their bill, they walked to their cars where Jennifer said, "Please stay in touch. I'm afraid he'll want to shield his little girl from the complete story, and me, three hours away."

"I'll do that, and if you remember something I might use in the book, email me. You'd better get on the road. I'll bet your little girl will be happy for Mama to be home."

Ava watched her drive away and wished they had more time together. The stories she shared were helpful, and she enjoyed her company.

Back at the cabin, Ava opened the computer to work. She hadn't taken notes at dinner and now faced recreating the stories she'd heard. It touched her how open and giving each person had been. Marvin surprised her the most.

*The Novel*

*"Max, are you ready? I told Smitty we'd be there by 6:00. Will you carry this bowl of macaroni salad to the car? I wonder if I made enough?"*

*"Good grief, Beth, it weighs a ton. How many people will be there?" Max faked struggling with the large bowl.*

*"He said around twenty. You know most of them."*

*He set the bowl on the back floorboard of his car and raised up to say, "Wait a minute. You know a crowd is not my thing."*

*"Oh, c'mon. It's a party. It'll be fun and some of them we haven't seen since the wedding. Anyway, Dr. Sheldon said you should socialize more. Right?"*

*He grinned and shook his head. "Yes, Mrs. Drill Sergeant. Put the address in the GPS. We're off."*

*When they arrived, Max felt the old uneasiness creeping in. "Don't leave me to talk with some jerk I don't even know. Promise?"*

*Beth kissed his cheek, then rubbed off the lipstick residue. "I promise."*

*Max relaxed some with a small group of men around the beer cooler. When the talk turned to how each felt about the continuing strife around the world, he listened to them talk about wasted tax dollars and the USA not needing to send more troops. Anger boiled within him. When he could stand no more, he had to say, "Have you been there? Do you even know what those men and women are fighting for? Have you met a gold star mother who's lost a son or daughter?"*

*A man Max had known since childhood answered first. "We get it, Max. We also know those men, like you, fought so we could have a relaxing day like this and discuss things openly."*

*Smitty joked. "Those mothers knew what they were sending their kids off to."*

*Max lunged toward him. "That's bullshit." He felt a firm hand pull him back as Beth whispered, "You've made your point, babe. Let's get a sandwich and enjoy the music."*

*His breath returned to normal. "I'm sorry. I've*

*embarrassed you."*

*"Not everyone feels or understands the pride of the country the same way you do. You were right to make your point. You might take the edge off the message next time, huh?" She hugged his arm as they walked.*

*The rest of the evening of food, music and beer went along smoothly until just after dark. Their host brought out fireworks. Someone in the crowd asked, "Aren't those things illegal in town, Smitty? It's not even Fourth of July."*

*"C'mon, you wuss. A few pops here and there. Nobody cares. Let's get this party lit up." The crowd cheered.*

*Max came out of the house after a trip to the restroom and jumped at the first explosion. "What the hell?"*

*It's incoming, old buddy. Get ready to fire on signal.*

*Max shrank down behind a lawn chair. In his head, screaming voices begged for help. We can't move in. There's women and children.*

*Enemy, that's all there is. It's them or you. Are you going to let down your fellow troops?*

*Max grabbed a plant stand and dumped dirt and geraniums as he ran into the crowd. "Shut up your crying, you bastards, you're done for." Max gasped as air left his chest and he fell to the ground, tackled with powerful arms around him. "Get off me, you lousy sand digger." He made his way to his feet and lunged at the man before him, the two hurtling through furniture and food. Glass bowls and platters crashed to the concrete.*

*Excellent job, Marine. Don't stop now. Kill him. What are you waiting for? He's coming at you.*

*Max felt the strength of several arms as they threw*

*him at an open flame. Suddenly his body was engulfed with...what? It wasn't fire. He struggled to right himself in the water. He floundered in the deep end of his friends' swimming pool.*

*The same men pulled him to dry land. "Are you all right, buddy? What happened to you? You were a crazy man."*

*Beth bent down over him, sprawled out on the grass. "It's okay, get up. We'll go home."*

*As he stood, he surveyed his friend's patio and yard. "It's not okay. I did all this?" He searched for his host to say, "I'm sorry, Smitty. I'll help clean it up."*

*"No, you've done quite enough." Smitty and the others were righting chairs and sweeping up glass. He looked at Beth and said, "I didn't think about the fireworks setting him off. I'll check on him tomorrow."*

*Beth glared at him and took Max, who still shook demonic laughter from his ears, by the arm. "We'll pay for damages. We've all got a lot to learn."*

Ava closed her laptop and went to bed early, recommitting herself to helping her friend Marvin.

Chapter 17

Ava got an early start on the manuscript without her morning hike. After around 2,000 more words written, she decided to see Marvin. As usual, the walk to his cabin refreshed and quickened her to the goal. As she approached, she called out, as had become her custom. Major came around the corner of the cabin first, then Marvin, who waved his welcome.

Ava waved back. "Am I interrupting your work?"

He removed a bandana from his back pocket and wiped the inside of his cap. "I'm ready to sit down for a bit. I'm caught up, but need to keep at it."

She thought for a second. "It keeps you from worrying about what's going on?"

"Yeah. It's tough, though, when deputies keep coming up here to harass me." He waved away the thought. "They're just doing their job. I wish I could help them find what they're looking for, but I'm at a loss, too."

"You mean there's more than the rifle?"

"Anything to tie me to this guy, but there just isn't anything. Like I told the sheriff, I guess he could have been the one to answer the door that day, but I wouldn't have recognized him again."

"What did you go up there for? I never heard."

"I know that grow farm is dumping stuff in the creeks around here. It's not right. I just wanted to talk to someone about it, but I was met at the door by a small group, some with pistols on their hips. When things got heated, a guy in the back, pulled one out. It set me off, and I went at them all. Three or four hit the ground. It may have pissed the gunman off when I picked up the pistol and emptied the cartridges on his stomach as he lay there. He called me a few choice words in Spanish as I walked off. Was that the guy they're talking about, or was he just one of the crowd? I don't know. That's their story, anyway. Honestly, I never thought anymore about them."

"Have you told the sheriff all this?"

He rolled his head around again and again. "So many times I've told them. I had no beef with those guys. It was his company and his boss."

Ava believed him. "And why would you go back with an over-powered rifle to do away with him? It doesn't make sense."

His eyes grew large. "You know what I keep at hand is a .22. I've pointed it at you before. The rifle in question is a collector's item for me. I keep it cleaned and usually in my safe. It's not for hunting or anything else."

"My dad had one he kept, too. I think I was actually jealous of the way he fawned over that thing. After he passed, my mother gave it to Uncle Frank." Silence engulfed them for a moment before Ava stood to leave. "We'd both better get back to work."

"Hey. I see you and Gerald are getting along well. He's sure a good one."

"I know. I'm enjoying getting to know him." She hesitated, wanting to ask his advice, like she would her father, but knew he had enough on his mind without her love life. "I'll see ya again soon."

On the walk back to her cabin, she decided on a trip into town. She strolled through the downtown area, thinking, before calling Gerald.

Ava's voice felt weak as breath through a hanky. "I wondered if you'd like to sit and talk over a scoop of ice cream."

"How could I resist that offer? Sure. Let me finish up my shift. I can be there in an hour."

That gave her enough time to visit Mr. Wyatt at the newspaper office.

When she walked in, she thought the bell on the door may have interrupted a nap.

"Hey there, Ava. Come sit a spell. How's that novel going?"

"I think it's going well. I had a few minutes and thought I'd see if you had another assignment for me."

"As a matter of fact, I do. Shelly Franklin is having her ninetieth birthday party on Friday. She's been such a big part of this community, and I thought a small article and pictures of the festivities would be nice."

"That sounds fun. Give me the details and I'll be there. I just noticed the awards you have hanging behind your desk. That's impressive."

"Thank you. I've been doing some cleaning in the basement and unearthed them. They're mostly from my father's days."

"A basement? That must be where you have archives and such?"

"Yes. I have at least one copy of every paper that's gone out of here from the beginning. Want to see?"

"Sounds interesting but I don't have time today. I'll be back."

When Gerald walked in to the ice cream parlor, she

tried to control her grin. "I was in the neighborhood and thought I'd see what my friend Gerald is up to."

He joined her at the small table and took her hand. "Glad you called. I should study for a test tomorrow, but this is a lot more fun. The other night, I enjoyed the gathering. Man, John is so interesting."

"Isn't he? I love his passion for his work. I won't keep you long if you should be studying."

"Don't worry about it. How's your day been?"

She let out a deep breath. "Interesting. I did some writing early and then hiked up to see Marvin. He tries to play it off, but I know he's worried."

"Who wouldn't be? Any fresh developments?"

"No. This is what I wanted to talk about. You can use some of that education. Is it possible for the voices in one's head to force them to do something they otherwise would not?"

"It has happened. Very hard to prove, though. That's what Jennifer was telling you, right?"

"Yes, but I can't let it go. I wish this all would go away for him. Not the way I want to get input for my story." She tossed her head to rid it of dark thoughts. "Enough about Marvin. Are these finals you're studying for?"

"Yes. I'm finishing my last semester. I can't wait to get started helping people."

"It must be nice to be clear about what you want."

"Your job isn't what you want?"

She savored the last spoonful of ice cream with a drink of soda. "It was a great start right out of college, but I deserve more now. I accepted the situation with little thought until I realized my life wasn't going anywhere. I'm just surviving. Here, I've been able to relax and live with my writing. And I have another assignment from Mr. Wyatt. I'm enjoying working with him a lot." Her shoulders straightened back. "I'm a good writer. I want to ride the wave as far as I can." She twisted her napkin until it crumbled. "Oh well, maybe I'll get it all figured out while I'm here."

He halted. "When do you leave?"

Her eyes met his. "Early September. Supposed to be."

He nodded, then said, never avoiding her stare, "I'll be sorry for the day."

Chapter 18

Ava entered the office talking. "Sheriff, listen up. I have something to discuss with you."

Jim Carson looked up from the papers on his desk in surprise. "Ms. Hardy, how did you get in here?" He looked beyond her to the deputy behind her with his hands palms up in frustration.

"I tried, boss."

"Don't blame him, Sheriff. I was determined." Ava didn't wait for an invitation to sit. "I want to know what's happening with the murder investigation."

He sucked on the end of his pencil. "As a seasoned newspaper reporter, you know my answer. I can't comment on an ongoing investigation. We're doing everything we can."

"Have you canvassed all the pawnshops in the area? Mr. Cameron says the rifle is a collector's item. It would have some value."

He chuckled and said with doubt in his voice, "Oh, so now you've given up on the idea of this mysterious perp tossing it away?"

"Your mocking attitude does nothing to garner trust in the professionalism of your investigation, sir."

He gave a lengthy stare. She delighted in his apparent discomfort.

"I assure you, Ms. Hardy, everything is being done. Now, I'm busy. Leave my office, please."

She stood with more to say before leaving, "I'm available for any assistance in this matter, Sheriff." She nodded a farewell to the deputy as she passed his desk on the way to her car.

Laughter filled her space. "Gotcha, you pompous jerk." She dialed Jennifer's number. "Hey, it's Ava. Got a minute?"

"Yes, but only. Is something wrong? Have they charged him?"

"No, they still have nothing. I just gave our illustrious sheriff a hard time about the whole thing, too."

"Be careful, Ava. We need him on our side. How's Dad?"

"He's a tough one. Working hard on his furniture to keep his mind occupied. My goal was to get the sheriff's attention."

"Ava, I love your tenacity but go easy on law enforcement. Go through his attorney if he'll help, but don't irritate Jasper, either. At least he answers my calls. Look, I have a meeting in five minutes. Is there something else?"

"Yes. Would you be willing to give me some actual episodes you remember with your dad? When you can."

"I've been making some notes already. The whole thing is kind of cathartic for me. I'll email them tonight."

"Thanks. And sorry. I won't call you at work anymore unless it's important."

"No worries. I'll send those notes."

Ava smiled at the silent phone, then headed over to The First Baptist Church to record Shelly Franklin's birthday party.

**\*\*\*\***

Ava and Major both jumped in fright when Marvin

slammed his hammer down on his workbench and yelled, "You did what? I told you not to get any more involved. Now he'll have his deputies out here snooping even more."

"I know. I feel foolish now, but I wanted to help." Ava turned her head so he wouldn't see her eyes well up.

After a few deep breaths as he leaned on the workbench, he acknowledged her discomfort.

"Don't you cry. I'm sorry I yelled. I know you mean well but, Ava, this is serious. When the deputies come, I've been able to get some of them to open up to me about each step they're taking. It will all work out because there is no evidence to find. Trust me."

"I do, and that's why I want to help. I want it all to be over, so we go back to the peace of our mountain."

He picked up his hammer and said, "Boy, so do I." He stopped to look at her. "You're liking it here, aren't you? How does Gerald fit in?" He shot her a sly grin as he got back to work.

"Well, since you brought it up, am I crazy to get involved, knowing I'm supposed to leave here soon?"

He turned back to her. "I'll tell you what I'd tell my daughter. Don't miss out on something that makes you happy. It doesn't come along too often."

"Same as Maggie tells me. I have some figuring out to do." She turned to leave.

"Maybe that'll keep you out of my business." His laugh echoed after her.

\*\*\*\*

On Saturday, she waved when her student drove up. "Hi, Davis. Thanks for being on time. I'm on a tight schedule today. Come on up, I even have snacks."

"Outstanding. Wow, are those lemon bars? You

must have been talking to my mom. They're my favorite." The teenager took three helpings.

"I may have asked for a little help. My small oven performed pretty well; don't you think? While you experience your sugar rush there, let's see what you have for me this time."

He handed her a blue folder with a B+ on a typed document inside. "I saw my last year's teacher at the movies last Friday. I asked her to read this. She said she sees improvement. Because you're helping me, Ms. Ava."

"The talent was already there, Davis. We're working together to bring it out."

"It's just a first chapter or something."

She read while he enjoyed his treat and paced the porch. After, she smiled as she said, "Well, young man." Ava waited while he took his seat again. "I have to agree with her B+ grade. Her comments are on point, too. One thing I would add. Distinguish for the reader when you are showing Billy's internal thoughts. Like at the beginning, when he's in his room."

"I didn't know how to do that." He looked down at his notebook.

"There are lots of ways. Like italics. You must be consistent, though. I noticed you had the same science fiction theme again."

"Yeah, I used the general idea of a story I wrote a while back, but thought this beginning was more fun. Ms. Ava, can you explain how you go about evaluating or editing the stories? Is there a formula of some kind?"

His enthusiasm and questions thrilled her. "Not so much a formula, but I tend to look for certain things."

Davis had his paper and pencil ready. "Like what?"

"Well, are the characters genuine? Will the reader engage with them? Do the scenes and chapters flow smoothly? Is it too wordy?"

He straightened up. "Oh yeah, we talked about that. Why use ten words when five will do?"

Ava couldn't hide her pride in his understanding. "That's right, Davis. See, the main thing is, does it read well? Is it a good story?"

"This is all beginning to make sense for me. Thank you so much."

Ava waved to him as he left with his next assignment and she said out loud, "By golly, I am a good teacher."

Later that evening, the cabin was astir with Ava's efforts to make it ready for company. Important company. Gerald planned to arrive around 5:00. She went simple with spaghetti and meat sauce. At 4:45, she heard his truck outside the cabin. She tossed the pasta into the boiling water and turned to evaluate the room. "Oh my gosh, my hair." She rushed to the comb she kept by the bed and ran it through the tangles as the knock came at the door. "Coming."

He called through the screen door. "I'm a little early. Wow, it smells good in there."

"Come on in. Dinner is almost ready." She fussed with straightening her clothes as he handed her a small bouquet of cut flowers. "They're lovely, Gerald. Thank you. I'll get them into water."

He looked around and said, "This is nice, Ava. Not sure what I expected after seeing Marvin's place. The only cabin I've been in up here." He giggled. "Honestly, his isn't so bad for a bachelor guy."

"Thanks." She put two soda bottles stuffed with

flowers and water on their small dinner table, then removed the pasta from the water. "Let's eat."

He saw the blooms dominate the small table. "I guess I should have gotten you something with a vase."

"No, this is fine. I use these for wildflowers all the time." She got up again. "I'll put one on the counter so I can see you across the table."

Conversation over dinner felt comfortable for Ava. "I met with Davis today. We worked on his latest writing. He shows such creative potential."

"I'm sure you've helped him. You should consider a teaching position."

Her hands went up in a stop sign way. "Look, I get this from my teenager friend all the time." She grinned and said, "I enjoy working with a young, eager mind, though."

"So, just in case." Gerald reached to remove something from his back pocket and spread it out on the table. "I read in the campus newspaper yesterday a long-time professor is retiring at the end of the year."

Before her hand pulled the paper to her, she said, "Yes, in the English department. Davis mentioned it to me. You must understand they'd say I'm not qualified. I mean, a professor, after all."

"Now you've seen it in print. The article says they'll post the position next month. You know, it's a small school and sometimes they have trouble getting people. What if they would bend the rules a little?"

She looked at him with wistful eyes. "Listen. While I'll admit staying here tugs at my heart, this may be a little far-fetched."

His eyes sparkled.

She rose from the table to change the subject.

"Would you like another glass of tea or some coffee?"

Gerald helped take the dishes to the sink. "Black coffee is fine."

"Stake out a spot on the porch and I'll be right out." Ava took down two mugs, lost in her thoughts.

She handed him his coffee and set hers on the table between them, then sat. "I love the nights here. So nice and cool after the hot days."

He took a sip of coffee and said, "This rocking chair is so comfortable."

Ava's eyes showed the excitement of a kid with a new prize. "Marvin made it for me. Doesn't he do fine work? I've paid him for a dollhouse for my niece, too. I can't wait for her to see it on Christmas morning."

"You have siblings?"

"One older sister, Barbara. We're as different as night and day, but I miss her. She's my best friend."

"I'm sure you have lots of friends in a big city like Tulsa." He moved his chair to face her better.

"Me? Just a few good friends. I work all the time. Then I try to write, but that's been a struggle. That's how I ended up here. I needed a change in more ways than one."

He took her hand. "Has it worked? For change I mean."

His touch brought a rush through her. She leaned toward him and as their lips met, she whispered, "In more ways than one."

He settled back. "So then, the teaching position?"

She stood and walked hard to the railing. "Are we really having this discussion right now?"

He stepped behind her, his arms pulling her close. "I'm sorry. I don't mean to push. Ava, I like you more than anyone I've met in a long time. I feel like we've started something nice here. You feel it, too, don't you?"

With her heart fighting to burst from her chest, she turned to meet his eyes. "Of course, I do. I'm not sure I have a right to. There's so much I have to deal with first. I don't know what else to say."

"You said all I needed to hear. I can be patient."

Chapter 19

After a morning of writing her story, Ava hiked up to see Maggie. A little friendly advice would come in handy right now. As she crossed the creek and jumped over fallen logs, her mind and heart raced about how soon she would leave these mountains. The solitude of her cabin was refreshing, and she enjoyed the ease with which she became so close to the people she met on the mountain. It felt like home.

She called as she neared the cabin. "Maggie? Hmm, the car is gone." She stepped onto the bottom step. "Anyone here?"

The screen door flew open with Maggie standing there wiping her hands on a denim apron. "Well, hi. Come on up. Let me clean up a bit in here and I'll be right with you."

Ava poured herself a glass of tea and found a place to sit. "Did I interrupt something important?"

Maggie's voice came from a back room. "I'm having fun playing in mud." There was that wonderful laugh.

Ava couldn't resist investigating and followed Maggie to the bedroom. There Maggie sat, clearing a lump of clay from a pottery wheel.

"Wow, Maggie, I had no idea you're a potter." Ava moved closer.

Maggie stood up and stretched her shoulders

backward. "John got me the wheel and some classes last Christmas. I've spent a lot of hours with my hands in the clay, but haven't finished too many. At least that I would show." She snickered and swung her arm around to point out the finished pieces on shelves.

Ava picked up a small tumbler. "These are wonderful. I'm sorry you stopped your work because of me. I'd love to watch you sometime."

"Don't be sorry. I've worked this clay so many times it's tired and so am I. I'm glad you came by. Let's sit on the porch. What's new, Ava? How's your handsome Gerald?"

"He's wonderful. That's part of my problem."

Maggie spun in her chair to face Ava. "How can a hunk like him be a problem? John and I enjoyed him at dinner that night."

"Yeah, John fascinated Gerald. The thing is, a romantic involvement was not part of my plan."

"Honey, you worry too much. Let life unfold as it's meant to."

"That sounds like a philosophy left over from the sixties. I'm a planner from when I'll wash my car to what I'll eat next Friday."

"The no-plan thing has worked for both of us, is all I can say. Like our big move from California to Tulsa. Everyone thought we were off our rockers, but we took a chance, and it worked out."

They looked toward the driveway as John drove in and parked the Subaru. He stepped from the car and took quick steps toward the women. "I'm glad you're here, Ava. I heard in town they've found the weapon."

Ava left her chair. "Where was it?"

"Inside an old fifty-five-gallon drum at the edge of

the lake. It was overturned but had enough water to cover the rifle. Of course, that destroyed any prints. They did ballistics tests and the serial number confirms it's registered to Marvin."

"He never denied it might be his, since it has been missing." Ava walked to John. "The test?"

He said outright, "It's the murder weapon."

Maggie gasped, "Oh no."

Ava clutched her abdomen. "Now what?"

John moved to wrap his fingers around her arm with care. "The sheriff says they have enough. He's getting a warrant for Marvin's arrest. I thought you'd want to call his daughter.

Ava ran down the steps two at a time and headed to Marvin's cabin as fast as her legs would carry her. Her yell as she reached his meadow sounded through the grasses and into his workshop. "Marvin, I'm coming in." Major rounded the cabin in a run. She didn't stop to pet him.

Their bodies collided as she met Marvin at the entrance to his shop. "Whoa. What's so urgent? Are you okay?"

She fell into his arms, tears soaking his shirt. She blurted out the words through heavy breathing, "They found it. The gun. Your rifle. The sheriff is getting a warrant."

"Slow down. Okay, good to know. First things first. You take Major to your place, if that's okay. Let's gather his things and get over there. Once I have him settled, I'll come back and wait. No, then I'll drive down to turn myself in."

"Why? I never thought you'd run, but if you turn yourself in, won't it seem like you're admitting guilt?"

"Or maybe it says I'm willing to cooperate because I'm innocent. Anyhow, I hope Jim sees it that way. Let's get going."

They got out of his truck at her place, then after he explained how to manage Major, he kneeled beside the dog on the floor, stroking his coat with every word. "Okay, your mission is to watch out for this nice lady. You know your duty. When I say stay at your post, you stick like glue. I'll be back as soon as I can." He stood and turned to the door. When the dog looked up and whimpered, Marvin held the palm of his hand up to him. Major didn't move to follow.

Ava waited until Marvin was finished. "He's amazing. He'll stay, won't he?"

"Keep him on a leash while he's outside. Chained when you leave him alone out there. Be careful when you're out with him. He's so strong and will wear you out. If he gets away, don't worry too much. He'll go back to our place. Thank you. I can't trust him with anyone else."

Ava's heart pounded as she watched him drive away. She texted the news to Jennifer, who answered right away.

—I'll arrive midday tomorrow—

\*\*\*\*

Ava greeted Jennifer at her door. "I'm glad you came. Can you help him?"

"I talked to his attorney, and he seems to think the DA has a case, but it's all circumstantial. He'll work on that angle."

Ava stiffened with resolve. "They won't find anything solid on him."

"If Dad wasn't such a loner, he might have an alibi.

He says he was working late in his shop all evening. Alone. I stopped by the jail to talk to him. He's taking it in stride, but he seemed glad to see me."

Ava moved around the room, scratching her head. "How can I help?"

"You're doing a lot by taking in his dog. He's quite the watchdog."

"Marvin gave him his orders to protect me. He's doing his job. He's really quite sweet when he trusts you. You'll stay for dinner, won't you?"

"Thank you. I haven't eaten since breakfast. Will you help me create a storyboard of sorts? Things like who's who around here. Dad's friends, enemies. Also, his habits. When he goes to town for supplies or to the markets where he sells. That kind of thing. I need to know him better than I do to be more involved in his defense. I'm ready to go to work."

"Can you be away from your family and practice for a while?" Ava checked the refrigerator for sandwich makings, then spread them on the counter.

"I cleared this week and most of next. I'll have to go back for two court dates and give my mother a break from keeping my daughter for a few days. She's been great about it. I know she's worried about Dad, too."

"And your husband?"

"Robert already says I work too much, and now I add being away. I'll make it up to him. Deep down, he understands. He became estranged from his father and didn't get the chance to fix the relationship before the man died. He doesn't want the same to happen to me."

Ava sensed the past with her father wash over her again. "I understand. As close as my dad and I were, we had our struggles. I'm thinking he had some form of

PTSD, too. Only now do some of the odd scenarios between us make sense."

The women worked into the night, organizing what they knew about Marvin and the case. Ava offered Jennifer a place to stay.

Instead, she gathered her purse and briefcase to go. "Thanks, but I'll stay at Dad's. Want to go into town with me tomorrow? I'll interview Dad like I would any client. I can't shake the feeling there's more to this. His arraignment is at ten. "

"We should leave about nine. I'll feed Major and get him settled."

"Sounds right. I'll pick you up."

****

"You'd better drop me off downtown while you see Marvin. I'm not the sheriff's favorite person after my visit the other day."

Jennifer chuckled and said, "You might have been the slightest bit over the top, but the important thing is the sheriff sees Dad has support around the area. Including his arraignment, I'll be a couple of hours if I can get him to talking."

"Let me out in front of the dress boutique. I've got shopping to do, then I'll walk to the library. Text when you're finished."

The boutique didn't open until ten, so Ava walked to the coffee shop on the corner. She enjoyed a latte while checking email. Junk mail and bills, as usual, but also an invitation to a birthday party for her niece in two weeks. She sent best wishes for a fun day and regrets she couldn't attend. The first time she'd missed her birthday hit her hard. She thought, "This is the price for being away from family. I'll get something and send it to her."

Ava bought two new blouses for herself and a pair of dress slacks. The woman at the boutique directed her around the corner to a family-owned shoe store where she could get into something comfortable but more formal than sneakers and boots for time with Gerald or a court date. Across the street at a children's store, she found cute tops and hair ribbons for her niece. She paid extra to have them shipped.

After a brisk walk to the library, Ava found her favorite corner table and filled in more of Max's story.

*The Novel*

*Most of the time, Max and Beth lived a life of love, fun, and excitement. He was doing well in classes as a senior at UCLA and she was the newest member of a large realty firm selling elite locations across Los Angeles. His PTSD appeared subdued by medications and regular therapy.*

*This day they enjoyed Malibu Beach. She watched as he surfed the waters he loved. He ran toward her and shed the salty water from his board and body onto her before he flopped down on a beach towel.*

*"Hey, you're getting me all wet." Beth brushed water from her legs and stomach.*

*"You are at the beach, you know. Come get in with me." He pulled her up, and they ran to the edge where she poked one foot in to test the water temperature. He pulled her to him and they fell into the water as a wave rolled in.*

*As the water receded, they laughed and hugged each other. She pushed herself to the end of his fingertips and stood looking in his eyes. "I love you, Max. Are you still scared after four years of marriage?"*

*"I am. It will never be over, but I know together we*

*can face anything."*

*"Anything? How about diapers and late-night feedings, and..."*

*He didn't let her finish. "Beth. You mean? Don't kid me now. Don't you do it."*

*She smiled and nodded. He picked her up and swung her around, then stopped to kiss her until another wave came in to sweep them off their feet. They made their way back to their blanket-sized beach towel, where he pelted her with questions.*

*"Are you sure? How far along? A boy or a girl?"*

*Her laughter came from deep inside her. "Slow down. Three home tests can't be wrong, but I have an appointment next week. Can you get away to go with me?"*

*"I'll be there for every appointment. Beth, you've made me so happy. If only I can do the same for you."*

*She smiled and touched his face. "You make me happy every day. We'll be okay in our current apartment for a while. But I should start watching the market for something larger."*

*He laid back on the towel and told her again about his dreams for the future. "Beth, when I have my practice set up, a key focus will be helping veterans and others who can't afford big time lawyers. Somehow, though, I'll still get you the large beach house right here on Malibu. Fixed up like you've always dreamed of, and the kids and I can be on the water all the time."*

*She raised up and faked a high pitched, shaky voice to ask, "Kids, as in plural? How many?"*

*"We'll start with two, then see how it goes." He laughed. "A family, Beth."*

*"I know. It doesn't seem real, does it? I can't wait."*

*The sun went down on the horizon as they continued making plans.*

Ava's brain filled with thoughts of how her future might look, as she waited for Jennifer to arrive. Should she take a lesson from Max? Would Gerald have a part? Or was her life in Tulsa to be her fate?

Chapter 20

Jennifer turned to a fresh page on her legal pad in the interrogation room down the hall from Marvin's cell. "Okay, let's go through it again. You were in your workshop all evening."

Marvin stood to walk to the window. "Probably so."

"Dad, you have to be sure, or at least sound convincing."

His body jerked around to face her and his voice rose to fill the barren interview room. "I don't remember for sure. Why can't you understand? We've been doing this for over an hour, and it doesn't change." He flopped down in his chair.

Jennifer gripped her pen. "Do we need a break, Dad?" When he shook his head, she let out a deep sigh and gathered her thoughts. "There's got to be a way to recreate your day. Let's look at the calendar. It was a Tuesday. Does anything special happen on Tuesdays?" She thumbed through his checkbook.

Something came to his mind. "Wait. Look for something at Morgan's Feed Store. I think that was the day I went in to town to get a bag of dog food. It should be around forty dollars."

"Here it is. Morgan's, $38.27. Great. Do you remember what time of day? Here's another one on the same day. Freeman's, for $52.80. What's that?"

"I wanted a new pair of jeans to wear to market. This

was all before noon and I had lunch at Pam's Diner, then headed home."

"Who did you talk to? Will they remember you?"

"Of course. I've been buying dog food from Will since I moved here. I ate with Bill Jones and Jess Phillips. Turkey dinner was the special, and Jess offered to pay, but we all went Dutch. We played a game of dominoes waiting on our food. Is this helping?"

She threw up her hands for emphasis. "Does this sound like a man planning to go kill someone that evening? We've got to make your moral character an important witness. Keep going. Did you go straight home from there?"

"Give me a minute to breathe, Jennifer." He leaned toward her across the table. "I hate taking you away from your family. You're good at this, though."

"Don't worry about me, Dad. This is important. Okay, you didn't even stop at Simmons's store on the way?"

He got out of his chair and walked around the room. "I stopped for gas in town, but paid at the pump. No contact there. Come to think of it, clouds were forming, and I wanted to get the bag of dog food out of the back of my truck before the rain started, so no more stops."

Her hand moved the pen across the page with speed. "Rain? Why has nobody mentioned that before?"

"That's important, isn't it?"

"It could be. Muddy boots and tires, wet clothes, darkness, footprints. They all have to be researched."

"You know, maybe I wasn't in the shop. I don't work out there much when it's raining. The moisture in the air affects the wood."

Her face darkened. "That changes everything. If you

weren't in the shop, as you told the sheriff, where were you?"

"I imagine Major and I were in front of a fire, me buried in a book. He shook his head and fell silent while she packed her briefcase.

She looked into his sullen eyes. "I'm going to suggest to your lawyer that we team up on this. I can work on interviewing people around the area while he follows leads the sheriff finds."

He bowed his head , "I'm just sorry it took this for us to get together. Separation like ours is not right for a father and daughter."

She stood to hug him. "I know I could have made a better effort. I sent you pictures each time Ellie reached a milestone, though. Her first words, walking. Even potty training." They both laughed.

"Jen, I missed so many things with you. I wish it could have been different."

"You worked a lot, Dad. And then Mom moved us away."

"Don't blame her for that, honey. She did what she thought was right."

Jennifer pulled away and straightened her hair. "The past is done. By concentrating on the present, we'll make sure you're free to enjoy our future together. Sorry to go, but I've got to pick up Ava downtown."

"Well, what do you think of my chances?"

"Because we have to rely so much on your memory, there will be more interviews like this." She tried to smile. "The important thing is, the prosecutor doesn't have much either. I'll see you again tomorrow."

Jennifer texted Ava to meet her at the cafe across from the library for lunch. Her body collapsed into the booth across from Ava. "I'm sorry I took so long, but it was a productive time. I'm going to approach his lawyer about working together on Dad's defense."

Ava pushed a glass of tea in front of her new friend. "How great. I'm sure Marvin likes the idea, too."

Jennifer took a drink while raking fingers through her hair. "Who in law school would ever imagine you'd be defending your own father someday? I have to keep my emotions out of it, though."

"Maybe that emotional connection is what it takes to get him through this."

Jennifer looked over the menu. "Let's order, then I'll fill you in on what Dad remembered. If you've got time, I want to stop by the lawyer's office. I'll let him know he just got a new partner."

After lunch, Jennifer parked her car in front of the office of Jasper James, Attorney at Law. He stood to greet the two women as they entered his workspace.

"Mrs. Wells, good to see you again. What brings you in?" His questioning eyes turned to Ava as he motioned for them to take a seat across from his oversized mahogany desk.

Jennifer motioned to Ava. "This is my friend, Ava Hardy. I'm here to offer my services on Marvin Cameron's case."

The lines on his brow displayed his confusion. "We've already discussed this and agreed I would call if I needed your help, Mrs. Wells."

"Jennifer will be sufficient outside of the courtroom, Jasper. Let me reword what I said before. I am joining the defense team as of today. I'll begin by interviewing acquaintances and character witnesses. Now, let me share what I learned from the accused today."

\*\*\*\*

In the evening hours, Ava and Major lounged on the porch. "I know you miss him, but your man can't be home right now. He has a fighter in his corner, though. Things will start going his way." The canine whimpered, then laid his head between his feet.

She let the evening breeze flow over her as she leaned back in the rocker Marvin made for her and spoke to her canine friend. "I wish I could have known him better before all this. He reminds me of my father in some ways. Both strong, independent, and artisans. Marvin with wood and my dad with words. If only I could have stayed six years old and Dad the hero of my playful days. We had such fun together." The dog stretched out in slumber.

She took out the emails printed at the library earlier. Jennifer sent the promised stories of her past with Marvin. Ava held them, eyes closed, while deep breaths filled her lungs. She feared they held heart wrenching tales, all too familiar. After reading, her eyes and chest burned as she laid the papers aside. The boards of the porch creaked in rhythm with the rungs of the rocker as Ava formed the story in her head of another little girl and her father.

*The Novel*

*"Daddy, Daddy! Pick me up, Daddy."*

*Max brushed past the toddler as he entered the house. "Not now, Kaley. Daddy's tired."*

*Beth ran to comfort the disappointed child. "Max, what are you doing? She's waited all day to see you. Come on, Kaley, go play in your room."*

*Beth's flaming eyes stared at Max in disbelief. "I won't have you hurt her again because you've had a hard day. If having clients in need of the same help as you is too hard, you chose it, you change it. Whatever is bothering you, you'd better get it out before you get home next time."*

*"You don't understand." Max yelled.*

*With each outburst, the child alone in her room let out a whimper again.*

*Beth's arms flew around in frustration as she cried out, "Max, I'm sick of hearing that from you. I understand as much as you allow. You made me stop going to the sessions with you. How am I supposed to help?"*

*"You have no idea how humiliating it is for you to see me messed up, weak, and dependent. I'm the husband, the man here. I'm supposed to be the strong one."*

*"Then act like it. Cut out the macho crap. Show your daughter and me the strength it takes to face your fears. Don't you know it's all I've ever wanted?"*

When Major came over to lay his head in her lap, Ava realized she was shaking, with tears running down into her collar. Her hand reached to rub his head. "Let's go inside, boy. I can't finish this scene tonight."

Chapter 21

The next morning, writing scenes about conflict between father and daughter caused her stomach to churn, but Ava kept at it until noon. She left her laptop and trekked the familiar path, with Major on his leash, to the water's edge. Her hand caressed the smooth stones from the creek. They shone in the sunlight as they slid to form a heart in her palm. Her face glowed, and she thought of Gerald. They had scheduled dinner and a movie.

She texted him.

–Can we change plans 4 tonight Can eat here—

She waited for his response. Again, she smiled when his name and words appeared on the screen.

—Of course. BBQ and beer. All ok?—-

—Yes, haven't left Major after dark Best for now—

—Got it. About 6:30—

The smiley face emoji he sent matched the one on her face.

When Gerald arrived, Major gave a dutiful round of barking until he recognized him.

Gerald asked over the barking, "He's okay with me here?"

"Oh sure. He's just being protective. But remember, you're being watched." She giggled.

"Hmmm. Sounds like getting a goodnight kiss might be risky."

"Could be he'll trust you by then. Maybe if you slip him a small piece of the meat?"

Gerald snapped his finger with an idea. "A bribe. I can do that."

"Sit down, and thanks for bringing dinner. It smells delicious." With everything ready, they clinked their beer bottles together in a toast.

Major ate his dinner while Ava and Gerald finished their plates of pulled pork, slaw, white bread, and sweet potato pie. They put the paper plates and plastic utensils in the garbage and settled on the porch to talk over coffee.

Gerald asked about Marvin. "Any recent developments in the case?"

"Not too much, but Jennifer is here and on the defense team. That's huge. She's been able to get him to remember some things. The DA is pushing for a quick trial date. You know, election time this fall."

"Of course. Everyone looking out for themselves instead of true justice."

She raised an eyebrow. "I haven't heard you be so negative." She reached to take his hand. "You handle the world around you with such grace most of the time. Is there something in your native beliefs that helps ground you? I apologize if I'm getting too personal."

He chuckled. "I want us to share everything, including our beliefs. I have prayer and meditation on my side, but I'm just worried about my friend."

Ava walked to the railing. "I am, too. I wish there was something I could do. Gerald, the more I learn about PTSD, I think my dad must have been suffering all those years. Some of Jennifer's stories sound familiar to me." She turned to him. "To deal with that, I may want some help."

He surrounded her in a bear hug. "When you're ready, I know a few good therapists and I can hook you up with one." He kissed her cheek.

"I'm comfortable talking with you."

He faced her at arm's length. "You know I'll always be here for you. I can listen and discuss, but someone less connected to you may help you more."

She sank into his arms again. "This is enough. I enjoy having you around."

Gerald led her back to her chair, then took his own. "Any more definite plans about leaving?"

"I told my boss I'd be back by Labor Day, but I'm trying to figure things out. There are still a mountain of questions about my life. I like it here more than I expected."

He relaxed and sipped his coffee. "I like the sound of that. Oh look, it's raining." He rose to his full six-foot three height and looked across the yard to watch the sparkling water hit the ground.

She stood and looked into his eyes. "It's nasty out. Do you want to stay?"

"Wrong question. Of course, I want to, but let's not rush." Their lips met in a shared passion.

She let out a sigh. "I get it. Be careful out there. Text me when you get home."

"Will do" He waved as he drove away.

****

Jennifer and Jasper waited for their client at the sheriff's office. When the deputy led Marvin into the room, he removed the handcuffs, then shoved Marvin down into a chair across from his two lawyers. "Sheriff says you've got an hour, then it's back to your cage." He strutted out of the room, keys jingling on his hip.

Jennifer said, "Well, he's proud of himself, isn't he?"

Marvin rubbed his wrists and gave a response. "He's young. Leave him alone. He'll soon figure out he doesn't have as much power as he thinks."

"Dad, if you say one more time, they're just doing their jobs, I'll scream. He looked at you like you were a convicted man."

"Understand, they only press charges if they're pretty sure they can get a conviction. What have you got new?"

Jasper straightened his tie and pulled a file from his briefcase. "They still can't place you at the scene of the crime. Though there were thirty-four workers on duty at the farm that night, seems not one witness has come forward. I've interviewed most, and they say they don't know anything, but others? I'm not so sure."

"And what will you do about those others?" Marvin moved his hands back and forth on the table before him.

Jasper showed Marvin a list of names and their work positions. A red checkmark stood beside more than half of the names. Do you know any of these people I've marked?

Marvin took his time, running his finger down the list. "I can't pronounce most of these names, much less say I know them."

Jennifer joined in. "Jasper says the majority are from Asian countries or south of the border. I'm sure you saw the same when you worked vice."

Jasper nodded. "They all speak enough English to tell me they didn't see or hear anything. Seems strange to me. A rifle as powerful as the murder weapon would make quite a ruckus."

Marvin acted fast to ask, "So, a cover-up? Have you talked to the bosses there? You gotta get somebody to crack." Marvin let out a deep breath and shuddered. "I thought I was tough enough to take it in here, but you have to do something. I blew it last night."

Jennifer took notes. "What happened?"

He shook his head. "That deputy brought my dinner and left it just outside my reach. I tried but couldn't get it. He thought it was extra funny and started taunting me. I went wild, trying to bust down the gate of my cell. After a while, another deputy took the guy out and pushed the dinner to me."

Jasper slammed the file shut. "Oh no. That helps nothing. No wonder this deputy was so smart with you. You'd better hope it doesn't make things worse. I agree he was wrong, but you can't respond like that. Control yourself, man. I'll go see how the sheriff is handling it."

After he left the room, Jennifer moved closer to her father. "Dad, I'm sorry he treated you that way."

"I wish I could make people understand. Control is hard for me sometimes. I just lost it. Get me out of here, please. I can't believe they wouldn't set bail."

"It is a murder charge, after all. Besides, there appears to be a lot of pressure on the DA to wrap this one up. Someone is hiding something."

Marvin thought a minute. "Got to be more than political pressure. Maybe from the higher ups at the farm? Could this be some kind of organized crime operation and I'm the chosen fall guy?"

Jennifer continued to take notes. "I remember you said you went there to talk to them about polluting the waters around here. Have you done research to verify your claims?"

"No, but I knew they were the only industrial outfit close by. It has to be them. I hate it when I'm fishing and trash, scum, dead fish float by."

Jennifer stood and grabbed her briefcase. "Okay, I'm going to follow up on this idea. It could be the answer to why someone would choose you as the guy to take the blame. If someone wanted this guy knocked off, hearing about your confrontation with him made it easy to frame you."

Marvin was up and pacing. "You're onto something, Jennifer." He stopped to face her. "You be careful. If we're right, these are dangerous people."

"I promise, Dad."

Chapter 22

Ava drove into town the next day. Her mind swirled with thoughts of Marvin, her manuscript, Gerald, memories of her dad, and the fast-moving calendar. The stores all had back to school signs and displays. Fall festivals wouldn't be far behind, and her last days on the mountain. She sat outside the coffee shop with a latte in hand and called her sister.

"Hi, Barb. How's everything there?"

"Busy, of course. How about you? Ready to come home?"

Ava didn't answer. "If you have a few minutes, I'd like to talk about Dad. Something I'm writing has got me thinking."

"Sure. About what?"

She gripped the phone, causing her knuckles to turn white. "I'm writing about a man with PTSD."

Silence filled the pause before her sister's response. "And you want to talk about Dad?"

Something in her sister's voice told Ava she was deciding what or how much to say.

"You know something, don't you? C'mon, sis, you're not ten and me five anymore. Talk to me."

"What are you asking about, exactly?"

"I don't know. I'm experiencing shadowy memories, for one thing."

"Okay, listen. Dad had his issues. He was never

160

violent with any of us, but he and Mom argued pretty hard sometimes. Remember how often we spent time at Grandma's? Even on school nights? Those are the times when things got tough at home."

Ava released the near empty crumpled cup. Her eyes spilled over.

"Ava? You still there?"

"Yes. I loved Grandma and just thought it was a special treat. Why didn't I see it was something more?"

"You were so young for most of it. A few times, Uncle Frank came over to calm them down. You don't recall hiding under the bed when the screaming and fighting started? Maybe you blocked the truth under there, along with your fear. After all, he was your hero."

"My work on this manuscript and making friends with people with this diagnosis is calling those things to mind."

"Ava, are you going to be okay? Mom will have to fill in more facts for you. I can only share some things and what I remember."

"I've asked her, but I thought she held back something. Maybe to protect my image of Dad. I'll try again. I'm going to finish the book. Will you read the manuscript when I have it ready to edit?"

"I'd love to. Ava, I hate to go, but I've got cookies ready to come out of the oven for the parent teacher meeting tonight. School starts in a few weeks. Tell me I didn't upset you too much."

Ava shook away the dark thoughts. "No. I'm glad we talked. Tell the kids and Jack hello. I'll see you soon."

Ava stayed in the car to finish her cry. Then, while completing her errands in town, she thought about her sister's words.

On her way out of town, she passed the sheriff's station, which held her friend. She felt closer to him through a shared pain but couldn't face him yet.

Back at her cabin, she stopped to run her hands over Major's back and remove the chain from his collar. He followed her inside where he laid at her feet as she opened the laptop. She planned on something lighter.

*The Novel*

*Beth flopped down on the couch next to Max. "The kids are down, at last. How was your day?"*

*He offered her his beer. "It was okay. The case we've been working on for three months is going to court next Monday. The poor woman got evicted yesterday so she could use some good news."*

*Beth placed the remaining brew on the side table and moved closer to him. "That's awful. Where is she living?"*

*He turned the TV off. "At her mother's. Not a perfect situation there, but better than the street. Which is what she planned until Sandy convinced her otherwise."*

*"Your secretary?"*

*"Yeah, I have a small office, but the three of us are a mighty team."*

*Beth laid her head on his shoulder. "I'm so proud of you and how you're helping people. You're not working this weekend, are you?"*

*"I'll need to read over the briefs for this case, but I can work on them Sunday night. What do you have in mind?"*

*"We haven't had Johnnie and Charlotte over since Christmas. How about Saturday night? Mom and Dad will babysit." She saw his face darken. "You don't want to?"*

*"It would be nice, but they're having trouble, Beth. He lost another job, and she's talking divorce."*

*Beth turned to face him. "Oh, no. How did that happen?"*

*"He said a fellow employee blamed him for some missing stock and he decked the guy. Right in the manager's office. I don't know how to help him anymore."*

*"I thought he was doing so well this time. Now they have a baby on the way. I guess poor Charlotte has had enough."*

*Max pulled her to him. "She's not you, my rock of Gibraltar. How did I get so lucky?"*

*"I know he's your buddy, and I want you to support him, but like you said, how much more can you do?"*

*"Things he said today frightened me. Like there's no hope, and he's ready to give up."*

*"He wouldn't...Oh, Max. He can't do that to Charlotte and the baby."*

*"I'm going to the center with him on Monday. Maybe his counselor can help before it's too late."*

Ava stood to stare out the window, hands on the small of her back. "Well, that took a dark turn."

\*\*\*\*

Ava filled Major's dish and set it down next to her chair on the porch. She paced while he ate. "We're getting along pretty well, aren't we? I love having you here, but I wish Marvin was home." He looked up at the sound of his master's name, then returned to his meal. "The nightmare will be over soon." Just then, a familiar car pulled up to the cabin. Major walked to the top step with ears alert and nose twitching.

Jennifer lowered a window and called out. "Too

busy to take a ride?" Jennifer got out and offered her hand to Major. "The sheriff gave us a drawing of a quarter mile circle around the crime scene. He says they've completed their investigation up there. I want to go walk it. Will you go with me? Jasper said his kid has a soccer game, and I'm not sure he would've gone, anyway."

"I'd love to. Let me put my boots on and secure Major."

"I'll wait in the car. We'll stop by Dad's so I can change clothes, too."

As Jennifer drove, Ava looked over the sketches. "These are pretty detailed. How did you get them?"

"They have to disclose anything like this they may use in court. Are we still on the right road?"

"Yes, but we can only get so close by car. It'll be a lot of hiking in. What do you want to see?"

"First, I want to familiarize myself with the general terrain. I know nothing about this area. They found the victim away from the main building, out in the woods."

Ava pointed at an opening ahead. "Pull over. We'll walk from here."

Jennifer put on a ball cap as she exited the car. They hiked up through the trees until they came to an opening. "This is the first mark on the map."

"Yes, it says this is where they found him. Must be a hundred yards from the plant. We've got about three hours before we lose the light."

Jennifer reached into her back pocket. "I brought a flashlight, but I'm not sure being up here after dark is a good idea. The flashlight might draw attention from the farm, too. Let's get started. I want to see what the shooter saw at dusk when he took the shot. I may have to recreate the scene in court."

Ava shook her head as they walked again. "I get it, let's not tarry. Hey, here's the spot. It's still marked with police tape."

The two walked around the area and measured from side to side. Jennifer made notes while Ava called out finds.

Ava kicked at a mound of dirt. "What footprints didn't wash away in the rain look to be trampled. Where did these deputies take their training?"

"Calm down, Ava. Look. Here's a full footprint. It appears to be a man's sneaker. There are clumps of molding material. Says to me they made a cast. This is not in the sheriff's notes."

Ava rushed over to inspect the print. "I've never seen Marvin wear sneakers. That proves it wasn't him."

Jennifer stopped her. "Woah, not so fast. It only proves someone was here in sneakers. It doesn't tell us when or who."

"They can at least determine the shoe size and weight of the person from the casting."

Again, the attorney in Jennifer stayed wise. "But if it belongs to the killer, it means he took the shot, then came down here to check out his work instead of high tailing it out of here. Not likely. I'll take my own pictures of the area and ask the sheriff why he didn't include this print in their disclosure documents."

"Jen, we've been over all of this area."

"I know, Ava. What we need to do now is find the place where the killer took the shot. The map says east of here. It has to be up on that ridge. Come on."

"Hold on, Jen. It's a long way up there. Look, the map shows this dirt road will at least get us closer." She walked to the car. Jennifer took more photos, then followed.

As they drove to the end of the road, Ava asked, "What do you expect to see up here? Law enforcement must have combed every inch."

"I have to get this all in my head." Jennifer said. "What did it look like to the shooter? How would he get away fast? From the drawing, the road we're on may have been his path out."

"Let's look for tire tracks, Jen. On TV they do all kinds of scientific stuff with those."

Jennifer smiled. "Remember, this is a small town. They'll send evidence to the Oklahoma Bureau of Investigation. It could take a while to get answers. This looks like the end of the road. Where to from here?"

Ava ran her finger across the drawing until she found the point of interest. "Looks like it's about fifty yards on up this hill to the east."

The women hiked and climbed to their destination. On the ridge, they looked for an opening in the trees toward the crime site. Ava called out, "Over here." She stood by a large boulder that came up to her waist. Yellow crime scene tape surrounded it. "Looks like the sheriff had the same idea. The shooter must have kneeled here and steadied the gun on this big rock."

Jennifer searched the area at the base of the stone. "Footprints again. Boots and sneakers this time, though. Move out of the light so I can get photos."

Ava was skeptical. "Why weren't these sneaker prints in the report?"

Jennifer put binoculars to her eyes and said, "I've got to give them the benefit of the doubt until I can talk to the sheriff." She zoomed in on the site where the body laid in the open area below. "You'd have a clear shot from here as long as you had daylight, which would fit the time of death the coroner set. This was a trained sharp shooter to hit a target through such a small opening and this far away. The coming darkness must have created shadows, too. Yeah, they hired someone special for this."

Ava thought out loud. "Why was the murder victim out in those woods, anyway? If our theory of a sharp shooter is right, someone lured him to be in the exact spot."

A rustling in the woods behind and to the north startled them both. They stood still and listened for more movement. Then there was silence.

"Ava, we'd better get back to the cabin."

"It might only be a deer, but I'm with you. Let's go."

When they arrived at her cabin, Ava asked, "Will you come in for dinner?

"No, I want to get back to Dad's place to make some notes about our research. I'll have to go over it with Jasper in the morning before visiting the sheriff."

Ava took Major outside to relieve himself, then took off her boots to sit with him for a while. She wanted to talk to Gerald, but waited for their usual goodnight text at bedtime.

After she sliced cheese and salami for a snack, her phone buzzed on the counter, and she saw the screen light up with Jennifer's text.

*—Break in over here Can you come bring Major I'll text sheriff's office—*

Ava leashed the dog, and both headed to her car. "Yes, you get to go with me this time. You're on duty now. You know what I mean, don't you, boy?" His ears shot forward, and he glared at the road ahead.

Ava parked behind Jennifer's car. "Jennifer, where are you? Are you okay?"

Jennifer got out of her car and ran back to Ava and the canine, who lunged toward the cabin. "I didn't go in after I saw the screen door torn off and a window broken."

Major snarled and pulled at the leash. Ava said, "Let's let him go, then follow him in."

Jennifer stepped back. "Is that a gun in your hand?"

Ava held the weapon behind her thigh. "Yes. I keep my dad's pistol in case I run into varmints around the cabin. I'd say a big varmint was here."

Ava stepped over the screen and used Jennifer's key to open the door. The dog rushed in, then took on a stealthy pose as he searched the cabin. A few minutes later, he walked back to the women and stood looking up at them. "I guess he means it's clear. We'd better not touch anything until the law gets here."

The women locked themselves in Ava's car with Major, waiting another twenty minutes for a sheriff's vehicle to arrive. Ava put a hand on her friend's shoulder. "Are you okay? I know this must have scared you."

Jennifer rubbed her face with a shaking hand. "I wish I could see my husband and baby. I act all tough, but it would feel good to have his arms around me right now."

"Hang in there. You'll see them soon enough."

Headlights crossed the trees as a sheriff's SUV turned into the drive. A spotlight outside the driver's door shone around the property before a deputy stepped out and approached the women. Major barked and growled from the back seat.

The deputy bent down to speak to Jennifer. "You called for assistance, Ma'am? Have you been inside?"

Jennifer did the talking. "We sent the dog in." She was glad it wasn't the smart-ass deputy.

The young man shone his flashlight on the excited dog. "Yeah, Marvin's dog is something else. If he cleared the place, we should be okay, but let me go in first." Ten minutes later, he walked back to the car. "Seems okay. Was the door open when you got here?"

"No. The screen was already off, but we unlocked the door to let the dog inside. When they found the door locked, they must have broken the window to get in."

He removed his hat and scratched his head. "Any idea what brought this on?"

Ava spoke up. "No. Unless they knew Marvin was gone and wanted his guns."

He nodded. "I found the safe locked." His expression changed with his furrowed brow. "If nothing is missing, is it possible it was you they were looking for?"

Ava grabbed Jennifer's arm. "Do you think it has something to do with the charges against her father?"

"It's something to ponder. I'll make out my report and see how the sheriff wants to proceed. Not a good idea for you to stay here tonight, ma'am."

Ava said before Jennifer could respond, "She'll be staying with me."

He added their personal information to his notebook. As he put it away, he said, "I'll go in with you to get your things." When they returned to the car, he said, "You ladies have a good night." They drove behind him out of the driveway.

"Ava, I can't intrude on your small space. I'll get a

room in town."

"Nonsense. I'll make a pallet on the floor for tonight, and tomorrow we'll get an air mattress. I won't hear of anything else."

Chapter 23

The next day, Jennifer returned to Marvin's cabin. Gerald came by to install a heavier screen and lock and replaced the glass in the window. Ava returned to her usual routine of writing as Jennifer forged ahead with the investigation. Marvin's struggle, never far from her mind, continued to fuel her work.

*The Novel*

*Johnnie watched as Max signaled a left turn onto the street to their destination. "Thanks for driving me today. You're a good friend."*

*"No problem, buddy. You've done the same for me. Now, you're gonna be open with the counselor, right? Tell him everything."*

*"Sure, like how I can't hold a job to take care of my family. I snap at the slightest pressure. Oh, and I don't want to forget my wife is about to leave me. Yeah, marvelous stories."*

*Max parked the car and reached to shake his friend's shoulder. "You stop it. Your story is no different from a thousand other veterans who made it through. You'll make it, too, but you've got to stop the negative talk. It helps nothing."*

*Johnnie slumped farther into the seat and stared out the window at the medical building. "I'm just tired of fighting. It's too hard. All I wanted to do was serve my country, and look what it got me."*

*"You came home alive. Yes, it's up to you to manage the rest, but many people are pulling for you, including Charlotte. I don't think she'd give up if you don't. Let's get in there. I'm sure you'll feel better and then we'll grab some lunch."*

*After a half hour, Max heard yelling in the counselor's office. He jumped from his chair. The receptionist stopped him in his tracks. "Sit down, Mr. Archer. He'll be fine."*

*He looked from her to the office door and back, then took his seat again. "I know you're right. My sessions used to be pretty rough, too. Now, they're for support. I wish he could get there."*

*Later, the two men talked over a hearty lunch of beef sandwiches and fries. Max tried at first to keep the things light. "Man, they have the best food here. I'm glad you live close so we can hang out like this."*

*Johnnie wiped ketchup from his chin. "I am, too. Look, Max, I know I'm a handful sometimes. You and Beth have been such good friends to me and Charlotte."*

*Max considered keeping silent, but thought he could make an important point. "Johnnie, when I told Beth what you said the other day about being, well, you know, ready to give up, her first thoughts were of Charlotte and the baby. You need to keep them top of mind, too. Not the pressure of needing to provide for them, but the blessing of having them in your life."*

*With eyes about to overflow, Johnnie responded. "Yeah, the doc said something similar today. I'm going to try. If I have to stand in front of the mirror every morning and repeat, 'I have a lot to live for,' I'll try."*

*"I hope you believe it, buddy. I really do."*

Ava stared at the keyboard until at last she could

peel her fingers away and say out loud, "Why is this getting harder to write with each scene and chapter? My gut is churning like it did as a kid under my bed."

Around lunchtime, her phone buzzed with a text. Though she missed some words because of a weak signal, she determined Jennifer was having a bad day. She responded with,

*—Come over when you're finished—*

As Jennifer drove in, Ava finished garnishing the salads she had prepared and wiped her hands to greet her guest on the porch. "Hi. I hope you're hungry. There's a sirloin we can split."

"Sounds great. I wish I could share it with Dad."

Ava's voice rose, a look of shock on her face. "Are they not feeding him right?"

"More like he's not eating. Come on, let's eat before we dig into my day."

"Okay, get settled while I pour the merlot. I thought we could use something strong tonight."

"You guessed right." Jennifer took a deep breath. "We may need more than one bottle. Thank you, this looks amazing. Ava, you've lifted me up once again."

Talk over dinner centered on salad dressings and favorite restaurants while Ava held back her many questions. She insisted the dishes wait in the sink for her to clean later. They went to the chairs outside with another glass of wine.

Ava could wait no longer. "Okay, tell me all. What did you learn today? And how is Marvin?"

"I'm worried. The stress is showing on him. I met with Jasper first thing. I demanded to know what the sheriff had to say about our findings at the crime scene, or had he even asked him?"

"Oh, I bet he didn't like that." Ava giggled.

Jennifer continued with excitement. "Not a bit. Get this. He pushed back from his desk and crossed his legs all casual like and said, 'Now, now, we don't want to rile the sheriff.' He said he'd scheduled to meet with him this afternoon. I asked him what time I should be there, but of course that wasn't his plan."

"You went, didn't you?"

"You know I did. Seems I surprised the sheriff with what we found. He was pretty embarrassed. I guess his deputies led the investigation at the crime scene. We'll see what comes of it."

Ava poured more wine for them. "And your time with Marvin? How did that go?"

Jennifer took a deep breath. "Other than him not sleeping or eating, I guess he's doing the best he can. He said the pair of sneakers I found in his closet are the only ones he owns and never wears them. I can believe that as they were clean as a whistle. The sheriff said the reason the sneaker tracks weren't in the reports was that they could be from one of his men. He's still working that out."

Ava made her point, "Yeah, I always said Marvin doesn't strike me as the sneaker type."

"I showed him the map around the area. He said the terrain would be too rough for him and his bad leg to climb up there and especially with a rifle. That means only if tire tracks matched his would they be able to say he was there at any time."

Ava wasn't standing for any of it. "The whole so-called investigation has been sloppy."

Jennifer thought it through. "Well, remember it rained. What if mud covered the shell casing at the time or even floated over from somewhere else? I'm trying to give them the benefit of the doubt. The significant thing is, the bullet taken from the body matches Dad's rifle."

Ava's voice conveyed conviction. "My loyalty stands firm. I think they're still running on circumstantial evidence all the way."

"I heard something interesting today. Family members have filed missing persons reports on a couple of other guys from the facility."

"Related to the murder?"

"Can't be sure. If these people have a habit of removing men, it brings up questions. Does this mean there is something illegal going on up there? Did these missing men know too much? Maybe Dad's visit up there a couple of months ago stirred the pot a little too much. Things are getting crazy."

Ava emptied her glass. "What do you feel about this Jasper James fellow? Is he doing anything to help Marvin?"

Jennifer hesitated. "I hate to think bad of a fellow barrister, but I can't be sure. He's either a goofball or knows more than he's sharing with me."

"Why would he keep things from you?"

"I don't know. Being the outsider here, I'm staying positive, and in my lane, right now. Let me check with my contact in Oklahoma City to see what he's found out about the names I gave him. Not everyone at the grow farm can be blind. Someone has to know something about what they're hiding out there. It might be up to me to find it."

"I'm glad you've got some help that's not from the bunch around here."

"I know. That's important. I feel bad taking so much

of your time. How's your writing going?"

"Not bad. I had a good session today. I'm moving in the right direction. Your stories and comments have been helpful."

"I hope so. It's hard to live through some of it again, but knowing I'm helping you makes it worthwhile. I'd better get to the cabin and bed. I've got some busy days ahead to get some things settled in my mind before I have to go home for a few days."

"I understand. Let me know what I can do in your absence. Text me when you get to the cabin so I know you're safe."

Ava and Major watched her drive away. "Do your thing out here, boy, and let's go inside. I'm ready to hit the hay and face another day tomorrow." After deciding the dirty dishes could wait, she noticed her phone light up with a text from Gerald. She smiled as they chatted, then told him goodnight. Sleep didn't come for an hour or two. The scene she wrote earlier, and now, more information about her friend Marvin, filled her head.

**\*\*\*\***

The next day Ava started early on a new chapter. Her writing seemed sluggish and uninspired. She couldn't concentrate on anything but the world she had made for herself in the mountains. The idea of not going back to her old life pushed into her every thought. "I know it's not fair to Gerald, Matt, or myself to keep putting off talking about it. Oh well, there's time." She grabbed her notebook and writing implements. "Let's get some fresh air, Major." With the dog's leash in her back pocket, she and her companion took off for a hike. Since the break-in at Marvin's place, she had taken to locking the door when she left her property.

At the creek, she watched Major play in the cool water until he came to lie at her side. She stroked his head and said, "This place is beautiful, although our first meeting here wasn't so good. Remember fella?"

He raised his head with a whimper.

"Yeah, painful, huh? At least I got to meet Marvin that day. Look how far we've come, but time is ticking away. I guess I might as well get used to the idea of going back to my regular life before long." The dog laid his head in her lap as tears trickled down her cheek.

After a few minutes, she stood up. Major shook off dirt and leaves, then looked up at her as if for instructions.

"I wonder if we missed something at the crime scene? Let's drive up there. Maybe you'll sniff out a clue."

As she drove to the site, Major sat on alert, surveying the forest on both sides of the dirt road. When the car stopped at their destination, he pranced around in the seat until Ava opened the door and latched the leash to his collar. "Just to be sure you don't get so excited you take off. Other dogs have already looked everything over, but let's see what you find."

He stretched the leash and her arm as he pulled her around the area, his nose to the ground. Each time he stopped, she felt a rush of hope that he had located an important piece of evidence, but no. Twenty minutes later, he stood at her feet and looked up at her again.

Ava rewarded his work with a scratch behind his ears. "It's okay, boy. I knew it was a long shot. Let's move to the shooter's site."

Near the point where they believed the gunman had kneeled, she followed a line of sight with binoculars beyond the spot where the man fell and toward the main building of the facility. At the entrance, a man watched as two black limousines pulled up. A rear window in the lead car lowered so the waiting man could lean down and talk to the occupant. Two men the size of grizzly bears got out of the second car and went inside the building.

Ava turned and took quick steps back to her car. "Come on, let's get closer." Major took his post in the front seat as she drove as fast as possible, the car sliding on the loose gravel. When she reached the gate to the farm, she parked across the road in a stand of trees. "I hope we didn't miss them." She opened the door to let the excited canine jump to the ground. "I know you've been on plenty of these jobs, and I probably don't need to say this, but please stay quiet."

They walked to a vantage point in some thick foliage where she might hear what was going on. She whispered, "Look, the cars are still here. If I could only see the tag numbers. Just a little closer."

Just then, the muscled men exited the building, gripping the arms of a small Latino man between them. They threw him into the back seat of the second car. Dirt flew as the car sped away. Major let go a low guttural growl, feet marching in place as a splendid-looking man in a three-piece suit stepped from the other car and looked in Ava's direction. The first man pointed toward her. She felt Major quiver as she pulled the dog to her and tried to make herself smaller. Her heart thumping, she whispered in his ear. "Stay still." Both men continued to move closer. She felt exposed when the men stopped six feet from her.

Now she could see the man from the limousine kept his hand in one pocket. His voice was calm, but forceful.

"Come out of those bushes, whoever you are. Are you alone?"

Ava gripped Major's leash wrapped around her hand to keep him in check as she stood.

The man looked them over. "Who are you? What are you doing on this property? Does the dog bite?"

She tried for a firm voice. "He's s been known to." Canine teeth bared and a deep-throated snarl backed her statement.

He continued the interrogation. "You hold on to him and answer my questions. Who are you?"

She waited until enough air returned to her lungs to speak with ease. "I'm Ava Hardy with the *Tulsa Herald*. I wanted to get an interview about the murder investigation into the death of an employee here. Would I speak to you about that?" She didn't stop Major's growl, but kept him close.

A tight-lipped grin shown from the extra man. The speaker took a step toward her and said, "Not possible. The sheriff asked us not to comment while the investigation continues." His face darkened. "Now, it's best you leave and not return. You must not be a very good investigative reporter. Did you not think there would be security cameras at the entrance?"

Most often Ava would have bristled at his sarcasm, but thought better of it in her present predicament. She also thought it best not to ask about the poor man hustled into the other car. Enough bravery, or maybe foolishness, had left her mouth for one morning.

The fast walk back to her car was made on trembling legs. Major looked back and asserted his feelings about the meeting. A forceful tug on the leash each time kept them moving forward. As her car rolled and bounced away, she checked the rearview mirror every few seconds. It didn't look like anyone followed, but not going back to her cabin right away made sense to her. When she reached the first gas station in town, she pulled over to call Gerald.

## Chapter 24

Over the phone, Ava told Gerald enough of her adventure for him to exclaim, "You did what? Ava, no. Are you okay?"

"Now, calm down. I can explain. Can you meet me after work? I need to talk it through and see what sense I make of it."

She heard his deep breath before he said, "I can't wait to hear this. I'll see if I can leave a few minutes early."

He met her as planned and got in her car to comfort her. "Are you sure you're okay?

"I know you're mad, but I'm fine now. I probably shouldn't have bothered you."

"Nonsense, I'm glad you called, and it's never a bother. I can't believe you went up there. Exactly what happened?"

"I wanted to get closer so I could hear what they were talking about. I didn't expect them to discover me. And anyway, Major was with me."

"Someone confronted you? Ava, are you nuts?" He looked at the dog in the back seat. "And I thought you were looking after her." Major growled but laid down.

She pulled back from Gerald. "No, I'm not crazy. I'm a reporter. This is what I do for a story. You'd better get used to it." She blushed and said, "I mean, if you plan on being around me."

His smile told her he got it. "Come on, I'll follow you out to your place."

When they arrived, Ava unlocked the door and let Major in. "Sit while I get us some tea. I'll tell you all about it." The evening light faded as she finished her story. "What do you think?"

"You need to ask? You take too many chances." His raised hand stopped her expected response. "But I get it, and I agree they're hiding something up there. Did you see anything that could be considered a clue?"

"I can describe the men, but couldn't get a tag number off of either car."

"I wonder what happened to the guy they took out?" Gerald stood and leaned on the railing, facing Ava.

She set her drink down to say, "The way they manhandled him into the back seat, I'm pretty sure they weren't taking a friendly drive into town for tacos."

"What about telling the sheriff?"

Ava joined him at the rail. "Absolutely not. For one thing, the only law broken was me trespassing. Because the crime scene reports don't mention some items we found out there, we believe either the sheriff or Marvin's lawyer is holding out on us. Why? That or the deputies are just doing a lousy job."

"Good question. I've known Jim Carson most of my life, but this Jasper James is new to me. I guess anything is possible." He rubbed his abdomen and whined, "Hey, are you going to let me starve tonight?"

"Not if cold sandwiches are okay with you. Come on, we can finish this discussion inside. Maybe I can find something for dessert, too."

He put his arm around her waist. "I was hoping for something more exciting after dinner."

She grinned and felt her face flush. "I just bet you were."

"I know we said we'd wait, but it's getting tough." He hugged her to him.

"Gerald, you're on my mind all the time. Waiting is no fun for me either. You understand, that kind of commitment is huge for me. We're adults, not teenagers, letting things go too far in the back seat of your mama's sedan. I don't want either of us getting hurt."

He bent to touch his lips to hers. "I get it." He tickled her sides. "I'll behave."

When her giggling stopped, he surprised her with, "I'd like for you to meet my mom. She said she'll fix a traditional meal on Sunday, and she's a great cook. Will you come?"

Ava held a hand to her heaving chest. "That sounds wonderful, but will other family be there and make too much of our friendship?"

"I'll tell everyone to cool it. Of course, my little brother Chet is a big kidder. I can only pretend to control him."

Ava scurried around the kitchen to prepare their sandwiches without answering.

He walked up next to her. "Too much? We can do something private with Mom, if you'd be more comfortable. She likes the steak house over in McAlester. We could…"

She faced him with a grin and laid fingers on his mouth. "Hush. It's fine. I want to know all about you, and maybe they can fill me in."

He rubbed his neck. "What have I gotten myself in for?"

\*\*\*\*

The following Sunday, Ava met Gerald at a shopping center parking lot in town. She locked her car and sat in his truck for the ride to his family's home. That morning, like a nervous teenager on a blind date, shaky hands dropped her toothbrush and spilled coffee while getting ready.

"What if they don't like me, Gerald? I don't want you to be embarrassed by me."

"Nonsense. How could they not like you? Just be yourself. They may be over the top sometimes, but I know you can stand up to their liveliness."

As the truck turned onto a long tree-lined road, Ava clutched his thigh as if hanging on to a carnival ride. "This is your property?" The sun showcased a modest home in a grassy meadow. "It's beautiful."

Gerald smiled. "My family's home. We've lived here and worked the land for four generations."

As they rounded a curve, her eyes bugged out at what looked to her like a sea of cars and pickups parked to one side. "Are all these people here to see me?"

He laughed and squeezed her hand. "I told you. When Mama cooks a feast, they come out of the woodwork. Don't worry."

The men had set up tables and chairs in the front yard, awaiting the feast. Children ran around playing games. Ava clenched Gerald's arm as they mounted the porch and entered the house.

A man about Gerald's age reached to hug him. "Hey, cuz, you finally made it. Are you going to introduce me to this one?" He turned to Ava. "You know you're much too pretty for this guy."

Ava responded, "That's sweet." Loud voices and laughter overwhelmed her. "Gerald! There are so many people here."

Gerald stepped in. "You leave her alone. Ava, this is my cousin, Jake." He joked with the man. "The guy who stole Mary Bluehawk from me in eighth grade. I've got my eye on you today, Jake."

Gerald introduced each person as he led her to the kitchen. She tried to memorize names and faces, but didn't hold out much hope for remembering so many.

When they stopped in the doorway of his mother's kitchen domain, the small woman called out orders to others basting meat and stirring luscious smelling dishes in family sized pots. Teenaged girls brushed butter across trays of rolls, ready for the oven.

Gerald stepped forward. "Mama, we're here."

She turned and opened her arms wide to embrace her son. "My boy, my heart is full."

He left her embrace. "Mama, this is Ava I've been telling you about." His arm went around Ava's shoulders.

The woman took Ava's hands. "Halito, chim achukma? You are most welcome in my humble home."

Ava looked at Gerald and he said, "Mom said hello, are you well? It's the traditional Choctaw greeting."

Ava looked back at her host. "Thank you for having me. It smells wonderful in here."

One of the other women handed Ava an apron. "You'll need this. I'm Allison. That's Julie, Margaret, and Trina." Her hand swept the room. "Our daughters, Millie, Janice, Bette, and Marva. You'll have to fend for yourself to name the rest of the family. Hand me those onions."

Ava watched Gerald wave as he left the room. She handed over the onions and put on her apron. Suddenly she was busy assisting, learning, and joining in the conversations and bustling activity of making the meal.

When the ladies laid out the food on the long tables, Ava hadn't seen such a spread since the buffet at the last office Christmas party. Some items she didn't recognize, but she took small portions of most until her plate was full.

Gerald chuckled and leaned to her to whisper in her ear. "You need sideboards on your plate. Or, you know, you can come back for seconds."

"It all looks so good." They took their seats as she prompted, "Now, tell me what I have here."

He took his time describing each dish she questioned. "The greens are Koshiba, lamb's quarter. If it was spring to early summer, we'd be having poke salad."

"My grandmother used to grow that. What's this in the little package?"

"Banaha. It's a kind of bread. Mom's way is to mix field peas and corn meal, wrap them in corn husks, then they're boiled. The meat dish you picked is called Tanchi Labona. It's pork ribs cooked along with hominy. There's another hominy dish down the table called Ashela. It has turkey and is more of a stew."

"I recognize all the fruit, nuts, and squash."

Gerald laughed. "The small things you got three of there are desserts. They're called walashi or fruit dumplings."

"You may have to roll me away from here in a wheel barrow, but I'm going to try everything."

Later, quiet filled his pickup as they rolled along at sunset until they reached her parked car. "Did you have a good time? We weren't too much for you? I thought you held your own pretty well."

The happiness in her heart gushed out of her. "It was wonderful. So much love in her house. Fun, too. I don't know when I've laughed so much. Our family is small compared to yours, but we feel the love, too. I was just thinking about how much I miss them."

His hand stroked the steering wheel in nervous anticipation of her coming answer. "I guess you'll see them soon."

Ava stopped his hand. "Yes, I will. I have to go back. Whether I stay there is the question." Her insides trembled as he kissed her hand. "I still don't have all the answers, but I'm working on it. You're being so patient with me."

"It doesn't solve anything for me to crowd you. Selfishly, I want you near me, but I know that's asking a lot with no real promises from me."

"We're not at the promising stage. Let's just enjoy each other right now. I'm becoming a great believer that things work out like they're supposed to." She looked into his smiling eyes. "I'll admit to getting a little impatient for the answers myself."

Parked next to her car, he wrapped her in his arms. Their lips almost touched as his words flowed over her, "I understand the impatience. In more ways than one." Their kiss said it all.

Emotions from their day together flooded Ava's mind as she drove toward her cabin. As she turned onto the darkness of highway 270 out of town, she turned on her bright headlights to guide her on the deserted road. She continued talking to herself, "What are you doing, Ava? But then, why shouldn't I enjoy him while I'm here?" His family had been so accepting of her, she felt like one of the family already. "Oh, there you go again, getting ahead of yourself." I enjoy time with him and why not? I can handle—" Breath caught in her throat as her head snapped back with a jolt from behind. "What the heck?" Tall headlights flooded the rear-view mirror. Another hit. "Hey, jerk. Stop it." She glanced back to see what she thought was an oversized black SUV pulling around to her left side. Her foot let up from the accelerator to allow the car to pass. Instead, it sidled up to her door and lunged toward her. Her natural reflex was to veer to the right, away from the oncoming vehicle. Now, fear engulfed her and she let out a scream as she struggled to regain control in the gravel close to the guard rail. Through tears, she yelled at the two shadows inside the vehicle, laughing at her attempts to escape. "You think this is funny? Leave me alone, you assholes." Once again, she had to swerve to the right to avoid contact. She looked ahead to see the trunk of a tree as it grew closer. A jerk of the steering wheel and a series of bumps and thumps came to an end with Ava's car in the ditch just feet away from a deep ravine which led down to a creek.

Her heart pounded like a ceremonial drum in her ears. Her hand shook as she opened her door and stepped out on unsteady legs. Her head shook away the fogginess of her brain. "I've got to get out of here. What if they come back?" After a quick review of her car and a plan in her head, she got back in to engage the four-wheel drive. She rocked the car forward and back until the tires made good contact with the soil and then dug in. She backed onto the highway and took off toward her cabin. As she started up the mountain road, "I should have called 911. No, those jokers wouldn't do anything. This wasn't kids out for a good time. Could it have something to do with me helping Marvin?"

As she skidded to a stop at her porch, she heard Major barking inside. "My goodness, boy. I wasn't gone that long." Released to go outside, he ran around the yard sniffing. She followed him with fearful eyes. "Has someone been here? Good thing I left you inside to guard the place. He looked up to her and sat down.

"I guess that means all clear, huh? Well, do your business and let's get inside."

Inside, she pushed furniture in front of the door for added protection, placed the pistol on the bedside table, then climbed into the comfort of the big quilt. When she picked up the phone to text Gerald that she was home, she hesitated. No need to worry him tonight.

—*Made it home Goodnight Gerald*—

—*What took so long?*—

—*Slight detour Thanks for today See you soon*—

Chapter 25

Ava's phone buzzed, vibrated, and skidded across the bedside table until she gave in to see who was texting her so early. The day with Gerald's family and the excitement later had exhausted her. She raised up to retrieve the phone, and pushed her hair back. Sunlight streaming in the window surprised her. "My gosh, what time is it?" The screen lit up with the truth. She had slept past 9:00 a.m.

Her smile lit as bright as the screen at the sight of Gerald's text.

--*Mornin sunshine*--

--*Hi. Thanks 4 waking me Wasting morn in bed*--

--*Yesterday 2 much huh? Glad u came Mom loved u*--

--*Free for lunch?*--

She was standing now with robe and shoes on. The trip outside couldn't wait much longer.

--*Out last class noon U ok?*--

--*Yes just need 2 c u*--

Ava grabbed her towel and toiletries before running to the facilities, her face covered by a smile. Her voice rang through the forest. "He is too good to be true."

Shower complete, she fed Major and secured him outside, then began writing. In a short time, she had another chapter. The tapping of her fingers on the keyboard was music to her ears. It was time to give Max some excitement, too.

*The Novel*

*"Johnnie, open the door. We can talk through this."*
*Max stood outside his friend's apartment door at*
*midnight.*

*"Go away, Max. You don't want to be here."*

*"Come on, man, you called me, so I know this isn't*
*what you want. We can go down to the diner and get*
*some coffee and talk." He leaned his forehead on the*
*door frame.*

*Max put his ear to the door and listened to sniffling*
*and crying. This from the man who had helped him*
*through traumas more than once. "You know we've been*
*through worse. We can fix this, Johnnie. She'll be back.*
*You'll see. I'll help you be strong, so you're ready to*
*welcome her." He heard movement inside. "Johnnie,*
*talk to me, man. You've conquered bigger storms than*
*this. I'm thinking some bacon and eggs from the diner*
*sounds…"*

*Suddenly, a gunshot filled the night. Kaboom. Thud.*

*As every nerve in his body flamed, Max knew what*
*had just happened. A guttural scream came from the*
*deepest part of him. "Johnnie. Johnnie." His fist*
*pounded the door, and he tried to kick it open.*

*A man came out of the apartment next door. "Hey,*
*what's going on out here? People are trying to sleep.*
*Was that a gunshot? Did you hear it? Do you need*
*help?"*

*Max slumped to the floor as he whispered through*
*his tears, "Call 911."*

*The apartment manager arrived to investigate the*
*ruckus, and Max convinced her to open Johnnie's door.*
*Max rushed in to see his friend laying stretched out on*

*the beige carpet where crimson liquid pooled from what remained of Johnnie's head. Blood and physical matter left an interesting sprayed pattern on the living room wall. Max stepped back and steadied himself against the kitchen bar. He needed to throw up, but didn't want to give the situation satisfaction over his inner strength. Deep breaths. Deep breaths. He heard the wail of the ambulance and police getting closer and used the tail of his shirt to wipe his face. He would have to answer their questions and help make some sense of the scene.*

*What sense did it make, after all? How could anyone understand who had not endured what Johnnie and so many like him had experienced? He did his best to explain and watched his friend's body roll away in its black vinyl cocoon.*

*His eyes were dry as he drove home. Instead of an uncontrolled emotion, he resolved to dig in and do more. He wanted to stop the senseless suffering of veterans across the country. What was his role in what he called The War Against the Ravages of War? He beat the steering wheel as he yelled, "I know. A nationwide movement like the country has never seen. It has to start somewhere, and why not with me?" Right now, he had to pick up Beth and head over to comfort Johnnie's widow.*

*After a few days off to collect himself, and a trip to his therapist, Max began setting the groundwork of his dream. An action organization designed to give veterans the help and support they need. How would his initiative go beyond what the government offered at a VA hospital? It had to begin with educating new recruits, so they're prepared for what they'll be up against. More than just pills and group talks after they get back. It had to include help with higher education and job search.*

Ava liked what she saw on the page. "That's positive thinking, Max, and your words came to me with ease. Must be because you inspire me. I need to follow your lead in making the future what I want it to be."

She jumped up to change into blouse and dress slacks. When she freed Major from his leash by the tree, he ran to her car. "No, you can't go this time. I've got important business to handle. Besides, remember our agreement. Protect the place while I'm gone." He followed her inside and laid in front of the fan she turned on for him. "Here's a bowl of water for you. I'll be back soon. You have your assignment." His ears perked with the command.

A blast from Maggie's car horn startled her. While she was always glad to see her lively friend, on this day she had bigger plans.

"Hi, Maggie. You almost didn't catch me here."

"Perfect. If you're going into town, you can ride along with me. What are you up to?"

Ava wasn't ready to share too much about the events of the previous night. "I'm driving over to the college at Wilburton. How about you?"

"A little shopping and the library. Are you doing research? John can help get you in there."

"Uh, yeah, you might say that. Thanks, I've made arrangements already."

"I don't want to keep you from your work." Maggie grabbed Ava's arm. "Say, how is that sweet man of yours?" Her laughter rang through the woods.

Ava tried to hide her crimson cheeks. "He's amazing, as always. We're having lunch. I'm trying to take your advice and come up with some answers about how life is all going to work out."

Maggie shifted in her seat to look out the window. "Still a dilemma? Can I help?"

Ava rested her hand and arm on the car's roof as she bent to face Maggie. "Not unless you can explain how I could let myself fall for a guy I just met. A man I'm supposed to say goodbye to soon."

Maggie got out of her car and hugged Ava. "Aw, honey, don't fight it. You're in love. I don't know anyone who ever figured out love. You just go with it. If it's meant to be, it will work itself out."

"You're right, and I'm no longer fighting it. I had Sunday dinner with his family. His mother is so sweet."

"Oh my. I want to hear all the details."

"Another time, Mag. Maybe we can all get together soon. I've got an appointment to keep this afternoon after I meet with Gerald."

She waved as Maggie drove away. "Just going with it, right? See ya!"

****

Gerald raised a hand in greeting when he saw Ava in the back booth. "I had a hard time paying attention in class. I mean, I'm thrilled to see you, but your text this morning sounded a little strange. Wow. You look nice."

Ava took his hand. "I have something to tell you. Please don't get upset. It's over now."

Gerald sat back hard, as if Mohammad Ali had thrust a fist into his chest. "What do you mean? Over?"

A light went on in her muddled brain and she jumped up to move to his side of the booth. "Oh, no, no, no. Not us. Oh, I'm sorry. For someone who uses words for a living, I messed that up so bad. No, I had a little run-in, shall we say, on the way home last night."

"What? Are you okay? What happened? Wait, let me have some of this tea to calm my nerves. Now, explain."

Ava held his hand as she shared details of the incident. He had questions.

"You think it was kids out for some mischief? What did the officer say when he got there?"

"No, I don't think kids and I didn't call those idiots. What would they do after the car left the scene?"

"They could make an official record of it for insurance if nothing else."

"I'm not worried about a banged-up bumper. Anyway, like I said, it's over and I got home safe."

"You called someone before you went in the cabin? At least Jennifer to go in with you? Tell me you did."

She shrugged her shoulders. "I have Major and a pistol by my bed to keep me safe."

He shrank back and looked around the room before whispering, "A pistol by your bed? You have a gun? Who are you? What else don't I know about you?"

She moved back to the other side of the booth. "Oh, don't make a big deal. The pistol was my dad's, now it's mine, and licensed. I brought it for protection. Seems to me a good idea."

He used a more relaxed voice. "Ava, some independence is great, but anyone would have called for help. I'm just saying. Okay, finish the story."

Over an onion burger for her and a chicken fried steak for him. She finished the telling. "It has to be because of my association with Marvin. That big boss man at the grow farm didn't like me snooping around at all."

"I'm sure it has everything to do with that. This is

getting much too dangerous and now you're acting reckless. Can I convince you to stop this foolishness?"

"If you mean stop helping Marvin, no. Don't even ask me."

He let out a deep breath of frustration. "What am I going to do with you? Okay, I'll follow you home and check over the place."

"Uh, well, no. I have an appointment I can't change. I'd give you the key, but with Major's current frame of mind, you might lose a leg or worse. Besides, everything is just fine.

He leaned to kiss her cheek. "Why would I think otherwise?"

****

Ava stood before the receptionist for the English Department, tapping her foot as she spoke. She felt a droplet of nervous sweat sliding behind one ear and down her neck. "Good afternoon. I'm Ava Hardy, and I called earlier about seeing Professor Elliot." As she waited for the young woman to put her book down and deposit gum into a tissue, Ava shuffled her briefcase to her other hand and looked up at the oversized clock on the wall. "If I'm too early…"

"No, you're fine. She just finished her last class. Have a seat while I tell her you're here."

Chapter 26

The next day, Ava joined Jennifer at breakfast. "Thanks for inviting me to come into town with you. It will be good to see Marvin."

Jennifer used her paper napkin to wipe bacon grease from her mouth. "Yeah, but you need to stop taking me to these local cafes and diners. I've probably gained five pounds. The food is so good."

"Glad you like them. So, what is your plan for today?"

"We'll visit Dad first. Maybe seeing you will brighten his day and even spur memories. I'm groping for straws. And by the way, still no mention of my break-in. No need to worry him."

"I won't. Or my run-in, either. Nothing new then? I don't trust that head guy I met one bit. His eyes are too close together for me."

Jennifer propped both hands on the table and stared toward Ava. "Run-in? What? Wait, and you've met someone from out there? How did I miss all this?"

Ava put her fork down and sat back in the booth. "Uh oh. I guess I didn't tell you because I knew it would upset you." She related both stories with as much detail as she could remember. "I got home safe both times." She didn't have to wait for Jennifer's reaction.

"I can't believe you took that risk at the farm. What were you thinking? I'm convinced the intruders at Dad's

197

place were trying to scare me off. And now this."

"When I told Gerald, I knew it scared him as much as me. I promise I won't go alone again, and I'm leaving Major inside when I leave the cabin."

"That's a good idea." Jennifer took out a notepad. "Okay, start again at the beginning. Leave nothing out. First, give me descriptions of the men you saw."

"I think I felt safer than I should have just because I had Major along."

Jennifer shook her head. "Don't you get it? If these people killed a man, they wouldn't have a second thought about turning a gun on a dog. Come on. Tell what you know and let's get over to the jail."

The women waited in the interrogation room until his escort brought Marvin in. He gave them a big smile as the deputy removed his handcuffs. "Well, don't you ladies look nice this morning?"

Ava blushed while Jennifer responded. "Thanks. It appears you've lost another pound or two. Still not eating?"

"It would be fine if you like a lot of ground meat and starchy stuff. I'm used to wild game and plants I forage myself."

"Eat what's offered to keep your strength up," Ava stated.

He ran a hand through unruly hair. "I know. I guess it won't hurt me to eat unhealthy for a little while. How's Major at your place?"

"He's fine and such a protector. He's tired of being chained when outside and looks up each time a car goes by. I know he misses you. But we're doing okay."

"I'm not used to being without him, either." He turned to his daughter. "Anything new on my case?"

Jennifer opened her briefcase and spread documents across the table. "Not a lot. How long have you known Jasper James? Did you ask for his legal services?"

"No. The young deputy that's usually here suggested him. I'd never needed a lawyer before and didn't know who else to call around here. Are you thinking he's a bad seed?"

Ava moved closer to join the discussion. "I don't like him. He's so flippant about the whole thing."

Jennifer nodded agreement. "I'm not sure yet, Dad. Jasper won't even look me in the eye when he talks. Other than that, it's just a feeling. Please don't worry or say anything. I'll handle him."

Marvin stood and walked to look out of the window. "I've seen and talked to you more than him. I have to admit I don't click with him. Ya know?" He turned back around. "Not like you should with someone trying to save your life."

"One reason I brought Ava is so she can tell you what she found at the crime scene."

Marvin flopped down in the chair hard. "Oh no."

Jennifer stopped him. "I know. I've already told her how foolish that was. Let's let her tell the story. Then we'll go over the crime scene and the evidence listing one more time."

After leaving their meeting with Marvin, the women stopped by Jasper's office. Jennifer asked Ava to mind her manners. "Let me do the talking, but pay attention to how he acts. Be my second set of eyes and ears with him."

"He won't get past my eagle eye."

"Now, Ava, you heard me. I'll ask the questions." Jennifer approached the secretary's desk. "Hi. Jennifer

Wells, to see Mr. James. And this is Ava Hardy."

The woman pushed buttons on an intercom and told Jasper he had visitors. "You can go right in, ladies."

Jasper met them at the door with hand outstretched and a painted-on smile. "Come in ladies. How am I so lucky to have you both today? Coffee? Water?

Jennifer was quick to set the tone for the meeting. "No, thank you. We have lots of work today. I just stopped in to update you on a few things and ask some questions."

He returned to his chair and flopped down. "Now, what have we not discussed already, Mrs. Wells?"

"Jennifer is fine, Jasper."

Ava held her tongue, though she already wanted to slap him

Jennifer spoke with confidence, "I keep finding information on my own. Things you should know and share with me as co-counsel. That is, if you're working the case as hard as I am."

He squirmed in his chair. "Why, Jennifer, I believe you're accusing me of something. You must know your father's case concerns me as much as it does you."

She asked with sarcasm in her voice, "Why, Jasper, are you attempting to reduce my concerns to that of an emotional daughter?" She sat forward in her chair. "Marvin Cameron deserves the best from his attorneys. That's what I'm attempting to give him, but when I continue to hit resistance or a lack of concern, it's hard. I need to know you're in this with me all the way. Or do I just have to recognize that I need to do everything myself?"

Jasper stood and moved to position himself in front of his Harvard Law School diploma before turning to face his accuser. "I have never had my professional integrity questioned. When I took this case, I knew it would be tough, but I dove in and have stayed on top of things since. Do you have something new?"

"I do. Ava was able to talk to a man at the grow farm where the crime occurred. The situation was uncomfortable, to say the least. They threatened her and ran her off the property. She saw enough to know there is something strange going on up there." His face flushed, and he returned to his chair as Jennifer continued. "What have you learned since our last meeting? And by the way, when's the last time you visited the prisoner? Each time I go, he remembers more or brings up questions we should be asking."

He tapped his desk with a pencil before saying, "Unlike you, Jennifer, he is not my only client. I'll get by there tomorrow." He then asked with a sideways grin on his face, "Anything specific you want me to follow up on?"

Jennifer let go a small grin. "Just what I'm sure you would do in any other significant case." She rose from the chair and turned to go. Ava followed.

He stood to see them out. "Oh, by the way, the DA is pushing for a date with the judge this month. As early as two weeks."

Jennifer glared back at him before leaving his office.

Back in the car, Ava ranted about his incompetence. "Yeah, he takes the cake."

Jennifer nodded her agreement. "We're heading back to see Dad. He's our best help."

Marvin had a look of surprise on his face as the deputy led him into the room. "What's up? Anything wrong?"

"Listen quick. Ava needs to get back to Major and the young writer she's working with, but I had to come back to ask you to dig deep, Dad. The prosecutor is pushing things so we don't have much time, and I feel like I'm alone in your defense. If you were out there investigating this thing, what would you do next?"

They watched him scratch his head before he said, "If Jasper is not to be trusted, that changes things."

"Let's just say I don't trust him enough to put my father's life in his hands and walk away. Come on. Give me something to go on here, Dad."

Marvin stood to pace the room. "Well, I've always wondered why they were so quick to charge me with so little evidence. Follow up on Ava's visit to the farm. Has anyone subpoenaed the security films out there? They have to give you access to those. It'll take time, but look at every inch for a couple of days on both sides of the date. Who's out there? What goes on? Any other times they rousted someone away from there, like what she saw?"

"This is good, Dad. If your suspicions of illegal dumping are valid, the films won't show that, but maybe we catch a glimpse of disposal trucks around the building or something."

Ava joined in, excitement in her voice. "Yeah, what I saw may be a common occurrence. We might even see the murder victim being sent, lured, or outright taken to the scene of the crime."

Jennifer made notes as quick as she could. "That's right, Ava. They must have cameras all over the place. Anything else, Dad?"

"Look deeper into who owns and operates the place. Why did they choose the location? Check out their tax records, phone records. Everything." With both hands splayed on the table, he looked at her hard. "You're going to need help."

Jennifer put her notebook and pen back into her briefcase, then stood to put her hand on Ava's shoulder. "I know a bulldog reporter who loves solving mysteries." They turned to go.

"Be careful, both of you. With something fishy going on, we may be talking about more than one murder."

Chapter 27

"Davis, let's see what you have for me this week." Ava sipped her glass of tea. "Did you find the book about writing I mentioned?"

He handed her his folder of work. "Yes. I had to go into McAlester to find it. I get what they're saying about show don't tell, but I'm not sure I used it much in this story. It's hard."

"I'm sure this version will be better. Last time, I kept waiting for a big climax, but all of a sudden, his conflict was all fixed. I knew you could build the scene a lot more. Let's see. And don't worry, all writers struggle with show don't tell. It just takes practice. Give me a minute to read this."

He rubbed Major's coat as she flipped through the pages. Not able to stand the suspense, he got up to pace the porch. She wondered if hearing her red pencil scrape across the pages was too much for him. The folder lay open on her lap when she finished. "Come sit down. I pointed out some places for us to review."

"That bad, huh?" He slumped down in his chair.

"Not really. Just a few opportunities to make the story move with still more excitement."

After an hour's work, his smile returned. "I get it and you're right. This is much better. You're helping me so much. I told my school counselor I'm sure I want to be a writer. He's helping me look into schools.

Especially ones that have good English and writing programs for when I move on from the college here."

"That's wonderful. I'm sure you'll figure it out. Hard work and having the right professors will get you to your goal."

"Like you? You're an excellent teacher, Ms. Ava. Have you looked into the spot open at Eastern?"

She turned her head to hide her smile. "Let's keep this to talking about you, Mr. Simmons."

\*\*\*\*

Ava drove to the store where she picked out fresh fried pies to add to the Thai food Jennifer was bringing for dinner.

Major announced their friend and pranced around as she entered the cabin. "Hi, Ava. Thanks for hosting tonight. After we eat, I have a challenge for you. How's the writing coming along?"

"Pretty well. I've reached what they call the arc and need to figure out how I'm refining the ending." Ava poured their tea at the table she set earlier.

"I can't wait to read it. When will you be ready to share?"

"Soon. What I have so far is good but still kinda rough. Your input can only make it better. What did you do today?"

"A lot of research and planning. Let's eat before we go there. I'm starved."

With the expected discussion put aside, they ate to stuff their stomachs while filling their hearts with friendly chatter.

Then Ava could wait no longer. "Okay, how can I help? I presume that's what you want to talk about."

Jennifer reached for her briefcase, then laid out

notes and documents as she talked. "I worked all day in one of the meeting rooms at the library and formed a plan of attack. I believe I've got the facts we know in a reasonable order, and this is a list of things we question or need to investigate more."

"Wow. This is impressive. I don't see any tasks assigned to Jasper. Where does he fit in?"

Jennifer's voice deepened. "As far as I'm concerned, he doesn't. It's up to us if you're with me. Definite word came today that the prosecutor is pushing for a court date only two weeks out. I'll appeal, but it may be tough."

Ava stood to give a fist pump. "Yes. We can do this."

"I don't want it to interfere too much with your writing, but I need help. Like you heard me tell Dad, you're the right person for the job, but I don't want you taking chances.

"I'll do whatever it takes to get him out of there. This whole thing has been a nightmare. Did the people in your office find anything on the owners of the grow farm?"

"It's registered to what looks like a shell corporation. The name is there on the second page. Greenleaf Farms. I want you to dig deeper. Who are the people managing things locally? That sort of thing. Start with city offices like taxation and zoning."

"Out here it might be county. I can check there, too." Ava shook her head. "It's a shame. Marvin sitting in jail assuming his original attorney is working for him when actually he's done very little. I'd love to see him fired, but I guess that would raise suspicion."

Jennifer took a last bite of her fried pie and agreed. "Yes, he's done enough to make a show, and that's all.

I've got to get to bed. I'm exhausted. Here, I made a copy of the to do list for you. Text or call anytime you find something and I'll do the same."

Ava stayed up late pouring over the plan and making notes. She had her work cut out for her, but she was ready.

****

Ava finished dressing as the sunrise peeked through her window. She styled her hair and chose an outfit to wear. Major whined when she brought him inside for the day.

"Sorry, boy, but I need you here. I'll be back for lunch after my errands." His ears perked, and he looked as if at attention. "Good dog. Wish me well." He barked his encouragement as she locked the door.

Ava parked in front of City Hall and began her research inside. The woman she spoke to in the tax office wasn't much official help, but had some gossip to relate.

The woman's curly red hair bounced as she talked. "Now, I wouldn't want to be quoted or anything."

Ava winked. "No, anything you give me that's not public record will be between us."

The woman leaned forward to tell her story. "I was at a city council meeting one night where a stranger took a turn speaking. He was the owner or manager or something of that place and trying to get the city to pave a road all the way out there." She leaned back and made a face of disdain. "I didn't care for him. You know, a city slicker with his fine suit and fancy talk." She returned to her position on her elbows again. "Anyway, after he finished his speech, the chairperson told him he was talking to the wrong people. While the council appreciates the jobs and economic boost, they've brought to town, the rest of that road is under county jurisdiction. The man slapped his briefcase closed, didn't say a word of thanks, and high tailed it out of there."

"Did you catch his name, or can you describe him?"

The woman straightened her shoulders and used clear, staccato words to pronounce, "Bradford Allen Stilton." She tried to stifle her laughter with a hand over her mouth. "Don't that just beat all? He was a nice-looking guy. Maybe six foot or six-foot one, slim, and graying hair. And like I said, dressed to the nines."

Ava's heart beat faster with the description of the man who confronted her at the grow farm. "Thank you. You've been very helpful."

As she drove to the Lattimer County offices, Ava mused, "So, he was a big shot, after all. Why was he in such a hurry to get a reporter off the property? I'll check out newspaper articles about the place as well."

She waited for her name to be called, then took her turn at the County Clerk's window. "I'm Ava Hardy with the *Tulsa Herald*. We're running a series about the economy in your county. I need some information about the, she checked her notes, Green Leaf Farm. Can you help me?"

"Only with what would be public record. What do you need?"

Ava gathered what she could and thanked the man for his help. On the ride to the newspaper office, her head spun with few answers but more questions.

She called Jennifer. "Hey, it's me. We'd better meet for a working dinner. I'm going to see the editor of the newspaper and then I've got to get home to Major. Is chef's salad okay?"

"Sounds great. I'll stop off for some wine. Am I

right? It sounds like you've had a productive day?"

"Yes. I have some things to share. And more questions."

They discussed things over dinner. "Ava, have you always wanted to write?"

"Yes, I get it from my dad. He most often wrote freelance for magazines and journals, though he had one novel. It did okay, but he never came up with another."

"He must have been good at it to have raised a family with his writing."

"Well, I remember a few lean times when he'd pick up a part-time job. Especially around Christmas time, and Mom worked at Sears until they closed in our town. We never wanted for anything, but he had a hard time punching a clock, working for someone else, or being around a lot of people. Sounds like your dad when he was younger."

"Maybe so. Sometimes we just don't know what goes on with people around us. I'm glad my dad and I have reconnected."

"I am, too. Now, we have to get him clear of this mess so you can enjoy each other. I sure wish I had that chance with my dad. I went to the offices like you asked. It turns out the grow farm is in the county, but I had a friendly chat with a lady at the city offices while I was there. She described the man who I met out there as someone in charge and gave me his name."

"Good work, Ava. I want us to visit the sheriff tomorrow and we'll see if he can get any more info on the guy. I can't keep asking my office to do research for us, even though I'd be willing to pay for it. What else did you learn?"

"The County Clerk was very helpful. The business

had to sign a stack of papers and have tests of all kinds done on the property before they could open. Here's the kicker, though. The reports required follow-up tests and they're missing from the file. He was in shock. He knows he scheduled the tests and will contact the agency that would have completed them. So, were the tests done and the reports removed? Who took the reports from the file? Was there something they didn't want revealed?"

Jennifer's hand slapped the table. "Oh, wow. Now we know something is afoul. What could it be?"

Ava smiled at her friend's excitement. "I'll get back to him to see what he learns. I also talked with Mr. Wyatt at the newspaper who is going to let me go over micro fiche copies of old issues tomorrow. I'm not sure what I'm looking for, but it's worth a try. You said you want us both at the sheriff's office tomorrow?"

"Yes, we can do that before you go to the newspaper. Maybe I can help you there to speed things up."

Ava pushed back from the table. "Sounds like a plan. Let's get an early start. I'm not sure I'll sleep much, anyway."

Chapter 28

"Thank you for seeing us this morning, Sheriff Carson. You remember my friend Ava Hardy?" Jennifer motioned for Ava to hand her the folder of her work.

"I do. I'm afraid we may have gotten off on a wrong foot. Good morning, Ms. Hardy. I'm glad you ladies stopped by. Marvin is having breakfast right now, so we have a few minutes before you go back."

Ava looked at Jennifer to share her surprise at his friendliness. Seeing no change in her expression, she resolved to sit back and listen to Jennifer lead the discussion.

"You're who we're here to see this morning. We've done some extensive research into the murder charges against my client. There are some discrepancies in what information you've shared. Also, when Ava visited the county clerk, he said nobody else had been there to investigate the company. Frankly, I'm not comfortable with what appears to be a rush to judgement."

The man's jaw flexed and his brow furrowed until his eyebrows almost met. "I sent a deputy over there right after it happened. He put nothing negative in his report." Without taking his eyes from Jennifer's, he said, "Ms. Hardy, would you close the door, please?"

Ava got up to do as asked, then returned to sit on the edge of her chair.

He looked to the ceiling, then exhaled the deep

breath that filled his lungs. "What I'm about to say can't leave this office. Even to Marvin. Our discussion may not be appropriate or even legal, though I have run it past some trusted advisors. I'm going to take you both into my confidence."

Ava swallowed hard and looked at Jennifer before they both said, "Agreed."

"In my twenty-three years of law enforcement, I've never had to deal with something like this. I'm trusting you because I want you to know I'm working hard to decide whether I've locked up the right man or not. I need help and I'm not sure who I can trust here." His shoulders raised and lowered with another breath while he rolled his head around to flex his neck. "I have a small, tight-knit crew of eight here, but it may be there is a leak, a mole amongst us. Things I've assigned, I'm having to follow up on, which is unusual. Reports on my own investigations are missing. I'm glad you've taken such a hand in your father's defense. Not that I can put my finger on why, but Jasper bothers me."

Ava struggled for breath. "Wow." Was all she could utter.

Jennifer responded in more detail. "Those are things we were going to confront you with today. There are documents missing from the county offices, too. So, does your telling us this mean you don't think he's guilty?"

The sheriff shuffled papers on his desk. "I've always liked Marvin. I just can't believe that in his right mind he'd kill someone. But the evidence…" The room filled with silence for a full minute while he glared back at them.

Jennifer nodded. "What do we do now?"

His eyes grew large. "We work together. Share

everything. Not here. I don't want to scare off the culprit. We'll have to set up meetings." His clenched fist slammed the desk as he leaned toward them and whispered, "I want to charge the right murder suspect, but I also want to get my hands on the throat of a dirty officer."

Jennifer put the folder in her briefcase for another time. "Doesn't this mean there could be something foul higher up, too? The DA's office, maybe?"

His voice shook with tension. "That's why we have to be careful. This is a small community where everybody knows everybody's business. Plus, this Greenleaf Farms must be part of a bigger organization. If they can bribe or blackmail law enforcement into doing their bidding, there's no end to the possibilities. Like murder." He looked from Jennifer to Ava and cautioned, "You ladies be careful. Don't take risks. Understand that I don't want Marvin to know what we've discussed today. At least hold out as long as you can. He's smart and if he figures out my rat before I do, he may try to handle him in his own way."

Ava bristled and said, "One thing I know about Marvin is that he lives by the letter of the law."

Jennifer had to be the voice of reason. "Yes, but we also know Dad can lose it sometimes. We'll play it close to the vest, like you said, Sheriff. At least as long as we can."

"I'll be in Dallas for a law enforcement leaders' conference for a couple of days. I'll text you about meeting when I get back."

Ava stood to make her point. "In the meantime, an innocent man sits in jail."

He raised a hand to stop her. "Like I said, the DA

showed enough to charge him. Until we have what's needed to prove it wrong, letting him out would cause suspicion. We don't want to give ourselves away."

Jennifer understood. "I guess we'd better go see him. I have some questions for him, anyway. Shall we make it seem this wasn't such a friendly visit?"

Jim Carson grinned and then yelled out as he opened the office door. "I told you I'm doing everything I can. And I will not tell you again, Ms. Hardy. You'll either respect this office or I'll curtail your visitation rights. Now good day." He slammed the door after them.

Ava giggled and whispered to Jennifer, "I think he enjoyed that last part a little too much."

The always obnoxious deputy who walked them to the visitation room laughed. "Sounds like you pushed the boss's buttons today. Sit down and I'll go get the prisoner."

Ava watched him walk away to see if he might take his pistol out and twirl it on his walk down the hallway like an old west gunslinger. "I'll bet that guy has an autographed photo of Barney Fife on his bedroom wall."

"Easy, friend. Let's stay low key." Jennifer watched as the deputy shoved her father into a chair and jerked the handcuffs from his wrists. After he sauntered away, Jennifer spoke. "Hello, Dad. Ava's done some excellent research we wanted to share."

The trio reviewed discoveries and their plan to dig through the newspaper archives.

Marvin showed his excitement at what he heard. "That's a good idea. Look for names and a larger parent company if you can. I hate to see these mafia-like organizations move into our peaceful part of the country. You've heard of the nasty violence surrounding growers in places like Humboldt County in California. We don't need that mess here."

At the newspaper, Ava introduced Jennifer to the editor before he took them down to the basement.

"The old micro-fiche equipment is out dated, but it serves me. When my son visits, my oldest granddaughter comes in to save the copies. These kids nowadays start learning technology in grade school. I would imagine the new owners will want to get new equipment down here."

Jennifer made small talk. "Have you worked here long, Mr. Wyatt?"

He flipped on the light that swung from its cord above. "My daddy started the paper right out of WWII. I grew up playing on these dusty floors. Just naturally took over from him in seventy-four. Gonna miss the old place. You can start with the files over here. That one should cover what you need."

"That's quite a story. So, you plan to retire and give it up?" Jennifer wondered what the little town would do without the paper.

"My kids don't want it. Maybe I'll find a buyer with the passion to keep the news of a small town flowing." He glanced at Ava. "You know what that's like, I guess."

Ava looked around the room at the history of a community she was growing to love and its people. "I sure do. Thank you for letting us do this research."

"That's fine. You gals turn the light off before you leave." Ava felt a tingle in her chest as she watched him struggle up the stairs.

Jennifer shook her head. "He's a character. You two seemed to bond with the writing and telling the news."

Ava looked up the empty stairs. "Yes, we have."

The archives were extensive, and they took his

advice on where to start. The women worked at the micro-fiche machine for two hours with few results. Ava's phone rang, and she smiled at Gerald's name on the screen.

"Hi. Are you at school?"

"Yes, between classes. You've been quiet for a couple days. Everything all right?"

"I'm sorry. I've been helping Jennifer. Can you come out tonight? We'll catch up. Oh, and I haven't had time for cooking. Can you bring something?"

"A small price to pay to see you. I'll be there about six thirty."

Jennifer taunted her about the smile that came with the phone call. "Somebody is in love."

Ava's hand waved away the kidding. "Stop it. I can't deny he is special, though."

"Like I said, go with it. I really like him. My eyes are tired. I'm thinking these people were very careful not to leave tracks. Let's gather what we've printed out and go so you can get ready for your date."

"Yeah, I need to get back to Major, anyway. Will you join us for dinner?"

"Are you kidding? That wouldn't be very romantic. Besides, we need to take the night off from all this. Remember, we can't share what we heard from the sheriff today."

"I know. I'm sure Gerald will find a way to keep my mind off things." She couldn't hide the joy in her voice.

****

"Like I said, Gerald, I've been helping Jennifer. The prosecutor wants to get into court faster than we thought. It's getting pretty interesting for sure."

"What can I do to help?" He poured wine and

handed her a glass.

"Nothing right now, but I'll remember your offer. I wish I could tell you everything. The deeper we dig, the darker it gets."

His hand clinched hers. "I don't like the sound of that. You're being careful, aren't you? I know this is important to you, but you're special to me. I worry."

Her free hand touched his. He loosened his grip. "Well don't. I wouldn't do anything to miss out on you saying things like that to me for a long, long time to come. Let's dig into these burgers before they get any colder. I just want to relax and leave the world outside. Only you can stop my mind from spinning over everything. I need that. I need you."

She observed his eyes close while his hand clinched the back of a chair. He whispered, "Then let's sit down to the feast, my lady. I'm here for you."

****

The next day, Ava made progress on her manuscript until noon and then readied for a trip to town. "Come on, Major, do your business and come back in. I'll only be gone long enough to meet with Jennifer. How about I bring you a treat for your dinner tonight? Marvin won't mind too much. You deserve a burger, don't ya, boy?"

As she entered the cafe, Ava found her friend in a booth at the back of the room. "Hi. Sorry I'm late. I think Major was taking his time getting settled on purpose."

"No problem. I ordered sweet tea for us. Do you know what you want?"

"Salad for me today. I've got to watch it. I'm going to take a small burger for Major, though. Any news today?"

Jennifer looked around the room for overactive ears.

217

"I have an idea. The one person we haven't interviewed. The victim's wife."

"How will that help?"

"We've talked about maybe they killed him because he knew too much. What if he took some of his concerns home? Married people often share secrets."

"It's worth a try. What if she won't talk? She may see you as the enemy."

"All I can do is try my best. Tomorrow."

Ava leaned forward and reached for Jennifer's hand. "Can I go with you?"

Jennifer grinned. "Do you speak Spanish? I might need help."

"Two years in high school. I haven't used it much, though."

"Good, I took French. We'll meet here about ten o'clock."

\*\*\*\*

The women met as scheduled and discussed their strategy over coffee. In the car, Jennifer handed Ava an address scribbled on an index card. "Put this in the GPS. I'm not familiar with the area."

They stood like tin soldiers on the porch of the modest frame home as they awaited response to the doorbell. The door opened just enough to allow a small woman dressed in black with a large silver cross at her neck to peek out.

Jennifer began. "Hello, Mrs. Martinez. I'm Jennifer Wells." No response. "I'd like to talk to you for a minute." No response.

Ava stepped forward and pointed to Jennifer while repeating her name. Then, "Mi nombre es Ava. Habla usted ingles, Senora Martinez?"

The woman stood tall but still did not open the door more. "Enough." Her eyes bore into Jennifer's. "You are the lawyer?"

"Yes. I am trying to solve your husband's death. I don't believe Mr. Cameron killed your husband, Mrs. Martinez. Will you help me?"

The woman clasped the cross in a quivering hand. "They say I don't talk. The big man is good. He feeds my babies."

"Did he threaten you? Your family? Please, Mrs. Martinez, I'll protect you."

The mother called in the house to silence a crying child. "The other lawyer said they send us back to Mexico. I no talk."

Ava's stomach churned as she asked, "What lawyer? Someone with the big man?"

"My neighbor say he defends the murderer like you. You must go now. I am afraid."

Jennifer reached to restrain Ava while she handed a business card to the woman. She had to try again. "Just one question more. Did your husband tell you things about the farm that made him scared?"

"My querido Rinaldo was brave. I am not." With that, she took the card and shut the door.

"Call me anytime, Mrs. Martinez. Others may be in danger."

In the car, Ava beat one hand into the other. "That slimeball Jasper. If I could get my hands on him, I'd give him what for."

"You might as well calm down. The only thing we can do is let the sheriff know what we heard. I'm not sure what to do next."

Chapter 29

Sheriff Jim walked up to the checkout desk at the McAlester library and spoke to the smiling woman working there, "Excuse me. I'm meeting a couple of women here."

She pointed to a corner of the building. "They're back in meeting room C. Let me know if you folks need anything."

"Thank you, ma'am." He greeted Ava and Jennifer and set down the package he carried. "Good afternoon. Have any trouble finding the place?"

Jennifer moved her briefcase to the floor to make space for his bundle. "No. You're right, it's only about thirty miles over here to McAlester."

Ava asked, "Your crew won't question your trips in this direction? Not your jurisdiction, is it?"

"Right, but the staff knows my mother moved into a senior place over here and my sister, who looks after her, is in Kansas City for a couple of weeks on business. So, not unusual for me to visit during the day. I'm sorry we have to sneak around, but I think you understand."

Jennifer laid her hand on the paper bag. "You brought something for us?"

Jim stood up and dumped DVDs out of the bag and said, "Security recordings from the grow farm for two weeks before and until the murder. Viewing them all will take some time."

Ava stood to access the discs. "They have video equipment right here. With all of us working on it, we'll get it done." Ava took a few of them and turned toward the DVD player.

Jim removed his cap. "I'm afraid I can't stay too long. When we meet during my workday, my length of time away from the office will have to make sense."

Jennifer agreed. "And I'm leaving from here to go home for a day or so. Mom said my little girl had a fever this morning. She kept her home from day care, but I'd better go check on her. Is it okay I take some of these with me?"

"That reminds me." Jim removed a typed form from the inside pocket of his jacket and spread it in front of Jennifer. "As Marvin's attorney, I need you to sign for this evidence. Gotta keep everything on the up and up."

"Of course. Let's get started." She chuckled. "I see Ava has commandeered the machine in this room. Let's see where they have more."

Ava stayed later than the others, but left to get back to the cabin before dark. They agreed to meet at the same location two days later unless someone had a discovery that couldn't wait. The videos she watched were from the back of the greenhouses and didn't lend any clues. After feeding Major and herself, she rubbed her tired eyes and made an early night of it.

****

The morning sun on her body and birds singing in the trees as she hiked along the path invigorated her. On returning, she took the porch steps two at a time. While her laptop started up, she rolled her shoulders back. Now she was ready to write.

*The Novel*

"Beth! Where are my sunglasses? I left them right here on the kitchen counter."

"Ha. You mean here on the dresser? Max, you'd lose your head were it not tied on."

"Or at least if you weren't here to look after me. Have I told you today how much I love you?" His arms surrounded her.

"Max, don't mess up my hair. Have you got everything in the car?"

"Yes. How can two kids need so much stuff? This is only a weekend trip, right?"

Beth grinned. "Let's see, the boy in diapers and the girl a budding artist who needs all of her colors. That'll fill a car pretty quick."

Max shook his head. "And don't forget, he has to have his bunny rabbit blankie. I hope Mom doesn't buy them a bunch more toys. The play room is full."

"Don't scold her. These two are the only grandkids your parents have and they don't get to see them that much."

Max fastened Kaley into her car seat. "I still don't understand why they had to move to Santa Barbara. Who would leave Malibu?"

"Some of their friends retired there. Look at it this way: if they hadn't made us such a good deal on their house, we'd never be able to live right on the beach. Okay, everyone snuggled in for blastoff? Let's go."

Later that morning, Max faced the discussion that kept them from visiting more often. "Dad, my practice is in the neighborhood where most of my clients live."

Max's father still held big plans for his son. "You could have a better class of clientele in Malibu and not have the commute. What is it, forty-five minutes on a *good day?"*

*"Maybe thirty. Dad, I'm right where I want to be. Why can't you understand I like my life?"*

*"Seems to me you've settled. You could be so much more. Such a waste."*

*Beth came in from the kitchen. "He's doing what makes him happy. There are veterans and other people out there that need someone like him to step up for them. I'm proud of the path he's chosen. You should be, too."*

*"The guys in my day served their country and came back better men for it. They didn't need psychiatrists and cry meetings. They got on with life while going for bigger and better things."*

*Max stood and took a step toward his father, who rose up to face him. "You mean like me, Dad? I know you're disappointed in me. I'm sorry I can't put all the pictures behind me of kids laying broken, drowning in their own blood. The knowledge of me pulling the trigger over and over is almost more than I can bear."*

*Beth joined the battle. "He's a fine man and father, but you just can't see that and be happy for him. Shame on you, Mr. Archer."*

*Max pulled her back from the fracas as his mother did the same to his father.*

*"Maxwell, this is your son. I'm tired of you making light of his troubles. Beth is right. Can't you be proud that he fought and made it home? He's helping people now. We must stand by him in whatever he needs. Now, the children are here for such a short time. Please tell him you're sorry so we can sit down to lunch."*

*Max's father turned his flushed face away from the group to brush a tear from his cheek.*

*Max put his arm on the shoulder of the man he most*

*wanted to please. "I'm doing my best, Dad." The two men embraced then shared memories and dreams throughout the day.*

*That night, Beth lay in his arms with the children's room between them and his parents and said, "I'm so proud of the way you handled your dad today. You stood up to him, but not over the top." She turned her lips up to his cheek.*

*Max chuckled. "Yeah, no need with you there. The weekend is turning out pretty good after all. Say, have you ever had, you know, in your parents' guest room?"*

*"Why, Maxwell Archer, Jr., what has gotten into you?"*

*He turned out the bedside lamp and rolled toward her embrace.*

Ava laid the laptop aside and stretched her arms to the ceiling, smiling. "Wow. Max is getting it together. I'm going to follow your lead, Max. Today I move forward. My writing, my job, Gerald. Everything is coming into the light. I must stay focused and take deliberate steps each day."

She dedicated that afternoon to the local library and finishing her review of the crime scene. Midway through the last disc, she halted. "What is that?" She ran the video back, then started it again. And again. And again. "Oh man, wait 'til they see this." She sent a group text to Jennifer and Sheriff Jim.

*--got something Can't wait 2 show u--*

Jennifer responded first.

*--That's gr8! No luck here. See you 2morro.--*

*--Me 2 Big news 2morrow at 3--* Jim added a smiley face emoji.

Ava realized she had worked through lunch. The ice

cream parlor came to mind. She parked around the corner from the shop and before she could exit the car, she heard her phone ding with a text from Gerald.

*--Hi Dinner?--*

She thought for a minute, then dialed his number. "Hi, it just so happens I'm in town. Are you going to spoil my ice cream treat?"

"Never, but how about dinner first? I'm starving right now. Wanna go to The Grill for steaks?"

"Okay, I'll head over and get us a table."

Ava couldn't hide her smile as he entered the restaurant. She waved him over to their table in a front corner. "Sit down. How have you been?"

He leaned down to place a kiss on her waiting lips. "I've been busy. I finished my last final today. What have you been up to?"

She looked down at her menu. "Working. Writing."

"Is something wrong? You seem quiet."

She grasped his hand and looked into his eyes. "Nothing. Well, maybe I'm missing my ice cream. Let's order so we can get over there for dessert." They laughed together, but she had to shake off the feeling she was holding something from him.

\*\*\*\*

Ava, Jennifer, and Jim Carson met at their usual place. "I have something I think you'll find interesting." "The last video I watched, of course. Oh, how is your little girl?"

Jennifer opened her briefcase to access the discs she had reviewed. "She's fine. Kids are always picking up some bug at daycare. I just didn't want Mom having to handle it alone."

Jim spoke next and laid out his evidence. "I've got

something, too. What did you find, Ava?"

She moved to the video player and inserted the disc. "Let's see, disc five. Let me fast forward to the right spot. There it is. Now watch what pulls up to the greenhouse."

Jennifer moved closer. "Is that a tanker of some kind?"

"Yes, and the driver jumps out to attach a hose to something on the side of the building."

"I can't read what it says on the door of the truck." Jennifer said.

"That's no problem, I got it." Jim jumped in. "The grow farms have chemicals and by products to be disposed of. But there are legal places approved to accept the stuff. Is that where it went or not? I got a couple of shots of trucks in the lights of the main entrance to the building. Both times you see the driver get out and enter the building. Then about eight minutes later, he comes out. Looks like he's carrying an envelope of some kind."

Ava slapped her hand on the desk. "Money?"

Jim removed his cap to scratch his head. "Can't be sure. The video is too grainy. Of course, a company would get paid for their service. I doubt the driver would take payment, though. A reputable firm would send an invoice. At least I saw the company's name, though. Waverly Pumpers. I checked them out and they've been cleaning out septic tanks and such around the area for over thirty years."

Jennifer took out a notepad and pen to jot down the name. "Okay, this is all good, but it doesn't tell us what they were pumping out of there or what they did with it. Jim, do you think you can get any information from someone at the trucking company?"

"I figured to stop by their offices after we talked. On

one of the discs I watched, I saw another instance of a man shoved into a car and driven away."

"Another Latino?" Jennifer made more notes.

"I couldn't really tell."

Ava stood to circle the table and hit her hand with a fist. "I knew it. If Marvin is right about them dumping into the water ways around here, someone endangered themselves by knowing too much. Maybe they get rid of possible whistle blowers."

Jennifer's legal acumen kept her level-headed. "Like I said, we have something to investigate, but nothing we can prove yet. And we still don't know why they would frame Dad for anything. Ava, I want you to focus on your writing unless I call. You've done so much already." She stopped Ava's objections. "Don't worry, I'm sure I'll need you along the way. There's still a lot of work to do."

Chapter 30

Ava did her morning writing at a city park for a change, then returned books to the library. She checked email and found one she had been waiting on. It was from the professor who interviewed her at the college. Ava took in a deep breath and released it with the greeting inside. "Hi, Ms. Hardy. I enjoyed our meeting and have forwarded your application. Dean Allison wants to meet with you next Tuesday at 10:00 a.m. Report to my office fifteen minutes early and we'll walk over together. Let me know if this works for you." Phyliss Elliott.

Fear and exhilaration flowed through her as her heart sped up over what she was about to do. She sent her positive response with race car speed and started planning what she would wear. She also scheduled a haircut.

Ava's next thought was to call Gerald, but she returned the phone to her pocket. She sat in her car to call her sister. "Hi, Barb. I need a level head to listen to me for a bit and maybe tell me what you think."

"Well, hello to you, too. This sounds ominous. What's up?"

"You know, part of the reason I took this time off was to make some decisions about my life."

"I knew something was up, but didn't know what exactly. Are you okay?"

"Yes, I'm fine. Confused, but fine. Have you ever wanted to just change everything about your life?"

Her sister laughed. "Only when the kids act up or Jack is late for dinner four nights in a row. How can I help? Tell me what's going on."

"I've got a good job, but am I happy? No. My love life has been nothing since Jeff and I split four years ago. Writing gets harder all the time."

Her sister interrupted with a big question. "Have you found a new home? You don't know how much we've missed you this summer."

"I'm not sure, sis. I know I've found something here. Maybe somebody. I told you about Gerald. I think it could be serious."

"Stop right there, Ava. Happiness doesn't come around all that often. If you find what and who makes you happy, I'm behind you one hundred percent. The thing is, I always wondered if our father having his issues made you afraid to commit to a man."

A light bulb went off for Ava. "You think so? I hadn't put two and two together on that."

"You've been close a couple of time, but always pulled away. This sounds like you may be working through that. Make sure about a move, though. You're talking tremendous changes."

"Don't I know it? I'm trying to make good decisions. I'll let you go. Thanks for letting me unload, and say nothing to Mom. I'm only at the what if stage. Lot's going around in my head. We'll talk soon."

She looked out the car window, elbow on the armrest of her door, fingers tapping her cheek. "Now that I've admitted how I feel about him, it's time I make sure he knows." After a quick text to Jennifer and a few minutes of nervous procrastination, she called his number.

His phone rang several times before he picked up. "Hi there, pretty lady. I'm walking across campus thinking about you."

Her smile felt good, and she didn't try to contain it. "I'm in town. How about a movie tonight? I realize I skipped lunch and all I want to do is jump into a big bucket of popcorn."

"That kind of day, huh? I'm in. You don't need to go check on Major?"

"Jennifer said she'll take care of him. He loves her. Maybe he knows she's a part of Marvin."

"Could be. Okay, see you there."

The proper snacks, the latest comedy, and hand holding at the back of the theater filled their evening. After, he walked her to her car, where she asked him to join her.

"This was fun. You always lift my spirits." She leaned over to kiss him.

He took her hand in his. "Something is on your mind. Everything okay?"

"Definitely. Well, I could use some clarity on a few items, but at least one thing is clear as a new sheet of glass. I know how I feel about you. I-I…"

His fingers touched her lips. "I know. I've known for a while. What we have is solid. Future comes to mind, but there's no need to rush until you have all your answers. Just know I'm here beside you all the way. Let me help you." A kiss sealed their pact.

Ava took a deep breath and went on. "I've applied for the job in the English department at the college."

His face lit up with excitement. "That's amazing. I

think you'll be perfect for it. When will you know?"

"I have a second interview next week. Understand, it doesn't mean I'll get it or even accept if I do. I have another possibility in mind, too. I would have a lot to work out in Tulsa."

"That you took the step makes me so happy." His lips found her neck, face, and lips, where they lingered longer than usual.

To catch her breath, she pulled away. "The way I'm feeling tonight, we'd better each head home sooner than later."

\*\*\*\*

Ava sipped her second cup of coffee in her pajamas and robe, enjoying the cool morning air, when Jennifer pulled up to the porch and parked. Major moved to the stairs, tail wagging. Ava went inside for another cup.

Jennifer ran her hands through the dog's coat and patted his back. "Hello, friend."

Ava handed her a steaming cup of coffee. "I'm glad you stopped by. What are you working on today?"

"Hang on." Her friend took a drink and leaned back; eyes closed. "This hits the spot. I was up late. Today, I need your help. I'm going to visit Mrs. Martinez again."

"You think she'll talk this time?"

"I've got to try. What did he know? Did he tell her anything? The story has to come together. We're running out of time."

"I'm with you. Of course, I need to get dressed."

"No problem. I'll sit right here with this luscious cup while you do."

Standing at the entrance to the Martinez home, the women waited for an answer to their knocks on the door. It opened a few inches and the woman they came to see peeked out. She shook her head and closed the door.

"Mrs. Martinez, please give me just a minute. I want to help you." Jennifer pleaded, her face close to the door. "I think your husband was trying to do something good. You can help us finish what he started."

The door opened again, a little wider. "I told you stay away. I am afraid."

Ava stepped forward. "Do you know who belongs to the black SUV parked across the street?"

The woman's eyes pooled, and she made slight head movements from side to side. "Go por favor." The door stopped the conversation a final time.

Jennifer slipped her business card inside the screen door as Ava turned to stare at the SUV. "I think that's the car that ran me off the road."

"Stop, Ava. You can't see in those tinted windows anyway, but they can see you. I hope we haven't endangered this family by coming."

Jennifer put her car in gear to drive away. "I'll let Jim know she may need a patrol by the house in case something is going on. I'm running out of ideas."

Ava sneered, "When have you talked to Jasper?"

"Yesterday."

"Is he doing anything?"

"He says he's all over it."

"Ha. Not likely."

"He claims he's interviewing employees out there again and checking into backgrounds. Both actions are hard to verify. When I talk to Jim, I'll see if we can meet to go over what we have. I may need to develop an opening statement and such. I got the court date delayed only a week."

Ava's body stiffened. "We can't give up."

"Absolutely not. I'm just being realistic."

**\*\*\*\***

The next day, the trio used their library meeting place for Sheriff Jim to share news. "I've been busy, and I hope we'll soon have some answers. A science professor friend of mine at the college has been a big help. I wanted to understand more about the processing at the farm in case Marvin is right about pollution issues."

Jennifer took notes. "So, you still think there could be chemical dumping of some kind?"

"It's about the byproducts of growing and harvesting the cannabis plants. Yes, there could be pesticides or something, but even water runoff or things like what they use in making essential oils. A lot of it is the stems and other parts of the plants that need disposal."

Ava chuckled. "I guess I thought they just smoked it all."

"No. I tell you it was quite an education for me. My friend has also tested the water where Marvin says he likes to fish and a couple of other locations. When he gets those results back, we'll know for sure what we're dealing with."

Jennifer continued writing. "Make sure I get his name and contact information. We can use him as an expert witness. When will he have the tests back? You know, time is getting short."

"He understands and put a rush on it. I'm hoping only two or three days more."

"This is great work, Jim. Have you determined where your leak is?"

Ava couldn't resist. "I bet it's that skinny little twerp

I can't stand."

Jim nodded. "Turns out, you may be right. I can't show my cards yet, though. It could spoil the entire investigation."

"Or, he could breakdown under pressure and give us all we need. I'll bet he'd squeal like the mouse he is." Ava made a squeaking noise.

"You ladies have to understand that as goofy as he seems, he's been an outstanding officer. I have to make sure. Trust me, I'm working on it."

Chapter 31

A car horn honking and Major barking woke Ava from a deep sleep. She got out of bed to answer the knocking and then banging on the door.

Major got there first. "Get back, boy. It's only Jennifer." She shielded her eyes from the sun and stepped aside as her guest rushed in. "Always glad to see you, but what time is it?"

"10:00. You're still in bed? Get dressed. We're having company."

"I worked late. Got a lot done, too. Wait. What do you mean?"

"Mrs. Martinez wants to talk. She's bringing a friend who also has a story. I thought it would be okay to meet here."

"Of course. When?"

"About 11:30. She has to get her mother to watch her kids first."

"Oh crap. Let me grab a quick shower. Why don't you get down some glasses for tea and cut up the apple strudel in the package on the counter? I'll feed Major and put him on his chain at the tree before they get here. "

They put the small dinner table in the center of the room and laid out the snacks, then waited. As the women pulled into the drive, Major pulled against his chain and barked until Ava commanded him to stop.

"Come on in, ladies. He can't get loose."

Once inside, Mrs. Martinez introduced the woman accompanying her. "Mrs. Gloria Jemez. Her Tony worked at farm, found dead two nights ago."

Jennifer started the discussion. "I'm so sorry, Mrs. Jemez. I thank you both for coming. You're very brave. May I call you by your first name, Mrs. Martinez?"

"I am Carmen."

"Fine, Carmen. You have something to tell me?"

"Gloria helps me."

The second woman spoke up. "Her English is not so good as mine. I will fill in where she cannot explain."

Jennifer nodded as Carmen told how her husband came home from work many times, upset at how they did things at the farm. "He said they told him to keep quiet and threatened him when he spoke to other workers about this."

Ava couldn't hold her questions any longer. "What kinds of things? The way they got rid of chemicals?"

Jennifer touched her arm. "Hold on, Ava. Let them talk. Go ahead Carmen."

Carmen told more. "They had shipments at night, and boxes went out Rinaldo could not explain. When he asked about them, they beat him and said to mind his own business."

Gloria related her story. "My husband worked raising the plants. When he asked what was in the boxes that went out that were not the weed, the boss man slapped him. Called him names. The next night he did not come home." She lowered her face to her hands as she wept.

Carmen continued the tale. "My Rinaldo and Tony think maybe drugs. Bad things."

Jennifer quieted Ava before she responded. "If they

asked about it, that could be why they didn't come home. I'm sorry, but they were very brave and now you are, too."

Ava heard Major growling and barking and stood to investigate. The door flew open as two men bolted in, brandishing pistols and yelling as they toppled the table. "Get down on the floor. Face down. Get down, now."

Ava thought of her pistol but couldn't get to it under her bed pillow. She glared at the men and heard Jennifer ask questions over the other women's screams.

"What do you want? Who are you?"

Ava joined her. "Why are you here? This is my home. Get out."

The larger of the two bent and grabbed Ava by the hair and pulled her close to his foul breath. "You shut your pretty face." He looked the women over. "Well, isn't this a bevy of beauties?" Ava let out a scream as he threw her to the floor. She rubbed her shoulder and glared at him when she stood again.

The other man asked, "What do we do with them, Hank?"

"Shut up, Billy. You know what the boss man will want done with them. Secure them with the tape." He stepped toward Carmen and her friend. "Stop the crying, or I'll have him tape your mouths, too."

Billy stepped back. "Hey, now. I didn't sign on for women. I mean, those men, border rats, were one thing, but no, not this."

Hank asked with his hands on his hips. "So, what would you do?"

"I don't know. Drop 'em in his lap. He can figure it out."

"Get to wrappin' them up. I'm gonna go pull the car

up closer while I think about this."

As they marched the women to the car, Ava recognized the black SUV they saw at Mrs. Martinez's house. She was sure it was the one that chased her down. She looked at Jennifer, who nodded that she understood.

At the grow farm, the women waited in the car and heard yelling from the office.

"You did what? Are you both out of your minds?" The man stood and put his suit coat on.

"You said if Martinez made a move with those women, we should stop her." The big guy's shirt carried wet circles under the arms.

The other chewed his filthy nails as he talked. "Yeah, she left the house, we tailed her like you said, and then, jackpot. Four of 'em."

"And you thought it a good idea to bring them here. Do you not have a brain between you?" The man straightened his tie tossed papers from the massive desk. "Bring them in and stash them in the basement storage room. I'll have to be the one to solve this, too. As always. Things around here are getting tight. The law was out here again today and I'm surrounded by idiots."

The men he berated trudged off to retrieve the women from the guarded SUV. Hank shouted orders. "C'mon, get out of there and follow him. Hurry up senoritas. And stop the sniffling." He gave Carmen's shoulder a shove.

Jennifer reached back to comfort her. "Be strong, Carmen. Someone will come for us."

Ava whispered. "I'll distract them. You three can make it to the woods."

Jennifer snapped, "No. Get back in line. You'll get us all killed."

Hank's gruff voice called out, "Shut your mouth up there." He stepped beside Ava. "You're gonna be a problem, aren't you? I knew it on the road that night."

"More than you can handle." She looked him in the eyes.

He spit at Ava's feet and growled out, "You just try me, little one. You'll see."

Jennifer grabbed Ava's arm and pulled her along. Her finger nails bit into the skin.

After removing the tape restraining them, Billy slammed the door to the storeroom that became their jail. The scraping of something heavy being shoved in front of the only exit to freedom gave way to silence. A beam of sunlight from one small window became the only illumination to the space. Carmen and Gloria huddled in one corner.

Jennifer glared at Ava and whispered close to her face, "We have a slight chance of getting out of this mess and you and your mouth are going to ruin it for us all."

Ava didn't back down. "So, you want me to just sit back and take it? That's not my style."

"These women came to us for help. I'll be damned if we cost them their lives. I'm saying control yourself. We'll put our heads together and figure out something."

Ava rubbed her wrists where the tape had been. "I'm sorry, Jen. You're right."

Jennifer patted Ava's shoulder. "I'm going to get them calmed down. You climb up there to see if you can open that window."

"Got it." Ava stacked three heavy wooden cases under the window and climbed on top to investigate.

When she jumped down, Jennifer joined her. "Well, what do you think?"

Ava brushed dust from her pants. "Shut tight and those half inch bars don't budge. It must be around 3:00. We've got a few hours before dark. but look for a light switch."

They ran their hands along the wall until Jennifer called out, "Thank the Lord for small favors. She flipped the overhead lights on." She turned around to survey the area. "I wonder what's in all these boxes and barrels?"

Ava struggled to turn a barrel and reveal its label. "It's coconut oil for making the essential oils like Jim said."

"Hey, look back in this corner. A partial box of peanut butter and cracker packages. And a bunch of empty wrappers. Why here, in with all these production supplies? I'll bet they don't give the employees breaks and one man stashed them here to catch a bite when he could." She tossed one to each of the others.

"Thanks." Ava ripped at the package. "Remember, I didn't have breakfast except for a few bites of apple strudel. But we'll need something to drink." She put the snack in her pocket.

"Are you ladies okay?" Jennifer moved to them. "If we work together, we'll be fine until someone rescues us, or maybe we can find a way to escape. You must remember the strength of your loved ones."

"Hey, Jen, something we're going to need pretty quick. I don't know about you, but I gotta pee something awful."

Jennifer agreed. "I know, Ava. Look for a bucket or even just a drain."

Ava called back to her. "There's a small sink in this workbench, and a drain below. We can use this empty can to make this work."

After each relieved themselves, Ava spoke to Jennifer, "Gerald was supposed to come over tonight. I left a clue, and besides, he'll see something is up and go for help. Jim will know what the clue means. He said we were in danger and he was right."

"Ava, I hope your clue works. Let's continue to look through this stuff for anything that might help us."

Chapter 32

Gerald parked his pickup at the base of Ava's porch that evening. "Huh. Jennifer is here and someone else. Whose car is that? What's wrong with Major? He's hysterical." He got out and moved toward the dog until bared teeth and frantic barking stopped him. "Wow, he's not going to let me close. Something's not right." He called toward the cabin. "Ava? Ava, you in there?" He bounded up the steps to find the door ajar. He went back to the truck for his tire iron under the seat and returned to the porch with slow, deliberate steps. When he pushed open the door, he saw the table overturned and nobody in sight. He ran to the railing and yelled into the forest at the top of his lungs. "Ava. Ava. Can you hear me, Ava?"

He took off in the truck, headed to the sheriff's station. When he arrived, he almost broke down the door to get inside. "Help. I need help. She's missing. Something has happened to her."

Jim Carson came to the door of his office. "Gerald, come in here. What's wrong?"

Gerald rocked back and forth in the chair across from the sheriff. "They're gone, Ava and Jennifer both."

"Slow down. Start at the beginning."

"I was supposed to have dinner at Ava's. When I got there, it didn't feel right. I went in and there were signs of a struggle. The table overturned and stuff tossed around. Oh yeah, and there's another car there. I took

242

down the tag number." He handed it to Jim, who called for a deputy.

"Run this plate, quick. Do a full workup on whoever it belongs to. Go ahead Gerald. Are you sure they didn't just take a walk in the woods?"

"I called and called. They're gone. I know it. I told them to be careful with this Marvin thing. Jim, I forgot to say, someone scratched the word weed on the tabletop."

Jim, took a deep breath, and called out, "Tyler, have you got that report?"

The deputy laid the papers on the desk. "That car is registered to Rinaldo Martinez. The murder victim."

Jim rose from his chair and reached for his jacket. "You ready to roll, Tyler? Tell Helen to stay close to the switchboard and phone." He turned to see his deputy frozen in place and white as a sheet. "What is it? Why aren't you moving?"

"Boss. I have something to tell you. I can't live with what I've done anymore."

Gerald lunged at him. "Do you know where they are? If you hurt Ava---"

Jim strong armed him back in place. "Back off, Gerald. What do you mean, Tyler?"

"I've been working for the man who had Martinez killed. I'm so sorry. I hope the women are okay. I'm so sorry."

"Why? You've been one of my best. Why?"

The young man melted to his knees, his face in his hands. "It was so much money, boss. I knew it was drug money, but I never thought things would go this far."

Jim had a snarl in his voice. "Drugs? After all the work we've done to solve the opioid problem around here?" He pulled the deputy up by his uniform shirt and shoved him against the wall while calling for help. "Deputy Phillips. Get this guy out of my office and into a cell. Nobody opens it until I'm back. Call in Janson and Berryman. It's all hands on deck." He stomped outside.

Phillips yelled after him. "But, Sheriff, where do I tell them to meet you?"

Jim shouted, "That God forsaken marijuana farm! Gerald, you take your vehicle, too. We may need to split up for the search."

Before Gerald could reach his pickup, an explosion to the east shook the entire area.

"What was that?" Gerald stared as smoke rose in billowing black clouds.

Jim shook his head. "It could be where we're headed. Does Ava still have Marvin's dog? We may need him."

"Yes, but he was so mad I couldn't get near him. Only she and Marvin can handle him when he gets like that."

"All the more reason to let Marvin go." Jim slammed his car door and re-entered the office, where he instructed Helen to call the fire departments in the area, county for a helicopter, ambulances, and at least two search dogs. He unlocked Marvin's cell and, as the men passed Helen's desk, he added. "Remember, Tyler stays in there until I get back."

The men parked at the start of Ava's drive to keep from spoiling the crime scene. Major gave every attempt to break his restraint until he saw Marvin step from the patrol vehicle. His demeanor changed to a K-9 reunited with his long-lost master. Marvin kneeled to greet him and accept the kisses his companion gave. Major's tail wagged so fast his body shook. After retrieving a leash from the cabin, the man and his dog returned to the car for the drive toward the blast. The eastern sky already glowed orange.

****

Jennifer crawled toward her friend. "Ava, are you hurt? I can't hear anything. Ava?"

Carmen removed boxes from her body and rolled over toward Gloria. She pressed her ears again and again, trying to stop the ringing.

Ava called out, though she heard only muffled words in her head. "Jen, where are you? Can you hear me?"

"I'm right behind you. My ears are clearing."

"So are mine." Ava saw the other two across the room.

Carmen tried to move the large wooden beam that lay across Gloria's legs amidst the woman's screams.

Ava and Jennifer, both sore and cut, moved toward the women. Jennifer called out. "Don't try to move the beam by yourself, Carmen. If you drop it, there'll be even more damage to her leg."

Ava couldn't stand Gloria's cries of pain. "We can move it together, don't you think? We have to. I think if we move all these boxes first, we'll have sure footing."

Jennifer moved boxes from the area. "Right. Bear with us, Gloria. This will take a few minutes. Let's stack over on this wall, out of the way."

They worked for a quarter hour before they felt it safe to address the oversized beam. Ava had an idea. "We'll space ourselves at thirds of the pole, lifting at the same time. When we've cleared her body, we give it a good toss with all our might. Even six inches away from her is good."

Jennifer motioned to Carmen to take the center position. "Together and all at once is the only way. Ready? One, two, three, and go!"

The three women lifted with their legs and gave a yell in unison as they shoved the beam aside. It fell dead in the dust. That's when they heard Gloria's guttural cry and saw her go limp.

Carmen reached her first, with Ava close behind. "She's ok, Carmen. She passed out from the pain of the broken leg."

"The poor girl." Jennifer searched for something to cover the injured woman. She pulled a tarp from a pallet of boxes. "Here, this is better than nothing to keep her warm." She sat down, rubbing her own head. "Hey, I think I'm bleeding."

"Let me see." Ava moved the blonde strands of hair away from the cut. "Needs stitches, but we have to clean it, at least. I dug out a case of water just before the blast. The headache pills I carry in my pocket should be enough for all of us."

"Ava, look at what the tarp was hiding. Cases and cases of pill bottles and little zip-lock bags."

"That's it. Drugs are what they've been shipping out of here. The legal marijuana is just a cover."

\*\*\*\*

As the sheriff, Marvin, and Gerald arrived at the facility, they could see flames stretching up through the smoke at the far end of the building. The stench from the burning plants mixed with the smoke.

As they got out of the cars, Jim gave orders. "Be careful. We don't know what chemicals might be in there. The heat could bring on another blast. We just don't know."

Gerald faced the flames. "Do you think they're in there? Let's go. I've got to find her."

Jim stopped him. "We'll let the dog go over everything first. I guess he can do this, Marvin?"

"He wasn't an official search and rescue dog, but he had some training. If Ava and my daughter are in there, he'll find them."

Marvin kneeled down to let Major sniff a tee shirt he took from Ava's when he went in for the leash. "You know what to do. It's your job to find my daughter and Ava." He held the shirt to the dog's snout again. "Go, boy. Search. Find." Marvin raised up and watched him go into action. Neighbors drove in and offered to help.

Gerald paced as Major roamed over the rubble. "I can't just stand by like this. When will more help get here?"

Jim tried to get Gerald to sit down. "Any time now. We'll have troops from around the area when word gets out. You know, I forgot Jennifer is his family. This has to be tough on Marvin."

"Yeah, and they just got back together. No, I've gotta do something." Gerald ran toward the pile, yelling. "Ava, Jennifer. Ava, can you hear me?" He watched as Major halted at a spot, dug a little, then moved on. This went on until the deputies arrived, along with the search and rescue crew. With a command center established, they all had their assignments. The billowing flames helped light their work.

## Chapter 33

"What do you think happened, Jen? Don't say industrial accident. I won't buy that."

"How can we know, Ava? I've thought of a hundred scenarios, but nothing makes sense except maybe they wanted to destroy evidence. One thing is for sure, they knew we were in here. How will anyone ever find us?" She wiped away tears.

Jennifer grabbed Ava's arm. "Don't you start. Those two are all I can take. There's got to be a way to dig out. And it's getting hot in here. Don't you think?"

"If we dig, we might shift everything on top of us," Jennifer shook her head, then reached for the torn spot under her hair. "I guess we're lucky. It sounded like the explosion was at the other end of the building. There must have been workers trapped. It shook everything enough to bring this part down."

Current time was a mystery, as the men had destroyed their phones and none of the women wore watches. Ava suggested, "It must be dark now. How about we sleep in shifts? That way, the one on watch listens for any sounds up above. I'll give Gloria some more pain killer, get them settled down, and take the first shift."

Jennifer tried to make herself comfortable. "Are you sure help is on the way?"

"I'm sure people heard the blast all over the area."

She smiled. "Besides, don't forget the clue I left for Gerald. Get some rest."

The ones who could, took turns sitting up. Ava, then Jennifer, then Carmen. After hours of getting what rest they could, Ava and Jennifer stayed close together, Jennifer talking about her family.

"Maybe because of the way I grew up, family is so important to me. My husband is understanding about my long work hours. Of course, come tax time, his office keeps the lights on late, too. We do a lot of carry out. How about you, Ava?"

"I'm at my mom's for Sunday dinner as much as I can. My sister and her family are busy with sports and cheerleading, so I don't get to see her as much as I'd like. We're still close, though. She was my comfort in hard times. You know, like when Dad was going through something."

"I didn't have that help, but my mother did her best."

Carmen called to them in an almost whisper. "You hear? Up there." She pointed up.

They moved to the spot, following Carmen's finger. Breaths stopped as they listened.

Ava jumped and gave a fist pump. "They're here. I knew we'd be okay."

Jennifer kept listening. "Hold on. Quiet." She took her cupped hand away from her ear and looked at Ava. "I can't tell. It could just be all this stuff shifting."

Ava refused to believe that. "No. Don't you hear that thumping? They're digging." She yelled. "Hey. We're here. Hey you guys."

They all yelled, screamed, and cried for a full five minutes. They stopped again to listen. Only the increased thumping sounds answered them. Carmen used a box lid to fan herself and Gloria.

Ava watched them for a minute then said, "Jen, it's getting boiling hot in here."

"Yes. I'm thinking it's fire from the explosion moving toward us. I don't know how much air we have left. The rescuers better hurry."

"For sure. If the brick and rubble hadn't covered the window, we could break it out for a breeze. Let's keep this quiet from these two. Hysteria won't help."

They survived on the crackers and water until midafternoon. Gloria asked for more water, but Jennifer worried about their supply. She and Ava gave Gloria some of their share, then Jennifer said, "It's getting hotter all the time. We have to keep her as comfortable as we can."

On the surface, Gerald was frantic. "Can't we do something to help?"

Jim tried to calm him. "The search and rescue teams know what they're doing. We have to stay out of the way."

"What if they aren't even here? Ava could be somewhere else, hurt and scared."

"Gerald, you're the one saw Ava's clue. It was clear she was saying this is where they were taking them. This is our best bet."

Marvin joined them. "I've been talking to the commander. They're worried about the fire moving closer to the area where their equipment detects life moving around down there. I called Jen's husband. He should be here any time now. This waiting is torture. Even Major is chomping at the bit to get out there."

Jim kept his cool. "Look, guys, we did all we could until the team got here. They'll let us know if they need us."

Later, a young dark-haired man tried to break through the line of deputies. They restrained him until Marvin called out, "He's Robert Wells, Jennifer's husband. Let him through." He walked to meet his son-in-law as the young man ran to Marvin.

"What's happening? Have they found her?" Robert put his glasses in a shirt pocket, revealing the redness of his eyes.

"Not yet, but they think they've heard sounds below. It can be a slow process. Come over to the coffee tent and sit down."

Gerald watched Marvin attempting to reassure the man who shared his fears. "Even though Ava and I aren't married, I know how he feels. Jim, I don't know what I'll do if anything happens to her." He turned his head away.

"Stop it, Gerald. We have to stay positive. These people are the best at what they do. They'll get them out."

A yell rose from the workers, which prompted Robert and Gerald to run to the mountain of debris. Workers stood, arms waving in a stop motion. The project manager came over to Jim.

"Sheriff Carson, I must have your help. Your people are doing a great job at the perimeter, but these family members on the inside have to stay back. Even walking in the wrong place can cause crumbling we may not be able to stop. Keep them back."

"I'm on it, sir. If I have to remove them from the area, I will."

The man wiped his sweaty brow. "Good. The yell you heard is because we have broken through to an air pocket. Looking at the blueprints of the building, we believe it is a basement room. It may be where they held them before the explosion. We can only hope."

"The fire. Is it still of concern?"

"Very much so. Search for victims at the other end of the structure is at a standstill. We have to work fast for any success in this area. We're trying to make contact with this room now. Tell the families their patience may pay off in a few hours more."

Ava and Jennifer moved away from the others to discuss viable options. They turned to a pecking noise by the debris-covered window. They called out together, "Carmen. Get down from there."

"I must try. Like my brave Rinaldo. I can maybe dig out."

Jennifer gazed at Ava and proclaimed. "We need fresh air. Okay, Carmen. We'll take turns. If you feel the dirt falling away, be careful. It might cascade in instead of out."

Ava armed herself with a length of pipe. "I'll take the next turn. Don't tire yourself too much, Carmen."

After two hours, their toil produced a small opening which allowed clean air to their waiting lungs. A short time later, they marveled as a ¾ inch hose came down through the debris. Little by little it floated to a stop at waist high level to them.

Ava grabbed it and thought she heard sounds. "Get me some cardboard so I can make a megaphone of sorts." Carmen ripped a piece from a box and handed it over. Ava rolled it to form a cone and held it to the hose. "We're here. Can you hear me?" She put the cone to her ear.

Muffled sounds came back through the makeshift earphone. "I hear noise but can't make out words." Ava turned to the others. "I'm sure they heard me." Yelling, laughing, and crying filled the room.

Jennifer motioned for them to stop. "We'd better be quiet so we can make out what they're saying if they try again." She looked over at Gloria. "See? We're going to be okay. You're very brave. They'll get you to the hospital soon."

Ava watched the opening created by the hose for any movement. She spoke into the cone every few minutes, but heard no response. Pounding and sounds of the rubble shifting frightened her, but also kept hope alive.

"Look." Ava yelled at the others. "I see more daylight." The opening around the hose grew in size, and the hose lifted. In its place came a cable with a two-way radio attached.

It squawked, then they heard, "Hello down there. This is Sheriff Carson. We're working as fast as we can. Who do we have there?"

Ava and Jennifer started talking as Jennifer pressed the button. "Get us out, please." Ava pointed to Jennifer and remained quiet to let her take the lead.

"This is Jennifer Wells. Ava Hardy, Carmen Martinez, and Gloria Jemez. Gloria has a broken leg. The rest of us are okay."

The Sheriff stated, "Stay back from the opening. It will be slow work to get you out safely."

"Thank you." Jennifer let the radio hang in place and they watched it go up again. "Okay, let's move away from where they're working. As they work through the debris, it may fall on us."

"I wonder how long it will take to get us out?" Ava asked. "Let's use these boards to make a cover for Gloria, since she can't move fast away from falling debris." The women huddled together and listened to the movement above. They coughed while brushing dust and small pieces from their clothes.

Hours later, concrete and wooden beams crashed down close by. Ava shouted, "They've broken through! Hey, we're down here."

One of the rescue team yelled down. "We'll lower a rope. Tie it around your waist and tug when you're ready."

Jennifer helped Carmen tie the rope around her waist and gave it a tug. "Tell them about Gloria. They need to make sure the hole is big enough to get her out on a stretcher. Understand? Say it, Carmen."

"Gloria hurt. Leg broken. Need stretcher." She grinned.

"That's perfect." Jennifer double checked the rope then gave it three good tugs. She and Ava stood back and watched Carmen float to safety.

A paramedic came down and looked Gloria over, then strapped her to the stretcher he brought down.

Ava heard the machinery above. "A crane is lifting her out?"

"Yes. We'll send down for you both when we get her settled."

Jennifer went next and cried with joy when she heard Marvin's voice. "Dad. You're here. I'm so glad to see you." Then she melted into the arms of her sobbing husband.

"I thought I lost you. Are you okay? Are you hurt?" He wrapped his arm around her and walked her to the waiting ambulance to be checked out.

Ava held onto the rope as it pulled her to safety. She dusted her clothes as she stood up. While thanking the person helping her to her feet, she saw the turquois bracelet on his arm. Her eyes rose to Gerald's, and she burst into tears. He lifted her off the ground and walked away from the mound to sit on a boulder. They kissed and hugged until she could stop crying to say, "I'm so glad you're here. All I could think of down there was telling you I love you."

He hugged her and whispered in her ear. "I prayed so hard for you so I could tell you I love you, too."

Sheriff Jim came over to say, "Thank heavens you're okay. I'm sorry I put you in danger. This case got out of hand, but it's coming to a close thanks to you and Jennifer. Arrests are being made as we speak."

"That's wonderful. I know Jen's happy to see her father out of jail. Thank you for finding us. I want to hear the complete story, but..." she looked at Gerald and proclaimed, "Right now, I want this guy to take me home."

Chapter 34

The aroma of biscuits and gravy and hot coffee caused Ava to roll over in the bed. She rubbed her eyes until Gerald came into view. His smile warmed her naked body under the sheet.

Gerald bent over to kiss her, "Good morning, sleepy head. I thought you might need some sustenance. He poured a cup of coffee for them both.

"After the last couple of days and…" she looked up from her cup with a smile. "And last night, you are right. You've been gone? I didn't even hear you get up."

"I went down to the little cafe out front of the motel and had my breakfast. You were sound asleep. I got us some toothbrushes and toothpaste from the front desk. We kind of came here in a hurry. You're not sorry about last night, are you?"

Ava leaned over close to his face. "Not one bit." Her lips caressed his. Her whole body shook before she returned to her breakfast.

"This coffee is wonderful." She said, running a bite of biscuit through the gravy. While savoring that morsel, she asked, "What time is it, anyway? When do we have to be out?"

"It's 10:00. I set us up for two nights here. Jim will call when they've cleared your cabin, but I figured that wouldn't be in time for checkout today."

"This afternoon, I'll get over to the hospital to see

about Gloria."

"I thought you might, so I took your clothes to the hotel laundry. They should be ready in about an hour."

"Hmmm." She grinned and poked a finger in his side. "Whatever shall we do until then?"

Gerald kicked his boots off and moved the food tray to the bedside table, then joined her under the covers.

\*\*\*\*

The sheriff's office was buzzing when Ava and Gerald arrived later in the afternoon.

Jim greeted them at his office door. "Come on in, you two. Have you gotten some rest since the ordeal?"

Ava took Gerald's hand before answering. "We sure have. I don't know what I would have done without this one."

Jim grinned and nodded. "We all need friends beside us. And, hey, big guy, you picked up on her clue right away. That was key."

Gerald commented, "You're sure busy here."

"Yeah, my cells are full and a ton of paperwork to do. This operation touched most every corner of the community. Tyler, my deputy, Jasper James, not to mention a couple of ladies in the county offices. It will take a long time to get all this through the court system."

"Women, too?" Ava sat forward to listen.

"They were taking documents from the files for the last nine months. It's a shame. This case has devastated their families. Speaking of families, Marvin, Jennifer, and her husband were in earlier. It was cute. She's sticking pretty close to that man of hers."

She wrapped Gerald's arm in hers. "I get that. We came close to losing everything and everybody. So, what more do you know about all this?"

Jim stretched back in his office chair to speak. "First, Marvin was right about the chemical dumping, but it was only once. My friend got his report back, and the water will still take time to clear. I guess they were trying to save money and hired the truck driver off the books. He was lazy and stopped at the first water he came to. After Marvin brought it to their attention, they let the guy go. Seems the big boss learned too late he had surrounded himself with idiots. The two guys that kidnapped you? After things got so out of hand, he told them to blow up the building to get rid of evidence. Their half-ass job of that cost them both their lives."

Ava shook her head. "But why the murders and blaming Marvin? You know, we found evidence of drug running out of there."

"I had been investigating drugs for some time. I never could get anything on them for sure. Turns out, it's one of the biggest operations in this part of the country. The murder victims must have figured it out."

Gerald asked, "What about this boss? Where is he now?"

"Locked up in Oklahoma City, where they caught him at Will Rogers Airport. He had enough cash in his bag to live large for a long time in South America, which was his destination."

Ava got it. "So, he was double crossing his higher ups, too."

"Yes. He grabbed cash out of the safe and took off. He's spilling his guts now about the whole deal. This will take a lot of drugs and bad guys off the streets." He sipped his coffee and said, "Ava, you'll be called to testify, of course. This is going to mean months of investigation and building a case."

"I guess you need a statement from me." Ava took a pen from the holder on the desk.

"Yes, take your time. Every detail is important. You know, like when you're writing for the paper. By the way, your editor, Matt, called, wanting to know how to get in touch with you. He took a statement from me about the incident."

Ava chuckled. "I'd better buy a new cell phone when we leave here. I guess he's right. There is a story and I'm not surprised it's already all over the state."

\*\*\*\*

Ava knocked on the screen door, then walked in to greet her friend. "Hi, Maggie. I came over to let you know I'm okay."

Maggie clenched her in a hug. "Girl, you scared us silly. Are you back at your cabin?"

"No, I can't stay there until they clear the crime scene. It will be at least tomorrow."

"John went over this morning and the officers were still there. You come stay with us where you'll be safe."

"Thanks, but I'm okay. I'm with Gerald." She braced herself for the expected screamed response. Which she got.

"Well, if this awful situation got you two together, I'm all for it. Where is he now?"

"He went to reassure his mother and pick up some things."

"Listen, Marvin and his family are coming over tonight for burgers. We'll expect you about five." Her laughter made Ava giggle.

That night when Gerald parked his pickup away from the crowd, Major came running up as Ava stepped down. She ran her hands through his coat and held his face to hers. "There's my hero. I have missed you so much. I'm sorry I had you chained that day. You would have given them what for, wouldn't you, boy?" She rose from the dog and ran to greet Jennifer. They stood in a hug while they asked how each was recovering. They weren't far from each other the rest of the night.

Jennifer took the arm of the man beside her. "Ava, this is Robert, and this is my friend Ava, honey."

They both said, "Nice to meet you." then Ava introduced Gerald.

Marvin came over to Ava and asked her to stand. "I feel like I owe you a big hug and then some. I never would have made it through it all without you two girls. You were beside me all the way, and I never thought I needed anyone. Now, I have my family, my friends, and you're all the best."

John spoke up, "Raise a glass to being there for each other." The clicking together of red solo cups was the music that mingled with forest sounds that night..

Jennifer already had a grin on her face. "Ava, how are you? And where are you staying?"

"I'm still a little sore and tired, but I am excellent. Gerald and I are at The Shady Mountain Motel until the sheriff finishes with my cabin."

"Together? That's wonderful, and it's about time, too. What's next?"

"We haven't talked about that. Right now, we're enjoying each other and he's taking good care of me."

"Hmm, okay, I'll go along with that. Ava, keep in touch when I leave."

"I hate the sound of you going home. I'll miss you. When will you leave?"

Jennifer looked over the yard where the men stood

talking. "Robert has to go back tomorrow, but I'm staying a few days to help Jim with the case. We'll share notes and ideas. And you? Do you have a departure date set?"

Ava's eyes dropped to the blueberry pie on the plate in her lap. "Not really. I told Matt I'd be at my desk the day after Labor Day."

"That's only two weeks away."

A deep breath and a catch in Ava's throat accompanied her response. "I know I have to face it, but it's going to be hard to leave." She turned to face her friend. "I'm not so sure I will, Jen."

"You're that serious with Gerald?"

"It's not just him. I've applied for a position at Eastern Oklahoma State College here and I may have something else up my sleeve, too. I'll know more about that in the next few days."

"Ah, a mystery. That's amazing. What a jump from your job at the paper."

"Yes. If, and that's a big if it works out, I'll have to go back to wrap things up in Tulsa. Not sure how all that will work out. I've only shared this with Gerald, and I told him there's always the chance nothing will change for me. No celebrations until I know for sure."

\*\*\*\*

Ava waited while her boss complained about her not calling. "Yes, Matt, I'm okay. I couldn't call you before because the guys tossed my phone."

"That's funny. I talked to other people there. Yours wasn't the only phone in that little berg. You need to get this story to me right away. Today. It's hot stuff all over the state. We've got the only reporter that can give a first-hand account."

"Give me a few hours. I have some thoughts about it, but I don't have my laptop back from the crime scene. Maybe I can use the computers at the library. You'll see it as soon as it's finished."

"Hmpf, so you've said. Are you packed and ready to come back after all this?"

Ava's gut wrenched. "You know my return date."

While in town, Ava worked as fast as she could, then transmitted the work as promised. Matt gave her a terse "Good work" and once again she felt it was his usual pat on the head reward. "Typical."

Ava stared through the windshield of her car outside the library and surveyed the mountain area where she had lived all summer. Comparing the forest to the newsroom in her mind made her wonder what awaited at her old job. "Will there be anything new?" She texted Gerald.

*--Meet diner tonight before hotel?--*

*--Yes! 6 sharp I miss you--* The flower emoji spread her smile wider.

She drove to the local newspaper and gathered the nerve to enter. "Mr. Wyatt, I hope I can spend some time with you talking about the newspaper business. There's still plenty I can learn from you."

"Sit down, young lady. You're the one working in the big city. I'm just a small-town editor."

"Your small town and its people appeal to me. You must know everyone for miles around."

"I guess you'd say I feel responsible for them. At least to keep them informed."

"That's wonderful. You said you'll be leaving it soon. That must be hard."

"I have to face facts. It's time."

Ava shuffled in her chair before asking, "Would you give me a tour and talk about how you make it all work for you?"

He cocked his head in question. "Are you saying you're interested? You'd leave the Tulsa paper?"

She stood. "So, you'll show me around?"

Chapter 35

Gerald entered the cabin, holding a small vase of flowers. He set them down and leaned over to kiss her. "Remember our first date here? I brought flowers then."

"You did, and these are as lovely. Thank you. How was your day?"

"Another full shift. I should get the grades from my finals this week. Leaving the grease monkey job for counseling can't come soon enough."

"You've worked so hard for that. You have something lined up at the veterans' center in Talihina?"

"Yes. I was offered a position at the center in Norman, too, but I want to stay around here. I spoke to the director in Talihina on the phone again today. The spot is waiting for me. I'll have that short commute each day, but maybe I'll be moving into my own place in town soon to make it a little closer."

"Oh, you're thinking of leaving your mom's place?"

"My sister will still be there to look after Mom, and anyway, maybe my lady will need a place in town, too?"

Ava blushed and dropped the knife she used to chop their salad. "Now, hold on. We haven't talked about that." She reached for his hand. "There's nothing settled about me staying here. I had my interview with the dean today, but nothing has been offered."

His face glowed. "They'd be lucky to have you."

"I'm thinking I may go back to Tulsa early just to

help me think. Here in this beautiful place and with you around, it will be hard to give both sides a fair chance."

He moved to help set the table. "Don't worry, I get it. I didn't mean to pressure you."

She moved closer to him. "My sister thinks I've had trouble with relationships because my memories of the folks fighting all the time made me leery of men. I don't think we have to worry about that." They kissed, and she changed the subject. "I went by the sheriff's office today. Jim says that the young deputy is really paying the price for his part in all this. Others there won't even talk to him. He has to check to make sure they feed him."

"Yeah, they have to feel betrayed. I'd hate to be in his shoes. How are you doing?"

She shrugged. "I'm still a little jittery is all. You helping get this place put back together was a lifesaver. How about a movie to get my mind off everything? Or we can stay here and count the stars."

Gerald grinned and they walked hand in hand to the porch. "One, two, three…"

**** 

Ava's walk to Marvin's the next morning filled her heart and helped clear her mind. She had options to weigh and wanted to share with her good friend. She called out to Marvin at the edge of his meadow and watched as Major ran to her. Her hands ruffled his coat. "Hey there, boy. I'm glad to see you." He pranced and played as they moved toward the cabin.

Marvin waved. "Hi, there. Come on up. I'll get another glass. Sweet tea, right?"

"Yes, thanks. How has it been getting back to work?"

"Invigorating. I can't believe how my hands

stiffened, though, no longer than I was away. But it feels good to be home. I wish Jennifer would stay with me, but she thought the motel would be better since she'd be working in town with the sheriff."

Ava sipped her tea. "You're over the ordeal, then? You look tired."

He stared off into the forest. "Last night I had awful dreams. It's funny; I didn't have them while in jail. Maybe I knew I had to be strong, and they were building up until last night they blew. I'm okay now, and I'm handling things better all the time. Maybe having people around me I care about keeps me focused on the good side of life."

"That's wonderful. Do you plan to join the meetings again?"

"Sometimes. I'm not an every-week kind of guy, but we'll see."

"I'll bet you love having Jennifer here."

"That means everything to me." He brushed something away from his eye. "She'll be leaving in a few days. I know she has family and a life in The City, but selfishly I want her with me. We've talked a lot about that."

"You've missed a lot of years together. She'll probably be just as happy to see you spending time with her daughter."

He sat tall. "That's going to happen, too. I'll make sure of it. So, when will you leave?"

"Not sure. I have a good first draft of my book going and maybe some direction in my life I couldn't see before. I'm pretty much over all the turmoil, and I'm trying to settle down and think smart."

"That sounds promising. We'll all miss you around

here. What does Gerald say?"

She blushed. "That he'll miss me, if I go, of course. You were right, Marvin. To just let things happen with him, I mean."

"Then you'll have him to consider, too."

"Yes, and I have told no one else, but I've been discussing the newspaper with Mr. Wyatt. What do you think about me taking over when he retires?"

"That's a great idea. Of course, I'm sure you wouldn't make as much money."

"I'm finding that's not the important thing for me. Doing something that makes me happy and to support this community seems pretty fulfilling."

"You sound like me a few years ago. Find what makes your heart sing. You're a smart girl. I know everything will work out."

Ice clinked in the bottom of her glass as she set it down. "Can we go out to your shop? I'd better get the doll house for my niece moved to my place. Wouldn't want to forget it. It should fit in my SUV. There are a couple of other pieces for me that caught my eye, but I'll wait in case I have a move this way in my future."

****

"Mr. Wyatt, I have that story for you. I think I got everyone's names right. I don't want to alienate any of my new readers." She handed the papers to him across his desk. "Wow, you've done some straightening here."

"Yes. After our talk the other day, I figure I'd better get ready for someone to take over. This old roll-top desk was holding quite a mess. Invoices from 2003 and story notes from 1992. My wife always did the cleaning. I guess you can see how long she's been gone."

"I think it says a man works hard here. Look over

267

what I wrote. I concentrated on how these crimes have affected the families involved."

"This looks fine. Very nice and respectful. I can't believe people I've known, some all their lives, would get involved in drug dealing. Here, you've got to let me write you a check this time."

"No, Mr. Wyatt. Like I've said before, this is me giving back to this community. If you want more from me, we'll work out an arrangement. I didn't ask you. Have you ever looked into remodeling the apartment upstairs?"

"Not really. It was fine for us and raising our son. I guess it could use a coat of paint for a nice young lady like you having guests over."

"Maybe. I'd probably have the second bedroom serve as a writing space as well. But I'm getting ahead of myself. You haven't decided when and if to retire, anyway."

"That's right. My son's family is coming for a week's visit before the smaller kids start school. We'll give it a good talk."

Ava's phone buzzed and she read the text from Gerald. "Well, I have to go, Mr. Wyatt. It seems I have a date. Let me know if you need something else on the story."

Chapter 36

Ava finished her breakfast watching the sunrise on her porch. Squirrels ran up the tree and reminded her of her first days at the cabin. "We've come a long way, haven't we, fellas? How many more mornings will we have?"

She went inside to her desk. "Well, Max. Long time no see. With so much going on, I've been neglecting you. Let's see what's happening in your life."

*The Novel*

*"Max, are you ready? I've got the kids dressed. We need to leave soon. We don't want to be late for the party."*

*"I know. It's not every day my folks celebrate a fiftieth wedding anniversary." He met her in the living room and took her arm. "Before I load the car, let's talk for a minute."*

*Beth moved a shock of hair off his forehead as they took to the couch. "Is something wrong?"*

*He shook his head and grinned. "At least I don't think so. I may have some news for the family tonight. Of course, I wanted to discuss it with you first. I'm glad your folks will be there, too."*

*"Good news? We can all use that. What is it?"*

*He stood to face her. "Two city council members came to the office today. They've been watching the work we've been doing with the veterans, activist rallies, and getting people off the streets. Me being vocal at their meetings didn't hurt either."*

*"I've always told you everyone is proud of your work. What is this about?"*

*"Yes, you have, but when they asked me to run for election to the council, I was shocked and even I was proud."*

*She jumped up and into his arms. They stood in an embrace that conveyed their love and support of one another.*

*Max backed up to ask, "So, does this mean you think I should do it?"*

*"For me? A big yes vote. Let's be sure, though. It will be a lot of added pressure. Do you feel ready?"*

*"Yes, I do, but I know what you're saying. Beth, you've seen me through so much and you know I can still lose it sometimes."*

*"Not so much anymore. I think you're doing great. You haven't broken any family heirlooms in a while."*
*She grinned.*

*"This will be more important than your grandmother's favorite Jello mold. I'm ready, Beth. When they left the office today, I felt so accomplished and confident about the future. Yes, I'm ready."*

*She thought a minute, then said, "I think they get paid a little, don't they? That should be enough extra income to buy a lot of diapers."*

*Max fell back onto the couch. "Diapers? Are you kidding? Beth, you mean number three? It's been a while." He grabbed her and they danced around the room like they did years ago with their decision to marry.*

"Well, get out the party china, Max and Beth. You inspire me so. I promise I'm going to do you proud, too.

Speaking of that, I'd better get busy. I've got business in town."

Ava parked in front of the First National Bank and used the rear-view mirror to straighten her hair one more time. "Okay, this is it." Inside, she asked the greeter who she would talk to about a business loan.

"Hello, I'm Richard. Come into my office."

"I'm Ava Hardy. Nice to meet you."

"Sit right there. Can I get you some water? How can I help you today?"

"A business loan is what I'm after. I searched on line for what you would need. Is this everything?" She laid a folder of paperwork on his desk.

"This is good to see. Most often people come and just say, 'Give me the money'." They had a good laugh. "I see you're looking at The Latimer County Eagle. I didn't know Dennis was selling. He and his father before him have kept the county well informed for a long time."

"Not that it's public knowledge yet, but we've been talking and he's ready."

"The bank will use the utmost discretion. The first thing is the full application. I'll look over your plan while you do that. Do you have a dollar amount in mind? Oh yes, I see it here."

"Mr. Wyatt talked it over with his son and what they came up with seems fair. I'll need some extra for renovations and updating some equipment."

"Fine, just fine. If there are no snags, you should have an answer today."

Ava's heart fluttered. "So fast? That would be great."

When she finished the documents, he suggested she go for lunch to give him time to complete the process.

She tried a salad at the diner, but pushed most of it aside. This was a big step in her life, and her nervous stomach wasn't playing along well.

She leaned back in the booth and called her mother. "Hi, Mom. I just finished lunch. How about you?"

"I had brunch with a few of the ladies from church. Let me turn the TV down. How are you? Have things settled down? I read your article about it in the paper. So sad for the residents there."

"Yes, it is, and I told you I'm fine. Anything new there?"

"I had to have a guy come out to get my computer working. When are you coming back so you can do those things like always?"

Ava shook her head. "Maybe soon, Mom. I'm not sure."

"My wandering girl. More like your father every day."

"And proud to be, if that means following my heart. Mom, we never finished our talk about what happened to him."

"Oh, honey, can't we let him rest?"

"But I can't rest without knowing everything about him. It wasn't a heart attack that took him like you told us, was it? I think I've figured it out."

"Barbara confronted me some years back and told me then I should talk to you about his suicide. I continued pushing it down. You understand, finding him alone at his cabin, the gun by his side, was almost more than I could handle. You girls needed me, and that kept me going."

Ava clenched her gut and fought to keep the tears from her voice. "I'm sorry, Mom. You made your life all about us. I shouldn't have made you go through it again. This helps me move on, though. Is that why we moved from Mannford to Sand Springs? You were afraid we'd hear something at school or church?"

"Yes, and Sand Springs is larger, so I thought you girls would have more opportunities. You know, honey, time marches on, and we're all adults now and should be able to talk about anything."

"Wilburton is only a little larger than Mannford. I think you'd like it. And the church is right off the town center."

"Sounds like you've enjoyed your stay. I love you, and will be glad to have you home."

"Right, Mom. We'll talk again."

Ava paid her bill and walked back toward the bank, stopping at shops along the way. Her favorite boutique had a sale running, and she had to check that out. As she charged a new dress, she got a text from Richard at the bank, saying he was ready.

"Thank you for working so fast. I guess you had everything you needed."

"Have a seat so we can talk."

Though he smiled, she thought she could tell what the answer was to be.

"After evaluating everything, Ms. Hardy, I'm afraid we won't be able to extend the loan."

Her heart fell. "I see."

"If you had been with the bank a while or had more collateral, like owning a home, it might have been different."

"That's okay. I knew it might be a long shot."

"Ms. Hardy, your credit is outstanding. You might try one of the other banks here. We're the largest, but still very conservative. You know, the print newspaper business might not be the best risk these days."

"I know, but I love this small paper and the community. I think I'll go to my bank in Tulsa and see what twenty years with them might mean. Thank you for your time. I'm not giving up." She felt deflated, though.

She also had the application in at the college, but wasn't sure when word would come about that. "Gee, it's the paper I want. I have to keep trying."

Chapter 37

Gerald held her hands across the table at the ice cream parlor. "You buying the Eagle sounds great. Right up your alley."

"Yes, and I'm pretty excited about it, but I failed to get a loan from the bank today."

"A bank here? I doubt that's unusual. Buying an established business or starting one is hard. The task is to get the powers that be to buy into your dream."

"Exactly, and that's why I'm probably heading to Tulsa in the next few days. I thought I'd wait to hear from the college. At least I'd know if I had that in my back pocket. Either would be fine, but I love that newspaper, and I could run it like I want."

"Am I hearing that you definitely want to stay?"

"I want to, Gerald. You know that. Whether I can make it work remains to be seen. Listen, I need to stop at Simmons' store to pick up a dessert for the gathering at John and Maggie's tonight. I hate to see Jennifer go, but we'll give her a good send off."

"Yes, we will. I'll go home to change out of my work clothes, then pick you up."

Ava's phone chimed with an incoming email. "Hold on. Let me see what this is. It's from Professor Elliott." She opened to read that she didn't get the post. "Well, I guess that answers that. She says I had a shot at it, but after much deliberation, they gave it to someone already on staff."

He tried to cheer her. "That's not too bad. It sounds like some were voting for you."

"Yeah, I feel pretty good about that. I'll get an official letter from the dean, but she knew I was waiting. She's really nice. So now my total focus is on the newspaper."

\*\*\*\*

That night, the group of friends gathered to bid Jennifer farewell, with hamburgers, hot dogs and all the fixins. John, Maggie, Ava, Gerald, Mr. and Mrs. Simmons, and Marvin and Jennifer talked and laughed through dinner, then watched the sunset together. Major slept through it all.

Marvin rose to speak. "Jennifer wants to get an early start tomorrow, so we'd better get going. First, though, I want to thank everyone for taking my little girl under your wings."

Jennifer poked his arm. "Oh, Dad."

"Well, you are my little girl. These folks are the best, wouldn't you say?"

Jennifer looked around the group. "Absolutely. I'll be back to see you as often as I can."

Ava whispered in her ear as they hugged, "I'll call you. I may have some news soon."

After they waved and watched the trio disappear into the forest, Gerald leaned over to Ava. "Don't you have something to share?"

"Yes, but I didn't want to take Jen's spotlight." She decided it was time. "Everyone, I have something to tell you. First, I applied for a teaching position at the college."

Surprise ran through the group and Maggie said,

"That's wonderful. So, you are staying here?"

"I'm trying, but the job didn't come through for me."

The crowd gave a collective, disappointed "Oh no."

"I still have hope. No, more than that. I am going to purchase the newspaper from Mr. Wyatt. He's retiring in October."

A cheer went up in unison.

"I tried to get the loan here, but that didn't work out. In Tulsa I'll have a better chance. That means I'll leave right away."

John asked, "Not to get too much into your business, but loans like that aren't easy to get, are they?"

"No, but when I decide on something, I'm hard to stop. If I have to take money out of my 401K for a down payment, I'll do it."

It was Charles's turn to quiz her. "What about your job at the *Tulsa Herald*? Won't you be giving up a lot?"

Ava smiled. "Living around all of you and being able to be my own boss sounds darn nice to me. It will be a tough discussion with my boss, but I think the job has run its course for me. The time has come to spread my wings."

"And your mother?" Of course, Maggie would think of her.

Ava's shoulders rose with a deep breath. She let out a long sigh. "Another talk I dread, but I think she'll come around. She taught my sister and me to dream big and that's what I'm doing."

Gerald put his arm around Ava. "Time you get some rest if you're going to be packing to leave."

"You're right. Goodnight, all. I'll stay in touch about everything." They walked to Gerald's pickup for the return to her cabin one more time.

****

Ava began her chores early. She packed and cleaned until noon, then took the familiar hike to Marvin's. Her usual call brought Major running. "Boy, am I going to miss you?" She moved on to the porch steps and called again. She waited until Marvin opened the screen and peered out. His hair looked like he had been in bed and disheveled clothes said he'd slept in them.

He said, "I'm not good company today."

She took a step up. "I'll be the judge. You sick?"

"Something like that. I don't even have tea made."

"That's not like you. It's after lunch time. What's wrong?" She moved up a step.

"Rough night and Jennifer leaving this morning hit me harder than I expected. I think it's best I'm alone today. I'm just barely keeping it together. Days like this are why I don't keep whiskey around."

She stood to go. "I'll respect your wish to be alone, but I'm leaving for Tulsa tomorrow. I'd like to know you're okay."

"You're leaving, too? Isn't that just fine? You should be glad to be rid of me."

"On the contrary and anyway, you know you can't get rid of me that easily. I'll be back as soon as I have things settled back home. You get some rest."

She hugged Major and left. On the way, she stopped at the creek and enjoyed meditation on her favorite boulder. Fall had brought a special nip to the cold water surrounding her feet.

That evening, Gerald brought barbeque and beer. After they finished eating, they went to the porch to talk in the moonlight.

His voice carried the passion he had for her. "I know you need to go, but being here without you will be harder than the day I stepped onto that transport plane that dropped us in the desert. I didn't know what I was in for then, and I don't know now."

"You know I'll be back. I won't let anything get in my way now. I'll go to my personal bank first, then I have a list of others. Someone has to see that I will make this work."

"No doubts from me. I hate to leave early, but I have to be at the VA Center at the crack of dawn tomorrow. Can't be late my first day. I want to get started."

"I'm so proud of you. Be sure to call and tell me all about your first day."

They stood to embrace, and their kiss was one to remember.

Inside, she gathered the debris from their dinner and headed to the dumpster by the road. On her way back, sounds from the trees frightened her. She ran the rest of the way to the cabin and her pistol.

With her second step up to the porch, she heard Marvin's voice. "Hey, wait. It's me."

She peered into the darkness to see him and Major coming nearer.

"Do you know you scared me half to death? What are you doing here so late?"

"I'm sorry. I should have called out like you do at my place."

"Well, yeah, or something. You just missed Gerald. Come sit."

"Where is the chair I made for you? Do you have it packed in the car already?"

"No, Gerald took it tonight. He'll keep it until I

come back. Kind of makes it feel definite for me."

"You came to share your news with me today, and I need to apologize for how I received you. What is your plan?"

She relayed all the details she had repeated many times in her mind. Her organization impressed him.

"Sounds like a solid plan."

"Thanks. I take it you got to feeling better."

"Your visit helped. You know, I wish my wife and everyone else could have treated me like you do." He gave a hatchet motion with his hand. "Firm and straight forward. No nonsense. Just, 'get up and get yourself together, Marine'. Then you leave me to figure it out myself."

She could only smile.

"Like I said, I came to apologize. I'm glad you were able to figure things out. Major and I will be here when you return."

That night, Ava sat up in bed with a shudder and threw the quilt back. There stood the dream-like image of her smiling father.

His familiar voice comforted her. "Hi, Tator Tot. You've been a busy girl."

She shook her head but was glad to see him still there. "Aw, Dad, you haven't called me that in a long time."

"I'm sorry I left you the way I did."

"I understand now."

"Remember, I'm always with you, and I'm proud of you."

Ava awoke the next morning, eyes caked with dried tears, ready to take on the world.

Chapter 38

Ava yelled to her brother-in-law in another room. "Jack, bring me that can of lavender paint." The apartment was full of family and friends working to get the place ready for Ava's new life.

He deposited the paint next to the pile of brushes. "What a sissy color. Doesn't look like you at all."

"No, but it's Mom's favorite. I want her to be comfortable in this extra bedroom when she comes to visit. Maybe she'll even come to live with me someday. Right, Mom?"

"I love my house in Sand Springs and all my friends. I'm not quite ready for the home just yet, young lady."

Marvin spoke up. "So, extra bedroom slash writing office?"

"Yes, I want my personal writing to be away from the workday of the paper downstairs. At least I hope it works. I don't want to be like my old boss saying he wishes he could have gotten his novel written."

Barbara chimed in. "You're going to make it all work, sis. It is going to be a lot of work, though."

"Davis, the student I've been working with, is going to intern with me to get things started. It will be wonderful experience for him."

Mrs. Simmons said with a smile. "He's so excited about it. He and his girlfriend, Brandy, will join us all later for dinner."

Jennifer added, "And Robert and I will be here for you every step of the way."

"Jen, having you as my lawyer will keep me in line for what the first amendment allows the paper to say and do. I'll push the envelope, but I don't need any lawsuits. It took every penny I could scrape up to make this happen."

Jennifer had to chuckle. "You listen to the rules? After your time in the business, you'll be just fine."

Robert made himself clear. "And I'll be keeping your books in line, don't forget."

Ava had to kid him. "Ha, ha. I hope you're a better CPA than you are a painter. It looks like there's more paint in your hair than on the bathroom wall you were working on." The group laughed and poked fun until Gerald interrupted.

"Jack, why don't you and I go down and get the pizza and drinks? Maybe our boss lady will give us a break for lunch."

The conversation was lively as everyone sat on boxes and the floor to eat. Gerald brought in a chair for Ava's mother. "Mrs. Hardy, I'd love for you to meet my mother while you're here."

"That sounds fine, but I rode with Barbara and Jack. They need to head back tomorrow."

Ava proclaimed, "I can take you home whenever, Mom."

Her mother smiled at Gerald. "Then it's a date."

Maggie asked, "Mrs. Hardy, I know you'll miss your girl."

"Yes, and you call me Shirley. I always wanted my girls to have full and happy lives. I never was too quick to kick them out of the nest, but it is time for this one."

Maggie's eyes sparkled, and she laughed. "John and I will be in Tulsa at least this one more school session. Maybe you and I can have lunch or go shopping sometimes."

"That would be nice. I know a nice tea room there in Tulsa."

Maggie let out her signature laugh. "I love it. I'll call you."

John asked, "Ava, I know it must have been tough getting all your business taken care of in Tulsa, but you've been gone for over a month."

Ava swallowed her last bite of pizza and reached for her soda. "I went to the sixth bank before I secured the loan. I was thinking they had some network going. Like, 'Hey, she's on her way to you next. Don't loan her money!' " The room filled with laughter. "My boss was none too happy when I resigned, either. He tried everything to get me to stay. Too little too late." She looked at Gerald and took his hand. "I had all of you to come back to, the paper, and this lovely area. Packing the apartment told me I had way too much stuff for this place. I gave away and sold a bunch, but you'll see when the movers get here tomorrow, I still have work to do there."

Gerald offered, "Archery season opened October 1st. There's plenty of deer out my way. Marvin and I are going out at sunrise. Anybody else want to join us?"

John raised his hand. "Count me in. I got my tag the other day. Superb meat for the winter if you can bag one."

Ava teased them. "That will get enough of you guys out of the way so we ladies can get the place put together and decorated. The moving truck will be here at 11:00.

This paint will dry overnight."

Barbara looked around the room. "Speaking of decorating, I love what you have planned for the place. When can you get the kitchen done?"

"Not for a month or two. The contractor is busy, and he has to order the counter tops. It's livable until then. I got enough extra on the loan to do the few things up here, but most of the money will go for new equipment downstairs. Mr. Wyatt gave me ideas, so I'd ask for enough. He's staying at a friend's house for a month so he can help me get a few issues out before he leaves for Enid, where his son lives. Just another example of how everyone has been so good to me and were the light on my pathway to figuring it all out."

Maggie giggled. "We love you tons, and you've given back just as much."

They all agreed, and Marvin added, "You sure did. I can never repay you."

Ava locked eyes with him. "We had a rough start, but then you took me under your wing. Like a friend, and you helped me understand more about my father." She glanced at her mother, who only smiled back.

Jennifer lightened it up again by asking, "How about your novel, Ava?"

"I sent it off to my editor before I left Tulsa. There will still be some work to do, but it felt good to write 'the end' on it. My mind has ideas percolating for the next one, too. Of course, I've got so much going on, let's just get this one published before moving on. Is everyone ready to get this finished up? I told Mary over at the diner this big group would be there about 6:30. She's setting up the meeting room in the back. Mom, you'll love their onion burgers."

Gerald chuckled. "And your daughter is the expert on those, Mrs. Hardy."

After dinner, her friends and family went back to their homes and motel rooms. Ava and Gerald listened to music in his truck outside the room she shared with her mother. "What a day. I have good friends, don't I?"

He agreed. "Yes, you do. You know, I could have taken my degree anywhere, but this place gets under your skin. I feel like I'm giving back by helping veterans at the center right close to home." He looked out at the flashing neon lights. "Remember when we stayed here?"

She snuggled closer to him. "Of course I do. A special time, for sure. We'd better change the subject. Remember, my mother is in my room tonight." She grinned and reached up to give him a kiss on the cheek.

"All I know is, we've got something special, and I can't wait to see what the future holds."

"We'll find out together. Our story is just beginning."

As Ava got into her bed that night, her mother said, "Don't turn the light out yet. Is there anything else you wanted to ask about your father?"

Ava rose up on her elbow to face her mother. "That's okay, Mom. Dad and I have worked it out."

The older woman nodded. "You talk to him, too?"

"Yes, and I think I've just started to listen. Marvin and Jennifer have helped me so much, and my main character, too. Writing it all out made me face things that must have been there all along. Even though he couldn't stick around, Dad taught me to be tough and bounce back. I understand him more now. We have a glorious life, don't we, Mom? And my future is bright."

"It is. I'm glad you found yourself and this place. I

won't worry knowing you're with these good people."

"And Gerald, Mom. What do you think?"

Her mother grinned and said, "I'd say if you break up, you do what you want, I'll keep him."

They laughed and chatted about all things good for another hour, then Ava finished with, "I came here in June with a mountain of questions to answer and a book to write. In three months, I managed all that, met friendly folks, smoothed out some old scars, and had a harrowing adventure. I wasn't sure where my life was going. Now I'm convinced, when you're in the right place, with the right people, there's no mountain you can't climb."

## A word about the author...

An Oklahoma native, Gency takes a down to earth look at life and can exist comfortably on the page with the fictional characters she creates. A career in retail management across America gave her a life enriched by a variety of personalities and cultures. Since retirement in the Albuquerque, NM, area, those characters and stories have jumped from memory to the written page. She is a member of Southwest Writers, Oklahoma Writers Federation, Inc., Women Fiction Writers Of America, and The Author's Guild. In 2024, her debut novel, A Right Fine Life, was awarded first place in general fiction from the New Mexico Presswomen. Pet sitting, live music, golf, and fly fishing fill her leisure time. gencybrown.com

Thank you for purchasing
this publication of The Wild Rose Press, Inc.

For questions or more information
contact us at
info@thewildrosepress.com.

The Wild Rose Press, Inc.
www.thewildrosepress.com